Sadie King was born in [...] in Lancashire. After gra[...] history from Lancaster [...] West Lothian, Scotland, [...] her husband and children. When she's not writing Sadie loves long country walks, romantic ruins, Thai food and travelling with her family. She also writes historical fiction and contemporary mysteries as Sarah L. King.

Also by Sadie King

Spinster with a Scandalous Past
Rescuing the Runaway Heiress

Look out for more books by Sadie King coming soon!

Discover more at millsandboon.co.uk.

HASTILY WED TO THE DUKE

Sadie King

MILLS & BOON

All rights reserved including the right of reproduction in whole or in part in any form. This edition is published by arrangement with Harlequin Enterprises ULC.

This is a work of fiction. Names, characters, places, locations and incidents are purely fictional and bear no relationship to any real life individuals, living or dead, or to any actual places, business establishments, locations, events or incidents. Any resemblance is entirely coincidental.

Without limiting the author's and publisher's exclusive rights, any unauthorized use of this publication to train generative artificial intelligence (AI) technologies is expressly prohibited. HarperCollins also exercise their rights under Article 4(3) of the Digital Single Market Directive 2019/790 and expressly reserve this publication from the text and data mining exception.

® and TM are trademarks owned and used by the trademark owner and/or its licensee. Trademarks marked with ® are registered with the United Kingdom Patent Office and/or the Office for Harmonisation in the Internal Market and in other countries.

First published in Great Britain 2025
by Mills & Boon, an imprint of HarperCollins*Publishers* Ltd,
1 London Bridge Street, London, SE1 9GF

www.harpercollins.co.uk

HarperCollins*Publishers*, Macken House, 39/40 Mayor Street Upper, Dublin 1, D01 C9W8, Ireland

Hastily Wed to the Duke © 2025 Sarah Louise King

ISBN: 978-0-263-34523-0

06/25

This book contains FSC™ certified paper and other controlled sources to ensure responsible forest management.

For more information visit www.harpercollins.co.uk/green.

Printed and Bound in the UK using 100% Renewable Electricity at CPI Group (UK) Ltd, Croydon, CR0 4YY

For Gemma, Joanne and Lynn.

Chapter One

Spring 1820

'Really, Mother, I am not prepared to have this conversation again.'

Ted drove an agitated hand through his thick chestnut-brown hair, regarding his mother with the severest gaze he could muster. It had been like this ever since he'd become the Duke of Falstone a little over a year ago—the same topics repeated over and over again, the same arguments made as both he and the Dowager Duchess failed to see eye to eye. As she reminded him of certain duties which had landed, unexpected and entirely uninvited, upon his shoulders, and he steadfastly refused to properly confront them. Steadfastly clung to the last vestiges of the life he'd made for himself and futilely tried to reject the one he'd inherited. Irritably he fiddled with the cuff of his shirt, before noticing the small bloodstain upon it.

He tucked his hands behind his back and said a silent prayer that his mother had not spotted it.

'I am merely telling you the news from London,' his mother replied, feigning nonchalance as she waved the letter which she held in her hand. 'I cannot believe that Cecily's daughters are betrothed already, and both of them to earls! They only came out last year.'

'I am sure the Viscountess Millington must be very pleased—making two excellent matches even while the *ton* is in mourning for the late King,' he replied, somewhat sardonically. 'Quite the triumph.'

'I believe that plans were afoot before the King's death,' the Dowager Duchess retorted, raising her eyebrows at her son's tone. 'Indeed, Cecily reports that both girls have had to wait patiently before matters could be formalised and the announcements made.'

Ted gave his mother an appeasing nod. 'Please extend my congratulations to the Viscountess and her daughters in your reply. Now, if you'll excuse me, Mother, I must change after my ride.'

He marched out of the parlour and into the hallway of Chatton House, hoping that was the end of today's deliberations on the news from the marriage mart. A hope, he quickly realised, which was in vain, since his mother followed swiftly behind him, her nose still buried in that damnable letter, her keen blue eyes still picking over its contents. He braced himself, knowing there was more to come.

'Cecily reports that the mood in London grows rather lighter now. Some of the ladies have even begun to wear a little white on their gowns,' the Dowager Duchess continued. 'I do not see why we could not have stayed in town a little longer, rather than returning to Chatton so soon after the King's funeral. Perhaps then…'

'Perhaps what, Mother?' Ted demanded, spinning around. He knew exactly what she was driving at—it was the same point, again and again, about the importance of being in society, of meeting eligible young ladies, of getting married. Of doing his duty. He bristled, feeling his shirt sticking to him uncomfortably beneath his coat, dampened by both the day's exertions and the drizzle which had beset his ride home. He squeezed his hands together, spying that bloodstain again. He really did need to change, to hide that particularly damning spot of evidence before his mother could notice it…

The Dowager Duchess held his eye, unblinking. 'You know that you must marry, Ted. You also know that London is where noblemen like yourself meet their wives. You are hardly likely to meet a suitable young lady up here in the wilds of Northumberland,' she added, waving her arms about in exasperation.

'I seem to recall that Perry spent a good deal of

time in London without any success on the marriage mart,' Ted countered.

The moment the words fell from his lips, Ted wished he could take them back. The look of hurt which flashed across his mother's face was palpable, drawing his attention to the lines etched upon her skin by the many months of grief and pain which she had endured in the wake of her eldest son's death.

'Forgive me, Mother, I spoke out of turn...' he began.

The Dowager Duchess simply shook her head, dismissing his apology. 'Your brother's attention tended to be on his other pursuits in town, as you well know,' she replied, giving him a meaningful look.

Ted gave a brisk nod. That much was true; Peregrine Scott's tenure as the Duke of Falstone had been as scandalous as it had been short. Eight whirlwind years of drinking and gambling, which had culminated in a fatal accident in London when Perry, drunk as usual, had driven his gig home through parkland at dawn. If only his older brother had shown as much dedication to being a peer of the realm as he had to his reckless ways of living then he might not have gone to his grave so early. He might have still been here, living at Chatton House with a wife and several heirs to secure the Dukedom and the dynasty. If Perry had lived, then Ted would never have received that dreadful letter on that frozen winter's day—the one which changed the course of his life and brought all his hopes and dreams crashing down around him.

He reached out, placing a reassuring hand on his mother's arm. 'We are back in Northumberland because there are matters here which I must attend to,' he said gently, not wishing to remind his mother yet again of how Perry's love of his other *pursuits* had left the family's lands and interests woefully neglected. 'But I promise, Mother, I will do my duty,' he swore, although even as the words fell from his lips he felt his heart sink. The thought of London, the marriage mart, and all the fawning misses competing to become his Duchess made him feel quite sick.

In his former life, as a younger son and a man with a profession, he'd been so relieved to avoid all that. To be far away from the ton, and perfectly invisible to the ambitious elite, had suited him just fine. Marriage, he had concluded long ago, was likely not for him in any case. Not when he'd had his work to occupy him, that vocation to which he'd been so devoted...

'Ted, why is there blood on your sleeve?'

Gripped by his thoughts, it took Ted longer than it should have done to digest his mother's question, or to realise that she was staring at his arm, her gaze fixed upon the brownish red blot which betrayed that he had, indeed, been doing far more than riding that afternoon. Panicked, he snatched his hand away as though he had been burned.

The Dowager Duchess furrowed her brow, examining him. 'There is more blood there, on your collar,' she added, pointing to his neck.

Was there? Damn—he'd missed that.

'What has happened?' his mother asked. 'Are you hurt?'

He shook his head, touching his collar gingerly. 'Do not fret, Mother, it is nothing.'

'Surely it is not nothing,' she insisted. She eyed him suspiciously. 'Where exactly have you been this afternoon?'

'Out riding,' he replied. 'I went into the village, paid a short visit to Ross...'

'The surgeon apothecary?'

'To my friend, Ross, who is a surgeon apothecary, as you know. And while I was there, I may have offered him some assistance with a patient...'

The Dowager Duchess's eyes grew so wide that Ted felt sure they might burst from her skull. 'A patient?' she repeated. 'What do you mean, a patient? Who were they? Is that their blood all over your shirt? Just what have you been doing?'

Ted hesitated. Despite her myriad of questions, he doubted very much that his mother really wanted to know all the grim details of his exploits that afternoon. How the luncheon he'd been enjoying in

Ross's parlour had been interrupted by loud banging on the door of the apothecary's shop which adjoined his friend's home. How Ross had been summoned to attend to a young boy of little more than ten years of age, who'd been injured after falling upon some farming tools while working on his family's smallholding. How Ted had followed his friend, instinct overtaking thought as he forgot himself and who he was meant to be now. How the wound which the boy had sustained on his leg had bled profusely, but mercifully had not required the young patient to endure the trauma of stitches. How, in truth, Ted had done little more than try to soothe the child, coaxing him to keep the bloodied limb still while his friend examined and dressed the wound, and yet…

The whole episode had taken him back to other places and other times. To a life he'd been called to but could no longer have. To a day, long ago, when he'd been that other ashen-faced child, cold with shock as he lay beneath a tree, hearing his friend Ross's cries echo across the meadow as he ran to fetch help.

This afternoon, the scar on his side had seemed to ache at the memory, just as his fingers had seemed to itch with recollections of their own. Recollections of the work he'd done, of the wounds he'd dressed, of the bodies he'd repaired. Of the lives he'd saved.

Alas, that was his life no longer.

'There is hardly blood all over my shirt, Mother,' he said after a long moment, dragging his thoughts back to the present. 'A child was injured. Should I have turned my back, leapt on to my horse and rode home? Is that what you would have counselled me to do?'

'I would have counselled you to leave the surgeon's work to the surgeon, and to remember that you are a duke now,' she bit back. 'I would have counselled you to remember how unseemly it is for a peer of the realm to…'

'To what?' he challenged, his temper flaring. 'To help people?'

'To play at being a doctor while your mother sits at home fretting about your family's future!' she cried. 'I know exactly how the late Queen Charlotte must have felt after the death of the Princess,' she continued, tears shimmering in her eyes. 'In fact, I believe our situation might be worse, since girls will not do. The Dukedom requires sons, Ted, and soon. You must marry, and you must have an heir for the sake of your family. I know you do not care for the marriage mart, but…'

'Do not care for it!' he growled. 'I do not believe there is anything I could care less about than that detestable business. Quite frankly, I think I'd rather marry the next eligible lady who walks through the door to Chatton House and have done with it, if it will placate you and put an end to these interminable conversations!'

Ted's hand shook as he pointed angrily towards the grand front door of his ancestral home. He stared at his mother, astonished to note that she had fallen into an uncharacteristic silence in the face of his threat. A silence which, when it was broken mere moments later, was not brought to an end by words, but by the loud creak of the door at which he still pointed flying open. By the clip-clop of outdoor boots, and by the death of laughter as two soaking wet faces realised they'd intruded upon something and looked at him in wondrous dread.

The face of his sister, Elspeth, and, to his eternal mortification, the very pretty face of her friend, Charlotte Pearson. He felt the heat of shame rise in his cheeks as two wide blue eyes regarded him, just long enough to make him feel every bit the ogre he must have appeared, before dropping their gaze demurely to the ground. Awkwardly, Ted cleared his throat, swiftly retracting the arm and the finger which, he realised, appeared to be pointing directly at the young lady's freckled visage. He glanced at his mother who, despite having been in the midst of an argument with him just moments ago, wore a look of thorough amusement upon her face. Amusement which he realised, much to his chagrin, was without doubt at his expense.

He cleared his throat again, tucking his hands and, with them, the offending bloodstained sleeve behind his back and well out of sight. 'Sister. Miss Pearson,' he greeted them with a formal nod of his head. 'Please, do excuse me.'

Then, without another word, he hurried towards his bedchamber, determined to wash and change before attempting to tackle yet more of the unholy mess Perry had left for him. Determined to wash away the stains of the day, blood and all, and to hope that a bowl of water and a fresh shirt might be sufficient to cleanse his thoughts as well. To make him forget about healing wounds and heated words. About idle threats made in anger. About eligible ladies with freckles across their noses and inquisitive sky-blue stares.

After all, he told himself, no good could come of ruminating on any of that. There was only the Dukedom and the duties which lay before him. Duties which had to be performed. Duties which did not give a jot what he thought about them, or how many hours he spent sitting at his desk, burying his head in his hands as he cursed his brother for dying for the thousandth time.

Chapter Two

'I'm sure there's little point in me drying off quite so thoroughly. I'm only going to get soaked again when I walk home.'

Charlotte was aware of how hollow her protest sounded even as she dabbed her face gently with the towel a maid had provided, and stretched her stockinged toes out in front of the fire which roared in the grand fireplace of Lady Elspeth's bedchamber. In truth, the warmth was welcome; the torrent of spring rain which had cut their walk short had drenched her clothing and left her chilled to the bone. Momentarily she glanced towards the window, a heavy dread pooling in her stomach as she saw the large raindrops which continued to fall outside. The walk back to her aunt's cottage in Kelda village had never seemed quite so daunting—which was saying something, considering how reluctant she always was to return home.

'You cannot possibly consider walking in that,' Elspeth replied, following Charlotte's gaze. 'I will send for one of the carriages to take you.'

Charlotte's heart lurched as she met her friend's steely dark eyes. Once Lady Elspeth Scott's mind was set upon something, it was near impossible to change it. 'Oh, no, there's really no need for that,' she replied. 'I'm sure the rain will pass, or at the very least the earlier drizzle will return. You know how much I like to walk. It clears the mind.'

She smiled reassuringly at her friend, her hands clutching the edge of the sofa as she prayed for her acquiescence. She could hardly explain how her turning up at home in one of the Duke of Falstone's carriages would prompt more questions than she'd ever care to answer. How her mother had absolutely no idea about her friendship with the Duke's sister, or her visits to Chatton House, and how she wanted desperately to keep it that way. How content she was for her mother to believe she was spending all of her days at *'that miserable little school'*, as she liked to call it—usually before sighing heavily and giving Charlotte one of those withering looks which reminded her what a disappointment she was.

'A clear mind is surely the last thing any young lady needs,' Elspeth countered, frowning as she lifted her teacup and took a considered sip. 'A busy, thoughtful and learned mind, however…'

Charlotte pulled her thoughts back from the abyss and forced herself to concentrate on her friend's words. Serious, meaningful words, and exactly the sort of words she'd come to expect from Lady Elspeth Scott. The Duke of Falstone's younger sister was a handful of years older than Charlotte, and a great deal more refined and better educated, and Charlotte would be the first to admit that they were the unlikeliest of friends.

Yet good friends was exactly what they had become, their bond first formed and then solidified over their shared interest in the local School of Industry. Established by the parish curate with the patronage of the Dowager Duchess, the school sought to educate the poorest girls from the village and the surrounding area, and with the curate's gentle encouragement on many a Sunday morning at church Charlotte had become a volunteer in that endeavour. Elspeth, meanwhile, was a frequent visitor and overseer of the girls' improvement, although Charlotte had long suspected that limiting their studies to a little basic reading, sewing and darning was a source of frustration to the scholarly Lady Elspeth Scott. Indeed, Charlotte had little doubt that if Elspeth had her way, every girl in Kelda would know the writings of Mary Wollstonecraft by heart.

Charlotte sipped her tea thoughtfully, mirroring her friend. 'Hmm, but you see, I have heard it said that too much learning is bad for the stomach,' she replied, consciously maintaining a grave voice and trying not to smile at her own mischief. 'I have heard, too, that this is especially true for ladies, who are particularly vulnerable to digestive malady.'

Elspeth raised a knowing eyebrow, apparently well aware that she was being teased. 'Then it seems I am condemned to be dyspeptic for ever,' she declared, pushing away the plate of small cakes which sat on the table for dramatic effect. She let out a small laugh, regarding Charlotte with an affectionate grin. 'Who on earth told you such nonsense?'

Charlotte returned her friend's smile with a shrug, unwilling to confess that the source of such *wisdom* had been her mother. It was a firmly held belief which had been repeated to her many times throughout her youth, and one which she held partly responsible for the very basic education her parents had seen fit to arrange for her. The other reason for the limits placed upon her learning was far more obvious: as a young lady born into wealth and gentility, her education had been designed to prepare her for an advantageous marriage, not for becoming a scholar. Her impressionable mind had been filled with the importance of being accomplished, but not clever. Of having elegant penmanship and flair on the pianoforte, but no knowledge of Latin or Greek. Of being pretty and pleasing, but not a great wit. For much of her life she had sailed along thus, her single aim of becoming the wife of someone wealthy and important conscientiously taken to heart. And, for the most part, her mind had been clear and her digestion thoroughly untroubled. At least, until that summer in Lowhaven…

Charlotte shuddered to recall the events of those fateful weeks. How she'd allowed herself to be swept off her feet by the charms of a dashing young gentleman, only to be told by her mother that marrying the younger brother of a baronet was simply not good enough. How, in her confusion, she'd attempted to defy her mother's wishes and had continued to encourage the attentions of Samuel Liddell. How, ultimately, her mother had confronted her with the grim and painful truth about the precarity of the Pearson finances and how, thanks to her father's spiralling gambling debts and poor investments, they were teetering on the edge of ruin. Her mother had spelt out the situation in no uncertain terms: for Charlotte, marrying well was no longer a mere ambition, but an absolute necessity. She had to save her family from disaster. She had to seek the very best match— a man with a title, land, and enough wealth to dig the Pearsons out of the enormous hole they'd found themselves in.

Those revelations had come as a shock. In their aftermath, she'd obeyed her mother, of course, even though that obedience had cost her dearly. Rejecting

Samuel had been painful, and she knew she'd hurt him badly. And going along with her mother's attempts to contrive a match with his older brother, the baronet, had been downright humiliating—not least because the man had so obviously fallen in love with Charlotte's friend, Louisa. A friend she'd lost during the whole sorry episode, too.

The highest price, however, came when her mother had whisked her off to London for a Season. The devil himself had come to charm her then, and because that devil was handsome and the heir to an earldom she'd been only too keen to be charmed. Driven by a potent mix of her mother's ambition and her own desperation to save her family, she'd been truly reckless—provoking the scandalised whispers of society with her flirtatious behaviour as she made her intention to secure Lord Crowgarth as plain as day, before allowing the rake himself to talk her into running away with him and convincing her of his intention to elope. In the end, she'd realised that his intention was only to ruin her and had fled from his clutches, but not before the damage was done.

Damage she'd had to live with and learn from. Damage which had ultimately caused her father's death and which continued to cast its long shadow over her life even now, hundreds of miles away in this remote corner of England. The only saving grace was that the devil could no longer cause her any harm.

He'd left for the Continent shortly after their dalliance with scandal, and had perished at sea in a shipwreck.

'I cannot recall who told me that,' Charlotte said, hauling her mind back from the brink yet again and forcing it to focus on their conversation. 'But doubtless you are right—it is nonsense.'

Elspeth sighed. 'Regrettably, such assertions about the dangers of a female education are commonplace. Indeed, the treatises of medical men are filled with all manner of absurd ideas…'

'The treatises of medical men?' Charlotte repeated. 'Whatever have you been reading now?'

Charlotte had always found that she lacked the necessary concentration and discipline to apply herself to the serious study of any book, yet for some unfathomable reason she always enjoyed their discussions of Lady Elspeth's unusual choices of reading material. Briefly, she contemplated how outraged her mother would be, if she knew her daughter was engaged in discussion about such *unfeminine pursuits*. The thought gave her a small thrill, feeding that rebellious streak she had been nursing ever since she'd arrived with her mother to live at Aunt Maud's house in Kelda. The one which had told her to answer the curate's call and volunteer at the school, and to consider that while those young village girls were gaining the benefit of her expertise in needlework, she might, in turn, improve herself through the experience of teaching.

Her newfound rebellious streak had also helped her to decide that it would be best not to tell her mother about her friendship with Lady Elspeth, or her visits to Chatton House. She'd little doubt that knowing her daughter was in the proximity of a duke would be a temptation too great for Mrs Pearson and her ruthless ambition. And, quite frankly, after Lowhaven and after London, Charlotte had had enough of her mother's machinations to last her several lifetimes. Although, she reminded herself, her mother was not the one who'd climbed into that carriage with Crowgarth, intent on reaching Gretna Green with him and securing the rake as her husband by any means necessary. Her mother might have schemed, but it was not the shock of her mother's reckless behaviour which had caused her father's heart to fail and turned their lives upside down.

Brushing off the darker turn her thoughts had once again taken, Charlotte reminded herself that there was nothing of consequence to tell her mother, in any case. She'd barely ever spoken to the Duke; indeed, on the occasions when they had met, he'd done little more than he had today when he'd greeted her politely but with all the disinterested aloofness of a great nobleman. Although today he had seemed different somehow. A little more dishevelled, a little more out of kilter, his deep brown eyes meeting hers for just a moment longer than they ever had before…

'The English Dance of Death,' Elspeth replied with a wry chuckle.

'Pardon?' Charlotte blinked at her friend, quietly chastising herself for the fanciful thoughts about the Duke and his eyes which had briefly occupied her mind. She ought to know better than to pay attention to such things.

'You asked me what I'm reading. It's called *The English Dance of Death*. It is not a medical book, though, but a satire comprised of illustrations and poetic verse in which a whole host of characters meet their fates in, well, the most outlandish of ways.'

'A satire about death?' Charlotte dared not imagine what her mother would say if she ever caught her reading a book like that. The consequences for her stomach would doubtless be considered grave indeed. 'Where did you get such a book?'

'Our library,' Elspeth answered. 'My oldest brother Perry rather neglected the family collection, but I must say that Teddy has begun to give it a new lease of life. I am for ever finding new reading material upon its shelves. I presume he must have brought the books back with him, when he returned last from Edinburgh.'

'His Grace was in Edinburgh?' Charlotte asked,

the memory of those stern dark eyes regarding her coming to the fore once again.

'Ah—yes, His Grace was,' Elspeth replied, correcting the previous informality with which she'd referred to her brother. 'He lived there, before Perry died and he inherited all of this. I'm not sure if you know this, but the Duke used to be a physician, although we are not supposed to discuss it,' she added in a hushed tone.

Charlotte nodded. Aunt Maud had once made a passing remark about the 'doctor turned duke', although she'd not mentioned that his work had taken him to Edinburgh. Nor, come to think of it, had she seemed to regard her knowledge of his profession as a secret.

'Why should you not discuss it?' Charlotte could not resist asking.

Until now, they had spoken little of the Duke—certainly not like this—and for some unfathomable reason Charlotte found that she wanted to discuss him. Perhaps it was because her curiosity had been piqued by the scene they'd walked in on earlier, with the Duke looking uncommonly ruffled and, dare she think it, unmistakably angry. She recalled the way he'd been pointing, seemingly in her direction, his face red with fury and his eyes blazing, before he'd cleared his throat and dampened the flames beneath the cloak of nobility and politeness…

'Oh, goodness knows,' Elspeth replied, rolling her eyes. 'After all, it is common knowledge that the Duke once had a profession, and what that profession was.'

'I suppose some people find the nature of a physician's work rather…provoking,' Charlotte pondered, trying to choose her words carefully lest she offend her friend. 'The idea that a duke once undertook such duties…'

Elspeth nodded. 'Indeed. All I know is we never speak of it, which is a shame as I am dreadfully curious about it all. Not about the intricacies of his medical work,' she added, wrinkling her nose delicately, 'but about his life in a city which is said to burst with genius. To think that my brother lived, studied and worked there, no doubt alongside the finest minds that Great Britain has to offer! Gentlemen simply do not appreciate their good fortune,' she concluded with a wistful sigh.

'I dare say it is not all good fortune. Indeed, His Grace appeared rather out of sorts today,' Charlotte countered as she finished her tea, finally unable to resist the temptation to acknowledge the scene they'd haplessly wandered into.

'Ah—yes.' Elspeth paused as she also swallowed the contents of her little teacup. 'We walked in at a rather inopportune moment, didn't we? I am sorry about that. I suspect Teddy and my mother had been arguing. Unfortunately, that has become a frequent occurrence at Chatton House and will likely remain so until my brother remedies the situation.'

Charlotte looked quizzically at her friend, not daring to be so bold as to ask about the nature of this *situation*, or indeed what its *remedy* might be.

It was clear, however, that Elspeth wanted to get whatever it was off her chest. 'He must marry,' she explained. 'He must have an heir. He knows it, I know it, and our mother certainly knows it.' She paused for a moment, shaking her head slightly, her deep brown curls moving as her usually bright expression grew uncharacteristically sombre. 'Perry's death was a shock to us all, although, given the way he conducted his life, perhaps it should not have been. But he is dead, and now it is up to Teddy to fulfil the duties of our older brother. Each and every one.'

Charlotte gave a nod of acknowledgement before dropping her gaze and selecting one of the cakes from the plate in front of her. Not that she truly wanted it, she realised, for her stomach felt suddenly unsettled. Doubtless it was the talk of marriage which was to blame. For most of her life, she'd been told that marrying and bearing the heir of a gentleman or, better yet, a nobleman, was her *remedy* too. It had been her purpose, her destiny—the answer to every question about her future she might ever have wished to pose. She supposed that hearing those words fall from

Elspeth's lips had troubled her, reminding her that she no longer knew what the future held for her. Not marriage, as her mother bitterly reminded her almost daily. She'd failed her family so spectacularly that she deserved only spinsterhood now.

'I am sure His Grace will find a lovely bride to be his Duchess in no time at all,' she replied with a cheeriness she did not truly feel.

Then she popped the cake in her mouth, chewed it and swallowed it down—along with uncomfortable thoughts of weddings which would never be, futures which were desperately uncertain and, above all, of furious brown eyes, holding her own.

Chapter Three

Ted leaned against the trunk of the sturdy oak tree and huffed out a frustrated sigh. Neither washing nor changing his clothes had served to make him feel any better and, worse still, his mood was such that he had not even managed to apply himself to addressing anything in that mountain of paperwork currently residing on his desk. He'd sat staring at that damnable pile for all of five minutes before throwing down his quill pen in defeat and seeking refuge in the vast grounds of Chatton House. Refuge from his responsibilities, and refuge from the anger which continued to bubble away in the pit of his stomach. Refuge from the niggling thought that the only reason he was so cross with his mother was because she was right. The future of his family and of the Dukedom rested squarely upon his shoulders and his duties to both were as plain as day. He had to have an heir and, to do that, he had to find a suitable lady to marry.

The problem was, the mere notion of *finding* such a lady set his teeth on edge…

Dragging his hands down his face, Ted allowed himself to groan aloud. In truth, he'd spent little time in the company of society ladies—except his mother and his sister, of course. Before inheriting the Dukedom, his life had been dominated by his work, and his work, by its very nature, had been dominated by his fellow medical men. As an unattached man in Edinburgh, he'd naturally enjoyed the occasional liaison with a woman—usually the sort which required little in the way of conversation, never mind courtship. In recent times, however, most of his interactions with women had been as their physician, where he'd rightly cultivated that aloof, professional manner with which he was most comfortable. He hadn't the first idea how to talk to a society lady—really talk to her—much less how to woo her. Indeed, the idea of doing any wooing made his toes curl…

Lord, what on earth was he going to do?

Certainly, continuing to argue with his mother about the matter was not going to achieve anything. Nor was it in any way helpful of him to make idle threats about marrying the next eligible lady to walk through Chatton's door. The memory of that particular moment made him groan anew, the heat of mortification climbing up his neck and on to his cheeks as the sight of Miss Pearson's face in the doorway crept unbidden into his mind. Her expression had been one of half-horror, half-curiosity, and he grimaced at just how disagreeable he must have seemed. Not exactly the sort of characteristic Miss Pearson would want in a prospective husband, he thought, shaking his head at himself. Not that he had any intention of asking for her hand! His threat, after all, had been an empty one, and entirely, unforgivably ridiculous.

At least the lady hadn't actually heard him utter it…

Or had she?

Discomfited by the thought that the wide-eyed look Miss Pearson had bestowed upon him might be attributable to what she'd overheard as well as what she'd seen, Ted detached himself from the old oak tree and began to wander home. He meandered out of the woodland, quickly reaching the stream which ran through the estate. He gave it a sideways glance as he strode along, briefly recalling the hot summer days of his childhood when he and his friend Ross would seek respite in its babbling waters. How simple life had been. How much liberty he'd had. He supposed he ought to be grateful that at least he'd been able to enjoy the boyhood of a younger sibling, free from the great expectations which came with being an heir. After all, Perry had seldom had the time to play in the stream.

His eyes cast down and his mind preoccupied with

his memories of the past, it was several moments before Ted glanced up and realised that there was someone else walking beside the stream. Someone who was walking slowly towards him, one hand holding her skirts up ever so slightly above her boots as she made her way through long grass, and the other hand clutching her bonnet. Her bright red curls, meanwhile, were entirely unrestrained, springing about wildly as she meandered along. Ted blinked, not once but twice, questioning whether his mind was playing tricks, whether through sheer guilt and embarrassment at his earlier behaviour he'd somehow managed to conjure the image of her.

As she drew close enough to converse and he realised that she was real, he also saw that those skirts she was grappling with were soaking wet, forcing the thin material of her gown to cling to the curves of her body. He swallowed hard as his wayward eyes raked over the shapely outline of her legs, hips and waist, before forcing them to fix firmly on her face. Fate had seen fit to give him the chance to redeem himself, to show Miss Pearson that he was no ogre—not to stand there ogling her. Really, what was the matter with him?

'Good day to you again, Miss Pearson,' he said, tipping his hat in greeting as his traitorous gaze wandered over her sodden gown once again. 'Are you quite well? Can I be of any assistance to you?'

He tried not to be disheartened by the look of sheer alarm which swept across her face as she shook her head vigorously at him. 'I…erm…good day, Your Grace.' She bobbed a curtsey, fiddling awkwardly with the bonnet which remained in her hand and casting her gaze down. 'I am well enough, thank you. I am walking home but my bonnet, you see, it is damp…'

She held up the offending item for his inspection, and Ted noticed that her hand was shaking and her bonnet, rather than being merely damp, looked as sodden as her skirts. Clearly, Miss Pearson found him so odious that she assumed he'd find her unwillingness to put on a soggy bonnet while walking to be an act of the most dreadful immodesty. In fact, if anything had struck him about seeing her without a bonnet it had not been immodesty. It had been how striking those red curls of hers looked against the grey afternoon light. And as for the sight of her in that clinging gown…

'Then you are absolutely correct not to be wearing it, Miss Pearson,' he said, trying to ignore the way his blood had seemed to heat and his heart had started to race. What on earth had got into him? 'But are you sure that you are all right? Please forgive the observation, but you look rather…wet.'

Miss Pearson gave him a distinctly watery smile as finally she allowed those bright blue eyes of hers to meet his. 'It rained quite heavily during my walk with Lady Elspeth earlier,' she confessed, shivering. 'Perhaps my clothes have not dried off quite as well as I'd hoped.'

Ted felt his frown deepen. 'I do apologise, Miss Pearson. Lady Elspeth should have offered to arrange a carriage for you,' he said, quietly surprised by his sister's neglect of her friend. Elspeth usually thought of everything. 'Come back to Chatton and I will arrange a carriage for you now.'

Miss Pearson stepped back from him, that wide-eyed look of horror returning to her face, which Ted felt certain had grown a shade paler. 'No—I mean, no thank you, Your Grace. Lady Elspeth did offer me a carriage but, as I told her, I do prefer to walk. It clears the mind.'

Ted nodded briskly at the truth in her words. After all, wasn't that what he'd been trying to do out there? Clear his mind, and quiet his racing thoughts? He wondered briefly what thoughts Miss Pearson was keen to dispense with, before reminding himself that it was none of his business.

'I quite agree, Miss Pearson, although a clear mind is of little use if it comes at the expense of your health. You will catch a chill, walking outside like that. At the very least, my sister should have offered to lend you some dry clothes.'

He watched as Miss Pearson appeared to redden

inexplicably at his suggestion before casting her eyes downwards once more. 'I am sure Lady Elspeth would have done that if necessary, but you see, my clothes were somewhat drier when I departed than they are now. As was my bonnet, although it was not dry enough to wear, which is why it was in my hand when...'

'When what?' Ted prompted her.

'When I slipped and stumbled into the stream,' she finished, her cheeks glowing scarlet now even as she shivered.

Instinctively, Ted stepped towards her. It made sense now—the wet skirts, the sodden bonnet, the shaking hands. She had indeed had a fright, but he had not been the cause of it. At least, not this time. 'Are you injured, Miss Pearson?'

She gave him another watery smile. 'Only my pride, fortunately. Thankfully, the water is not deep and holding my bonnet meant that it bore the brunt of my fall rather than my hand.' She shook her head at herself, clearly mortified by her confession. 'It was very clumsy of me.'

Ted shook his head in gentle protest. 'The path along here tends to be slippery, especially after rainfall. It is perhaps not advisable that you take this route back to the village in future.' He frowned. 'Indeed, why are you taking this route? It is not the most direct.'

He detected the slightest bristle before she answered. 'As I said, Your Grace, I find walking clears the mind. But I shall heed your advice and avoid this path unless the weather favours it.'

'All right.' He regarded her carefully, noticing that guarded, wary look had returned to her eyes once more. 'I really would like to insist that I escort you back to Chatton and summon a carriage to take you home. However, for reasons I do not truly understand, I suspect you will refuse, won't you?'

She nodded, clearly trying to master control over her chattering teeth. 'I really do prefer to walk, Your Grace.'

'Then I must insist upon walking with you.' Swiftly, he pulled off his woollen greatcoat and draped it over her shoulders. 'And I must insist you wear this.'

'But, Your Grace, you will be cold…'

'I will be fine,' he insisted. 'You, on the other hand, will not if you do not get warm. In fact…' He paused, removing his top hat and placing it upon her head. 'This will help, too.'

'I'm sure I must look ridiculous,' she replied, laughing as the hat slipped over her eyes. 'Also, I'm not sure I can see with this on my head, Your Grace. What if I end up back in the stream?'

'Ah—yes, good point,' Ted replied, retrieving his hat and setting it back upon his own head. 'I have another idea, if you will permit me…'

Miss Pearson nodded, a small smile still lingering on her lips as he reached over tentatively and pulled the collar on his greatcoat up high around her neck. All of a sudden, he became aware of his close proximity to her, of her subtle floral scent wafting towards him, of the warm softness of the skin on her throat as his fingers brushed against it. Of the way his heart had started to race again, his thoughts wandering to those luscious curves he'd spied, the ones which he was alarmed to realise were already indelibly etched on his memory. His eyes met hers, gazing into their blue depths just a moment longer than was proper, and more than long enough to see the laughter in them fade and her wary countenance return. An overwhelming awkwardness came over him and he cleared his throat, stepping back and forcing himself to regard her in that cool, steely physician's way.

'That's better,' he observed, conscious of how clipped his voice now sounded.

'Thank you, Your Grace,' Miss Pearson muttered hoarsely, reminding him at once of the danger to her health of her remaining too much longer outdoors. 'We'd better make haste. My mother will be expecting me.'

He nodded, clearing his throat again. 'Yes, of course. Let us make haste,' he said, repeating her sentiment and wondering why on earth his mouth felt suddenly so dry.

Together they began to walk towards the village, Ted clasping his hands stiffly behind his back and trying not to dwell on the way the cold, damp air had begun to seep into his bones. Kelda was not too far away, he reminded himself. He could bear a little discomfort for the sake of ensuring Miss Pearson did not succumb to illness. He could make polite conversation and be kind and considerate. He might even manage to be charming! Although perhaps that was expecting too much.

At the very least, he decided, he could show his sister's friend that the Duke of Falstone was not a monster. Furthermore, he could prove to himself that he could make conversation with a lady without wishing the ground would open up and swallow him whole.

Chapter Four

Charlotte walked cautiously at the Duke's side, as mindful of the words which might fall from her tongue as she was of not repeating her earlier mishap in the stream. She was conscious of the water which continued to seep up the skirts of her gown and the length of her pelisse, and of the squelching noise emanating from her sodden boots with every step she took. Everything about this was abjectly humiliating and, as usual, she only had herself to blame. If only she hadn't decided to take the longer route back to the village, she would not have fallen, and she would not have crossed paths with the Duke while resembling a drowned rat. If only she wasn't always so desperate to avoid going home...

Still, at least she was no longer quite so cold, thanks to the Duke's big woollen coat. She snuggled into it, breathing in the citrus scent which laced the sturdy fabric—a crisp masculine smell which was not at all unpleasant. Immediately she chastised herself for the thought; she had no business noticing what the Duke smelled like, much less enjoying it. Just as she'd had no business grinning at him like a ninny while she permitted him to turn up the collar on the coat, or allowing her eyes to lock with his as his hands had accidentally brushed against her skin.

Fortunately, she'd remembered herself quickly, reinstating that reserved, serious air she worked so hard to cultivate as she'd insisted that they ought to be on their way. A reserved air which she swore solemnly to maintain all the way home while she made only the politest of enquiries and kept her own counsel. After all, she doubted the aloof Duke of Falstone had any interest in her idle chatter. Indeed, the silence he'd fallen into since they'd set off spoke volumes. His insistence upon accompanying her home was a matter of honour, and nothing more.

Not that she intended to allow him to accompany her all the way home. She could not countenance that. Could not bear to imagine the questions or the discussions such an event would provoke.

'Your Grace, you do not have to walk into the village with me. I will be quite all right once we reach the lane,' Charlotte said, deciding that it was best to break the silence to tackle that particular issue sooner rather than later. 'It is only a short distance from there to my home. Besides, we do not want to provoke any…comments.'

The Duke looked at her quizzically. 'Comments?'

Charlotte nodded. 'From those who might observe us walking together and jump to absurd conclusions,' she replied, giving him a meaningful look.

Charlotte saw the Duke frown briefly, before the penny finally dropped. Clearly, he had not even considered how the two of them being spotted walking together might appear. For a man in his position, this was odd indeed.

'Ah, of course,' he said after a moment. 'I suppose small villages are inclined to gossip just as much as London society.'

'Indeed, although London society tends to move on more quickly. Small villages have far less gossip to feast upon, so when a juicy morsel comes their way, they tend to linger over it.' She glanced at him, and saw those dark eyes of his cast yet another inquisitive glance in her direction. 'You need only listen to the whispers in the pews on a Sunday morning to appreciate that,' she added swiftly, gripped by a momentary panic that he might take her words to mean that she spoke from personal experience of being gossiped about.

An experience which she'd thus far been spared in Kelda, but then, after London, she was determined never to be fodder for the gossips again.

The Duke gave her a wry smile. 'I dare say my family have given everyone plenty to chew over in recent years,' he observed. 'My brother's antics, in particular, were always more than sufficient to fill the column inches of the newspapers. I am sure that the press must miss him a great deal.'

'I did not know the previous Duke, but I am sorry for your loss,' Charlotte said quietly, not knowing quite what else she should say in response to his unexpected candour.

The Duke nodded his appreciation. 'Thank you. Unfortunately, the tale of Peregrine Scott's demise is an infamous one, as I'm sure you are aware. But I am sorry, too,' he added, tucking his hands once more behind his back. 'More sorry than you could know.'

Charlotte inclined her head politely, not wishing to consider just how thoroughly she could relate to the sentiment. Although she had not been close to her father in recent years, she felt the loss of him keenly. Felt the consequences of his sudden death rippling through her life every day. Most of the time, she tried not to examine the feeling too closely. Tried not to think about how much of it was attributable to grief, and how much was guilt.

'Have you spent much time in London, Miss Pearson?'

Charlotte felt her breath catch in her throat at the question. Her time in London had felt both astonishingly short and intolerably long, but this was not a sentiment she could ever share with the Duke. 'I spent part of a Season in London once,' she replied.

'And what did you think of it?'

Charlotte pressed her lips together and, for several long moments, memories of London ran unabated through her mind. The glittering ballrooms, the sumptuous gowns, the full dance cards. The quadrilles and waltzes: the art of performing well, even when the dance was simple because everyone knew what they were there for. The competitive looks exchanged by ladies as they each circled the same prey. The flirtatious glances given by rakes as they each calculated their chances of successful seduction. And, in the midst of it all, a red-haired young lady from the country, getting giddy on punch and ambition. Trying desperately to fulfil her promise to marry well, to dispense with girlish notions of love once and for all. To learn the lessons of her summer in Lowhaven and to follow her head, and never her heart. To do her duty, to save her family from ruin, and to pay attention only to wealth and titles at the expense of all other considerations. At the expense of examining a gentleman's character too closely, or heeding society's warnings about his dishonourable intentions…

What trouble and heartache her wilful ignorance had caused. It had been the worst lesson to learn, but she was, at least, determined to learn it and to carry that lesson with her until the end of her days. She knew now that neither her head nor her heart could be entirely trusted, and understanding that was a form of wisdom in itself. That was the Charlotte she was determined to be now—wise, sensible and focused on atoning for her past mistakes by accomplishing something worthwhile in her future. It was that determination which had ultimately drawn her towards volunteering at the local school. She might no longer be destined to be a wife and a mother, but she could be a good teacher to those little girls who benefited from her instruction. And she, in turn, could benefit from the reprieve that the school gave her, from how it sustained her spirit in the face of the constant reminders of her failings which she had to endure at home.

'In truth, I found London society a little overwhelming,' Charlotte replied, forcing her thoughts into order as she finally dared to speak. 'Before I went, I thought I would love it but…well, perhaps I am unsuited to life in large towns and cities.'

'I dare say it depends upon the town,' the Duke observed. 'I am no enthusiast for London or its society either, but there are other cities I like very much. Well—one, really. Somewhere I used to call home, not so very long ago.'

'Edinburgh?' Charlotte guessed, content to move the conversation away from herself and her own opinions. 'I believe you worked as a physician there, once?'

A broad smile broke across his face and Charlotte could not help but notice how it brightened his dark features, before quickly ordering herself to stop paying attention to such details.

'Lady Elspeth told you, no doubt. I must wonder what else my younger sister has been telling you.'

Although she could tell that he was teasing her, inexplicably Charlotte felt her face begin to redden. 'Lady Elspeth only mentioned it in passing. We were speaking about some books in your library, and she said that she believed you brought them back with you from Edinburgh.'

The Duke raised his eyebrows. 'And which books were these?'

Charlotte felt certain her blush had turned to a deep, unbecoming shade of scarlet. 'Oh, I cannot recall,' she replied, feigning nonchalance and praying the Duke wouldn't enquire further. The very last thing she wished to do was cause trouble for her friend.

The Duke smiled at her again. 'Yes, you can,' he said, clearly very amused by her sudden memory loss. 'But I think you are worried that I will think them entirely unsuitable reading material for a young lady.' He chuckled wryly, shaking his head. 'Doubtless they are, since they belong to me and my sister has shown an interest in them, but do not fret—I have never disapproved of Elspeth's ways.'

'Really?' The question fell from Charlotte's lips before she could prevent it.

'Really. My sister has a brilliant mind. If she were a man...' The Duke shook his head again, sighing, before regarding Charlotte once more. 'Perhaps keep this information about these books away from my mother's ears, though.'

'You have my word, Your Grace,' Charlotte replied, giving him an obliging nod.

They were almost at the lane now. Charlotte felt the knot tighten in her stomach as she stared towards the rough track which meandered down a gentle incline towards the village. That familiar cold dread ran through her veins at the prospect of the long evening ahead, of the sour company, of the constant criticism. Of the inevitable need to invent an explanation for why her skirts, boots and bonnet were so wet, and of the predictable scolding that would follow. If she was particularly unlucky, she would walk through the door to discover that she'd already been charged with some new crime, or found guilty of some fresh sin, *in absentia*. She huddled deeper into the Duke's coat, relishing the last few moments of its warmth and foolishly entertaining the wish that the robust fabric could somehow protect her from what lay ahead.

Clearly, the Duke had also noted that they must

part ways soon. 'Forgive me, Miss Pearson. I realise I have not asked you about your family. Elspeth tells me you are from Cumberland, but that you came here with your mother to live with your aunt. Is that correct?'

'It is, Your Grace. We came to Kelda after my father's death. He died suddenly, about a year ago.' Charlotte swallowed hard, wishing they could speak about anything else. Even offering a simple answer about how she came to be in Kelda felt like dangerous territory.

The Duke inclined his head briskly, but Charlotte could see the sympathy in his eyes. 'My condolences to you and your mother,' he said. 'It cannot be easy for you, having your lives uprooted and planted down elsewhere. Too often our society is not kind to widows,' he added, a remark which suggested he'd grasped something of the nature of their circumstances, and just how difficult they must be.

Of course, she reminded herself, whatever the Duke made of her situation, he could surely not imagine the half of it. Her father's debts had been settled, but only just. In truth, they'd lost everything, and only her mother's marriage settlement, which had mercifully remained in trust and untouched by her father's folly, had shielded them from complete destitution.

The Duke regarded her carefully, his brow furrowing. 'I do hope you have other family that you can call upon for assistance,' he continued. 'An uncle, or a brother, or…'

She nodded. 'My mother is from a Northumbrian family. She grew up here, on her family's estate. Her brother—my uncle—made the arrangements for us to come to Kelda to live with my aunt. He is very good to us.' She smiled broadly, hoping that would satisfy the Duke's enquiries. Hoping that she would not be drawn into discussing the fact that Uncle Matthew, for all his benevolence, resided on his estate on the other side of Northumberland, at a safe distance from his sisters.

Charlotte stepped on to the lane, glancing warily left and right to ensure no one was around. Swiftly, she removed the Duke's coat from around her shoulders and handed it to him. 'Thank you for accompanying me, Your Grace,' she said with the quickest of curtseys. 'And for giving me your coat. I ought to be on my way.'

The Duke stood stiffly, as though the moment of their parting, now it had arrived, had taken him quite by surprise. 'Of course. It was my pleasure.'

Charlotte inclined her head, hoping she appeared graceful even though her hair doubtless resembled a fiery bush by now, and started for home.

That was not so bad. You did not make too much of a fool of yourself in front of the Duke. Well, apart from the fact that he saw you looking like a drowned rat after falling in the stream...

'Miss Pearson?'

Charlotte startled as the Duke called out to her. She spun around to see him, still standing stiffly at the edge of the lane. 'Yes, Your Grace?'

He shuffled awkwardly for a moment, before tucking his hands tightly behind his back. 'It occurs to me that we have been remiss in not inviting you, your mother and aunt to dine with us at Chatton. I should like to rectify that this Friday, if you and your family will oblige?'

The knot which already resided permanently in Charlotte's stomach seemed to double in size. Her mind raced as her heart began to pound and her hands gripped her soggy bonnet so tightly she thought it would break beneath her fingers. These past months in Kelda, Charlotte had lived two lives: one inside her aunt's cottage, and one outside of it. One life with two reclusive and ageing ladies who barely left the house and who were avowedly disinterested in anything, unless it gave them cause for complaint, and another life within the community—going to church, working at the school, and visiting Chatton House. Two distinct and separate worlds which now, thanks to the Duke's invitation, threatened to collide in the most spectacular and catastrophic fashion. An invitation to dine at Chatton could not go unexplained;

her mother would demand to know everything and, upon learning the truth, she would understand just how thoroughly she had been deceived.

That was not even the worst of it, either, since Mrs Pearson was not a lady who allowed opportunity to pass her by. When she had finished admonishing her daughter for her deception, she would turn her attention to milking her newfound, unexpected connection with the Duke of Falstone for all it was worth. And it was worth a great deal, Charlotte knew, since the Duke was unwed and in need of a bride.

And you know exactly who she will push under his nose as the perfect candidate...

If she was not still standing a few feet away from the Duke, Charlotte would have groaned aloud. She could not countenance bringing her mother to Chatton House under any circumstances. And yet, in that moment, she could not find the words to refuse his invitation.

After a long moment Charlotte nodded, painting on a smile. 'That would be lovely, Your Grace. I'm sure my mother and aunt will be delighted.'

Without another word she hurried away, hoping the Duke had not seen through her smile and glimpsed the horror it had masked. Horror at the thought of just how delighted her mother was going to be. Horror at the schemes this invitation would provoke.

And horror at the clawing feeling that the life she'd constructed for herself outside of her aunt's cottage would be pulled apart at the seams.

Chapter Five

Ted dismissed his valet with mumbled thanks, staring at himself sternly in the mirror as his servant left the bedchamber and pulled the door closed behind him. Emitting a deep sigh and glad to be left alone for a few moments, he inspected his collar and cravat, trying to ignore the unsettled feeling in his stomach which overcame him every time his mind turned to the evening ahead. Formal dinners, balls and soirées had always had a tendency to make him feel on edge, and that feeling had only intensified since he had become the Duke. He disliked the attention: the sense of many eyes scrutinising him and determining his worth, especially now that he had a title and inherited wealth to his name. It was not that he did not like to be sociable, but as Dr Edward Scott he'd been most at home in a lowly city tavern, ruminating on medical matters with colleagues over a bottle of port. A simple pleasure, and yet another aspect of his life which he'd had to leave behind.

So why, given his aversion to such events, had he invited Miss Pearson and her family to dine at Chatton?

That question had circled around his mind ever since the invitation had fallen from his tongue, unrehearsed and unplanned, on that cold, damp afternoon earlier in the week. He supposed that extending such an invitation had been a matter of politeness; Miss Pearson had become a firm favourite of his sister, after all. Thus far that had been his explanation, to himself and to his mother and sister. He'd told them both about the dinner as casually as he could, describing how he'd crossed paths with Miss Pearson as she'd left Chatton and insisting that he'd extended the invitation only because he thought Elspeth would appreciate it. Both ladies had regarded him in astonishment, with the Dowager Duchess immediately making connections that were simply not there.

'This invitation doesn't have anything to do with your threat, does it, Ted?' she'd asked him.

'What threat?' Elspeth had asked before he could say a word.

'Earlier, Ted threatened to marry the next eligible lady who walked through our door,' his mother had explained, amusement shimmering in her pale blue eyes as she recounted the story. 'Moments later, who should walk in but you and your friend, Charlotte Pearson! The look on Ted's face was…'

'Yes, thank you, Mother…' he'd interjected, his face growing hot as fresh embarrassment clawed at him.

'You'd better not marry her!' Elspeth had said, rounding on him. 'I like Miss Pearson and value her company a great deal. I like to think we are kindred spirits—unmarried kindred spirits!'

'I've no intention of marrying your friend,' Ted had assured her, holding his hands up in surrender. 'So, if Mother would kindly stop making mischief, we've a dinner to plan.'

'All right,' Elspeth had relented. 'Although, I do hope you have not vexed Miss Pearson, by inviting her family to dine with us.'

'Why do you say that?' he'd asked, his heart beginning to thrum at the prospect that he might have inadvertently caused Miss Pearson some distress. Had she seemed perturbed by his invitation? It was hard to say. She had accepted it then fled so quickly…

Elspeth had shaken her head, her dark brown curls moving gently as she considered her answer. 'It's just that it's odd, isn't it? Miss Pearson and I are friends, and yet I've never met her family. Whenever I have mentioned inviting her mother and aunt here for tea, she has seemed reluctant. She says their health is poor, which is why they do not accompany her to church or the curate's school, either.'

'Miss Pearson said nothing about their health preventing them from dining at Chatton,' Ted had observed, frowning.

'Which is another reason why I am concerned that you will have vexed her,' Elspeth had concluded. 'You're a duke, Teddy. I've little doubt that Miss Pearson would have found declining your invitation impossible, no matter the circumstances.'

Ted turned away from the mirror, still replaying that conversation in his mind. He'd never realised she was unaccompanied at church. He'd spied her once or twice, sitting beside others from the village whom he'd presumed to be her family. For some reason, the thought of her being so often alone troubled him, just as it troubled him to think that his invitation to dine had been unwanted.

You'd better hope that Elspeth's concerns are unfounded, he thought to himself, opening the door to his bedchamber and walking out into the hall. *Because it would be just like you, Edward Scott, to hold a dinner at Chatton for a young lady who does not even want to attend.*

'They're here, Ted! Make haste!'

The sound of his mother imploring him startled Ted from his spiralling thoughts and he hurried downstairs to greet his guests. Slightly breathless, he tried to compose himself as he arrived just in time to see three ladies being ushered inside and out of the pouring rain, ably assisted by a footman and Ted's butler. Two older women led the way, almost identical in every detail from the sober manner of their dress to the sharp, birdlike features of their faces. Ted's breath caught in his throat as they both approached him at a pace, regarding him with matching keen blue stares like a pair of crows inspecting their supper. Near-identical smiles broke out across their lined faces and they both curtseyed more deeply than seemed possible, especially for the lady who walked with the aid of a cane.

'Your Grace,' the lady clutching the cane simpered. 'It is a great honour. Thank you for sending your carriage for us. It is indeed a terrible night.'

Ted held out his hand to her, partly because politeness required it and partly because he was concerned she might not manage to rise from the position she'd got herself into, so close to the floor. A thin, gloved hand gripped his as the lady pulled herself upright. A few paces behind her hovered Miss Pearson, painting quite the contrasting picture from her older relations in a deep green gown, her red curls as striking as ever. Ted watched as she stepped forward hesitantly, a distinctly nervous expression flickering across her face as she addressed him.

'Good evening, Your Grace,' she began, with a

swift and far less dramatic curtsey. 'Allow me to introduce my mother, Mrs Mary Pearson,' she said quietly, gesturing first to the lady with the cane. 'And also my aunt, Miss Maud Fenwick.'

Ted formally greeted them all, before introducing his mother and sister in a similar fashion. Once the introductions were complete, the Dowager Duchess embraced her role as hostess and beckoned the party towards the dining room, where Chatton's impeccably dressed table awaited them. As they began to walk along the hall, he found himself arriving at Miss Pearson's side, as though he had unthinkingly gravitated towards her. She continued to look as anxious as he felt, chewing on her lip, her bright blue eyes wide and alert as though she was anticipating something. His heart sank; it seemed that his sister's concerns had not been without foundation, after all. For whatever reason, it was clear that Miss Pearson's presence here tonight with her relatives was some sort of trial for her.

Gripped by the need to somehow reassure her, Ted reached out and offered her his arm. He watched as Miss Pearson seemed to hesitate, looking at the offending limb as though it might scald her. But then, to his surprise, she accepted, threading her arm through his and holding on rather tightly. Her sudden proximity made him grow inexplicably warm, and he tried his best not to notice how her hip brushed against him as they walked, or the way that her floral perfume wafted tantalisingly towards him with every step. Worse still, his damnable mind immediately set about conjuring that image of her, standing on the path with that soaking wet gown clinging to every perfect curve. An image, he had to admit, which had sprung into his thoughts more than once in recent days.

'It has been a while since we have entertained at Chatton,' he said, trying hard to focus on being a considerate host and to disregard his wholly inappropriate physical response to her. 'I am sure we will have a lovely evening.'

Miss Pearson nodded, offering him a smile which definitely did not reach her eyes. 'Yes, indeed—a lovely evening,' she repeated, as though trying to convince herself.

The Dowager Duchess had made all the arrangements for the dinner, including the seating plan. Upon entering the dining room and reviewing the place cards, he saw that he'd been placed beside Miss Pearson. Clearly, his mother was yet again having her amusement at his expense. However, for once he felt glad of it. He was responsible for inviting Miss Pearson and her family to his home, and if the occasion had given the lady cause to fret, then it was his responsibility to assuage her fears. He could only do that, he knew, if he remained close by her side.

The soup course passed without incident, with

polite enquiries exchanged around the table as everyone settled into their meal and each other's company. He noticed how his mother made a particular point of engaging with Mrs Pearson, asking her how she'd settled into life in Kelda, and how she found it compared to the other places she'd lived, and before long the conversation around the table had broadened to discussing the merits of rural Northumbrian life. He noticed, too, how Miss Pearson did not contribute to the conversation, preferring to sit quietly and occupy herself with her food. Several times she looked up but seemed to steadfastly avoid looking at anyone in particular, including him. By the time the fruits and sweetmeats were served, Ted could have sworn that Miss Pearson had uttered only a handful of words, and most of those in response to his sister, who had clearly also noted her friend's odd vow of silence. Across the table he saw Elspeth's brow wrinkle slightly as she regarded her friend with confusion.

Come on, Ted. You invited Miss Pearson here tonight. Talk to her just like you did when it was just the two of you, walking alongside the stream.

As his mother, Mrs Pearson and Miss Fenwick continued to chatter away, Ted cleared his throat and leaned towards Miss Pearson, praying that some witty and inspired words might fall from his lips. Something which might capture her interest and perhaps even make her smile. Hers was a lovely smile, after all...

Where on earth did that thought come from?

'Tell me, Miss Pearson, are our village girls making good progress in their studies?' he asked. 'My sister tells me that you are a diligent and reliable tutor.'

A safe and sensible question, surely, and whilst it had lacked the humour necessary to raise a smile, he was pleased to see Miss Pearson incline her head graciously at the compliment.

'They are all doing very well, thank you, Your Grace,' Miss Pearson replied, before returning to sip her wine. 'I do enjoy my work at the school—very much.'

'And what do you teach them, Miss Pearson?' he prompted when it was clear that she was not going to elaborate further.

Around him the room seemed to grow quieter, the conversation between the older women becoming muted as their attention was drawn to the exchange between the Duke and the young lady. He could not fail to notice that Mrs Pearson, in particular, seemed to be hanging on to every word.

'Sewing, embroidery and drawing, mainly,' she replied, her expression brightening now. 'And sometimes I help them with their letters...'

'Their letters? Oh, Charlotte, you exaggerate, surely!' Mrs Pearson interjected, shaking her head.

'To hear you talk, anyone would think you fancy yourself a bluestocking, or a governess in training.'

'The girls must learn to read, Mama. The curate teaches them to read passages from the Bible...'

'Exactly, Charlotte—the curate teaches them. Not you,' Mrs Pearson replied.

Beside him, Ted felt Miss Pearson shrink beneath her mother's severe gaze. The whole exchange took him completely aback. To hear a mother undermine her daughter like that, and in company...it was unfathomably unkind. He felt an unexpected heat rise in his gut as anger and indignation coursed through his veins, and it took every ounce of self-control he possessed to appear outwardly calm.

'I am certain Miss Pearson makes a valuable contribution at the school,' he interjected.

The look he gave Mrs Pearson must have been a stern one as the woman flinched, apparently recovering her senses and remembering where she was. 'Oh, well, of course, Your Grace,' she replied in a freshly honeyed voice. 'That little school has given Charlotte something to occupy herself with, at least. It is important for a young lady to busy herself with such Christian pursuits—until marriage, of course.'

Such a predictable remark.

'I dare say good works do not have to cease upon matrimony, Mrs Pearson,' he replied drily, turning back to Miss Pearson before her mother could answer.

'I am sure that our curate appreciates all that you do, Miss Pearson,' he said, giving her a broad smile.

'He does indeed,' the Dowager Duchess chimed in. 'As do we, as patrons of the school. The education of girls is too often neglected. You are teaching them valuable skills and, from what Elspeth tells me, you are particularly talented at needlework.'

The blush which crept on to Miss Pearson's face was startlingly becoming. 'Oh, Lady Elspeth is too kind,' she said with a gracious nod towards her friend. 'I suppose it is something I have always rather enjoyed.'

'Charlotte is accomplished in all domestic skills.' Again, her mother attempted to command the conversation. 'The gentleman who asks for her hand in marriage will be very fortunate indeed, for she shall make him an excellent wife.' A grin spread across her pale, thin face as she added, 'That gentleman, whoever he may be, had better make haste if he wishes to secure her. When we were in London last, her beauty was oft remarked upon.'

Ted wasn't sure what he found more excruciating to witness: the bold, unwavering stare Mrs Pearson cast in his direction as she laboured over those final, calculated words, or the fact that Miss Pearson's blush-stained cheeks now glowed scarlet. Truly, Mrs Pearson's behaviour was astounding—publicly belittling her daughter one moment, then praising her and unsubtly trying to marry her off the next! Little wonder that Miss Pearson had seemed so ill at ease this evening. Little wonder that she'd mostly held her tongue throughout the meal. Guilt flooded through him then: guilt for inviting her here tonight with her mother, and guilt for starting a conversation with her which had inadvertently placed her under scrutiny.

'I am sure Miss Pearson will excel, no matter what path she chooses to take in life,' he said, forcing a smile in her mother's direction and hoping that his answer would serve to end the conversation. He could not bear to see Miss Pearson suffer any further humiliation on account of her mother's blatant machinations. He thought the ambitious mamas of the *ton* were bad enough, but at least they tended to approach the task of securing a husband for their daughters with some delicacy.

Ted nodded at the Dowager Duchess before rising from the table, prompting her to invite their guests to the drawing room for tea and card games. As they walked away from the dining table, Ted reached out, touching Miss Pearson gently on the arm. His heart lurched for her as she startled, and he sensed every muscle in her body grow tense.

'Please forgive me, for all of this,' he whispered hurriedly, lest anyone overhear him. 'It will be over soon, I promise.'

She glanced up at him briefly, but long enough

for him to see the maelstrom of emotions gathering like storm clouds in her eyes. 'It is never over for me, Your Grace,' she said.

He frowned. 'What do you mean, Miss Pearson? Is there something I can…'

'Your Grace?'

The unwelcome intrusion of his butler's voice forced Ted to pause and, before he could say another word to her, Miss Pearson hurried away.

'Yes, Gregson?' Ted replied, suppressing a sigh.

'Forgive me, Your Grace, but you have received a note from Mr Deane.'

'From Ross?' Ted raised his eyebrows.

Gregson nodded as he handed Ted the note. 'I thought best to give it to you as soon as dinner was over, Your Grace, in case it is urgent.'

Gregson had worked for his family for years, and knew all about the close bond which existed between Ted and his childhood friend, Ross Deane. He was also well aware that in addition to their long history, both men had found their vocations in medicine and that a note from Kelda's surgeon apothecary might well contain matters which could not wait until morning.

Ted's eyes scanned the note rapidly. It was good news, thankfully. Ross reported that he had visited the boy with the injured leg again this evening and that the wound was healing well. He thanked Ted for his assistance and signed off by inviting him for luncheon in a few days' time. Inwardly, Ted breathed a sigh of relief. At least all was well where Ross and their young patient was concerned. How he wished the same could be said for Miss Pearson. After the events of this evening, he suspected that where that young lady was concerned, all was as far from being well as it was possible to be.

Ted thanked his butler and made his way directly to the drawing room, still clutching the note in his hand. He felt terrible; everything Miss Pearson had had to endure this evening was down to him and his damnable invite. He had to make amends to her somehow. Perhaps if they could finish their conversation, then he might understand how he could assist her.

She's not a patient, Ted. You cannot mend everyone—especially when you're no longer a physician...

'No, I'm a damned duke,' he muttered under his breath. 'There must be something I can do.'

He flung open the door to Chatton's large, opulent drawing room to see the group gathered on the sofas settling down to tea and cards in a blaze of candlelight. Four expectant female faces looked up at him: his mother, his sister, Mrs Pearson and Miss Fenwick. Four faces—not five. He glanced about him, furrowing his brow in confusion. Miss Pearson, he realised, was nowhere to be seen.

Chapter Six

Charlotte sank down on the floor of the greenhouse and hugged her knees under her chin as she promised herself she would not cry. At least she was warm and dry in there, hidden away in the darkness amongst Chatton's collection of exotic plants. The evening air she'd insisted she needed to take in the garden had been bitingly cold, and although the earlier rain had ceased in favour of a clear, moonlit night, she'd found that she could not endure more than a few moments outside in her fine but flimsy evening attire. And so she had wandered the short distance across Chatton's gardens to the greenhouse and slipped inside, seeking respite from the weather, and from her racing thoughts. From the stifling air of the drawing room. From her mother.

From her complete and utter humiliation and despair.

Tonight, the double life she'd carefully curated

for herself had come to an end. She'd known that it would, days ago when she'd accepted the Duke's invitation. When her errant mouth had said *yes* even as her head and her heart had screamed *no*. Why had she not had the presence of mind to refuse? She could have told him that her mother and aunt were too unwell to attend a dinner. That excuse had placated Lady Elspeth often enough, and it wasn't without basis—these past months, neither her mother nor her aunt had managed to attend so much as a church service, and both received near-constant care and a ready supply of tinctures from the local surgeon apothecary, Mr Deane. The fact that Charlotte suspected they both exaggerated their ailments and were in fierce competition with each other over worsening symptoms was neither here nor there. To the outside world, they were ailing ladies. She could have excused them all easily enough on this basis, and yet...

For some reason, she'd been unable to say the words. She'd been unable to refuse the Duke, and she'd been bearing the consequences of her failure ever since. She'd had to endure her mother's admonishment when she discovered that her daughter had been concealing a friendship with the Duke's sister. Worse still, she'd had to witness the moment when ambition inevitably overtook anger as Mrs Pearson set aside her daughter's deception and focused only on what this unexpected connection to an unwed duke could mean. Days of scheming and speculating had followed, so much so that by the time her mother had climbed into the Duke's carriage and they'd set off for Chatton, Mrs Pearson had only one thing on her mind—making Charlotte the Duke's bride.

Yet now, as Charlotte sat on that hard stone floor, she knew that wasn't even the worst of it. Because, as it turned out, being forced into the only passable evening gown she still owned and paraded in front of the Duke of Falstone as a potential wife was not half as humiliating as being cut down to size in front of him concerning her achievements at the school. Tonight at dinner, her mother had managed to both make her marriage machinations excruciatingly obvious and thoroughly belittle and diminish her daughter into the bargain.

At the memory of it, Charlotte balled her fists, a hot, indignant rage growing within her chest at the unfairness of it all. Was it not enough that she had to live with the shame of her past mistakes, with their consequences, and with her mother's daily reminders of how badly she'd failed? Did the life she'd managed to carve out for herself, the little bit of purpose and meaning she'd managed to find in her work at the school, really have to be trampled all over?

Was nothing beyond the reach of her mother's bitterness and resentment?

The only saving grace was that the Duke had

looked utterly unimpressed by her mother's behaviour. Indeed, though she knew him only a little, Charlotte believed that her mother could not have made her daughter sound less appealing to a man like the Duke of Falstone if she'd tried. He was an educated, thoughtful man who spoke about his own sister's intellectual achievements with admiration. He was not a man to be impressed by the prospect of being saddled with an empty-headed ninny who was not even capable of helping girls learn to read.

Not that Charlotte wanted him to be impressed by her! Of course not. But her heart had warmed to hear the way he'd seemed to come to her defence, however subtly, by acknowledging her contribution to the school. And then there was the way he'd offered her his arm before dinner—a gentlemanly gesture which had left her fingers tingling with awareness ever since...

No, Charlotte—stop it. Titled gentlemen are not for the likes of you. They never were. Remember the trouble you caused in London. And before that in Lowhaven...

As if she could forget. As if her mother ever allowed her to forget. Being forced to relive those sins and shortcomings each and every day was her penance, a bitter pill she was made to swallow as often as her mother indulged in her tinctures. Mrs Pearson never wasted an opportunity to remind her daughter of the damage she'd done, of the disappointment she was. Of how her behaviour and actions had turned their lives upside down. Of how, ultimately, she had caused them to lose her father.

And that, Charlotte knew as she squeezed her eyes shut, was the worst of it all. The guilt she felt over her father's death was palpable, threatening to crush her spirit in a way that no amount of bitterness, resentment or humiliation at her mother's hands ever could. Just as bad as that was the anger she felt towards him—anger that his gambling and his debts had placed them in such jeopardy, and that the burden of trying to rescue the family's fortunes had been hers to shoulder alone. Anger that his terrible choices had set her up to fail so dreadfully. Anger that he was dead and she was stuck here with her mother, trying to make the best of the bleakest prospects...

Despite her best efforts to suppress it, she felt a solitary tear slip down her cheek. It might be no more than she deserved but still, life in that stifling little cottage, being constantly picked apart, was growing increasingly intolerable. Tonight's events had left her in no doubt that she needed to escape from it somehow, because if she did not, what remained of her spirit would eventually be ground into nothing.

The sound of the greenhouse door opening startled Charlotte from her thoughts. She shivered as the cold air outside intruded briefly, remaining rooted to the floor as she heard the door close and the careful approach of footsteps. Hiding in the shadows behind pots of exotic foliage, she could not see who had just walked in. Perhaps whoever it was would not realise she was here. Perhaps they were not even looking for her at all—perhaps it was one of the Duke's gardeners, come to check the temperature or attend to the plants.

'Miss Pearson?'

The deep timbre of the Duke's voice broke the silence, putting paid to fanciful ideas about gardeners or about remaining hidden. Clearly, she'd absented herself from the drawing room for so long that her host had grown concerned and gone looking for her. She'd been so preoccupied with trying to calm her racing thoughts and regain control of her emotions that she had not even considered how excusing herself and wandering off to the greenhouse would look. How it would cause consternation when she was nowhere to be seen outside. How it would doubtless invite yet more scorn from her mother when they returned home tonight.

Charlotte dragged her hands down her face, praying she did not look as wretched as she felt. 'I'm here, Your Grace,' she called out as she got to her feet and began to walk with resignation towards the greenhouse door.

If she hadn't been so busy trying to calm herself

and appear cheerful, Charlotte would have heard the Duke's footsteps quicken towards her—an observation which, had it been made, might have prevented her from colliding with him as she rounded a corner and finally left her shield of greenery behind. As it was, Charlotte found herself walking straight into the solid wall of the Duke's chest, before the shock of it caused her to stumble backwards.

'Miss Pearson!'

She heard him call her name again as he caught hold of her, his strong arms adeptly circling her waist and preventing her from falling. Holding her, however unintentionally, close to him. For several quiet moments Charlotte was aware of her own rapid breath, of the furious beating of her heart, and the scattering of her wits as she stood pressed against the Duke in the near-darkness, apparently unable to take the necessary step back for the sake of propriety. She dared not look up at him, dared not meet his eye, and yet she could feel the heat of his gaze on her. Could feel that his breath, and his heartbeat, were both frantic, too.

At length, it was the Duke who broke the spell, clearing his throat as he let her go and stepped away. In the silvery light she watched as he rummaged around on a nearby table, feeling too dazed to properly ponder what he was doing until, after a moment, she saw him light an oil lamp.

'That's better,' he declared, positioning it carefully on the table before stepping back towards her. 'Miss Pearson, are you all right?' he asked, regarding her closely. 'Lady Elspeth said you'd stepped outside for some air, but we were concerned when you did not return promptly. What are you doing in the greenhouse?'

'It is warm in here, Your Grace, and the night so cold and blustery and the drawing room so stifling that I…'

Charlotte bit down hard on her lip, stemming the chaotic flow of her words and reminding herself of the need to consider her explanation carefully. Of the need to control that tumult of emotions currently bubbling away inside of her and to say no more than needed to be said.

'I did need some air, Your Grace,' she began again, 'but lingering outside in an evening gown is hardly advisable. The air in the greenhouse is much more agreeable. I am sorry if I have alarmed anyone. I did not realise I had been away for quite so long.'

The Duke nodded. 'Would you like me to escort you back inside? Or do you need a few moments longer?' he asked. It was clear to Charlotte from the tentative note in his voice that he suspected there was more to her hiding in his greenhouse than the simple need for some air.

She attempted a smile. 'Perhaps a few more moments in here,' she replied. 'Since the air is so agreeable.'

'Hmm.' A smile played at the corners of his mouth in response to the repeated sentiment. 'I am sure the plants would agree with you, Miss Pearson, if they could speak. Like you, they favour warmth over our chilly Northumbrian climate. In the coldest months, a fire is lit in the bothy at the rear of the greenhouse and the heat sent up through the floor.' He regarded her carefully. 'Although I presume from your earlier remark that the drawing room felt too warm for you. Unless that is not what you meant, when you said it was stifling.'

'I...um...' Charlotte's words dried up completely as she met the Duke's eye and watched him search her gaze.

'Only, you seemed upset after dinner,' he continued. 'I cannot help but think that I am partly to blame for your distress.'

'You, Your Grace?' She stepped towards him. 'Why would you think that?'

'I invited you and your family to dine at Chatton, and I began the conversation at the dining table which proved to be...discomfiting for you.' She sensed he was choosing his words carefully. He furrowed his brow again, deeper this time. 'What did you mean earlier, when you said to me that it is never over for you? What is never over, Miss Pearson?'

Charlotte felt the heat rise in her cheeks at hearing those ill-chosen words repeated back to her. 'Oh, please, Your Grace—forget it. I was a little overwhelmed, that is all. Really, you have nothing to reproach yourself for. It has been a lovely evening.' She feigned a laugh, trying not to wince at how hollow it sounded.

For a long moment, the Duke regarded her with a pained expression, as though unsure how best to proceed. Then, to her surprise, he emitted a lengthy sigh before dragging his hands down his face. 'May I speak plainly, Miss Pearson?' he asked.

'Of course, Your Grace.'

'It is clear to me that there are aspects of this evening's dinner which have vexed you greatly. I do not wish to interfere, and indeed, I do not pretend to have any real understanding of your circumstances beyond what you have told me, and what I have observed for myself. However, I cannot in all good conscience allow you to go home tonight without offering some assistance to you. If there is anything I can do for you, Miss Pearson, if I can be of service at all, you need only ask.'

His words were so earnestly spoken and kindly meant that it took every ounce of determination she had to prevent herself from crumpling in front of him.

'I'm afraid there is nothing you or anyone else can do for me, Your Grace,' she began, fighting to keep her tone matter-of-fact. 'I am resigned to my situation now…'

'So resigned that you have been hiding by yourself in my greenhouse tonight,' he interjected.

'Resignation does not mean happiness, does it?' Charlotte retorted, an indignant heat rising in her chest. 'Resignation means knowing that there is no way out and accepting a situation for what it is. It means understanding that sometimes life deals us a tricky hand. But if those cards are all we have, then we must play them.'

Something in her words appeared to strike a chord with him and he nodded slowly, those dark eyes of his regarding her intently. 'I suppose we all hold cards we'd prefer never to have been dealt,' he mused, a frown creasing his brow. 'You are unhappy with your situation, then? Only, you just said…'

Charlotte huffed out a sigh, wishing then that she'd said nothing of happiness. 'I am an unmarried woman, Your Grace. My natural place is with my mother and my aunt, until the end of their days or until the end of mine. My feelings on the matter are irrelevant.'

'But surely your feelings are relevant,' the Duke protested. 'Is that what you want, Miss Pearson—to remain with your mother and aunt here, in Kelda?'

Charlotte shook her head vigorously. 'It does not matter what I want.'

'Of course it matters.' The Duke stepped closer to her. 'What do you want?'

'I want to escape!'

No sooner had the words fallen from her lips than Charlotte wished she could take them back. Wished she could tick back the minutes so that this conversation might never have happened. But it was too late—the words were spoken now. She'd given voice to them, breathed life into them. She felt them hang heavily in the air between her and the Duke as his eyes searched hers and found that they were the truth.

'Forgive me, Your Grace,' she began, shaking her head at herself. 'My mother can be difficult to live with at times, and I think my spirits are just a little low tonight, so I…'

'Marry me.'

The Duke said the words so quickly that for a moment Charlotte believed she must have misheard him. Indeed, what other possible explanation could there be? There was no conceivable way that Edward Scott, the Duke of Falstone, had just asked for her hand in marriage…

'Marry me, Miss Pearson,' he said again, taking a tentative step towards her.

Charlotte felt her mouth fall open. This time there

was no denying what she had heard. 'But…why?' she stuttered.

The Duke shrugged. 'You need to escape, and I need a wife,' he replied simply, as though it was the most logical idea in the world.

'But…but you are a duke, Your Grace. You could go to London and marry any society lady of your choosing. A viscount's daughter, or…'

The Duke gave her a tight smile. 'I think you understand my feelings about London and its society well enough after our walk a few days ago. I have no inclination to offer myself up to the marriage mart. But it is the duty of a man in my position to marry, and so I believe this arrangement could suit both of us. We seem to get along with each other well enough, do we not? And I do not believe the difference in our ages is so very great, is it?' He paused, looking suddenly unsure of himself. 'I am not yet three-and-thirty…'

'No, the difference is not so great,' Charlotte replied. 'I am three-and-twenty.' She laughed bitterly. 'Positively an old maid, according to my mother.'

'Absurd,' he said, shaking his head before giving her a more hopeful look. 'What do you think, Miss Pearson? I believe that our life together could be very…companionable.'

Charlotte nodded slowly. An arrangement—that was what it would be. A way of living contentedly together—nothing more and nothing less. They did not know each other very well, but then, how many couples entering matrimony truly did? She'd seen enough of how matches were made on the marriage mart to understand that a man and a woman could walk down the aisle as perfect strangers, driven towards each other by worldly considerations like wealth and titles, and not by love and affection. If London had taught her anything, it was that marriage was transactional, and a transaction was exactly what the Duke was proposing. At least it was one from which they both stood to benefit. Bitter experience had taught her that there were other, far less desirable sorts of transactions. Ones which could come at an enormous personal cost…

For a moment, she considered whether she ought to tell the Duke about the deal she'd almost made with the devil, before quickly deciding against it. After all, what possible good could come from him knowing about the foolish, reckless young lady she used to be? And besides, it was not as though Lord Crowgarth could harm them from where he was now. The threat of scandal had died with him, and there was little point in resurrecting the ghosts of the past—especially the spectre of a man about whom she'd much rather forget.

'The idea does have some merit,' she pondered.

The Duke looked surprised. 'Well, if you truly think so, then perhaps we should…'

Charlotte stepped closer, nodding. 'Yes, perhaps we should…'

Her words were interrupted by the sound of the greenhouse door clattering open, and a bitter wind swept the shawl-clad figure of Mrs Pearson inside. Breathless, Charlotte's mother leaned heavily on her walking cane, her sharp gaze fixing itself immediately upon her daughter and the Duke as an unmistakably triumphant smile spread itself across her face.

'They're in here!' she called over her shoulder.

Charlotte felt her chest tighten as the Dowager Duchess and Lady Elspeth hurried in behind her, their mouths falling open in matching looks of astonishment as they spied Charlotte and the Duke, standing opposite each other. Charlotte knew what they were thinking; she could see it writ large across their faces. She knew all too well what anyone would make of finding a man and a woman, alone together in a greenhouse on a blustery night.

'Ah—good, you have found Miss Pearson,' the Dowager Duchess said, addressing her son and clearly trying her hardest to recover herself.

'Found?' Mrs Pearson repeated, and Charlotte could sense her mother building towards histrionics. 'Your Grace, is it not clear what is going on, when the two of them have been out here for so long, and alone? His Grace has seduced my daughter! Oh, the scandal this will cause! This is an outrage!' she went on, barely able to conceal her delight.

The Dowager Duchess looked alarmed. 'Mrs Pearson, I am sure my son would never…'

'All sons would!' Mrs Pearson cried, waving her walking cane at the Duke. 'Mark me—all sons would when tempted by such beauty! Well, I dare say there is nothing else for it now. They shall have to marry. It is the only way that my dear Charlotte's virtue can be saved!'

The look of satisfaction on Mrs Pearson's face was galling. Charlotte stared hard at her mother, the heat of anger coursing through her veins. How dare her mother try to shame the Duke into making her his Duchess? Did she really have no regard for her at all, no consideration of her feelings, of her pride? No regard for the lessons of the recent past—lessons which ought to have taught Mrs Pearson, as they'd taught Charlotte, that such scheming brought only misery and heartache?

You know the answer to that, Charlotte. And you know what the answer to the Duke's question ought to be, too.

Before she could think too hard about it, Charlotte stepped towards the Duke and reached for his hand, threading her fingers through his. His skin felt warm and reassuring against hers, a fact she tried not to dwell upon as she looked up to meet his eye. She watched as his confusion gave way to understanding, watched as he gave her a brisk nod—a small gesture, but all that was needed. Confirmation of a transaction made. Of an arrangement agreed.

'There is no need for any of this, Mama,' she said, still holding the Duke's gaze. 'The Duke has already asked me to marry him, and I have already said yes.'

Chapter Seven

Ted rode his horse at a gentle pace across the lush, rain-soaked greenery of the sprawling Chatton estate, enjoying a brief reprieve in which to gather his thoughts while he made his way to Kelda to visit his bride-to-be. It felt strange to even think those words but, given the speed at which it had all happened, he supposed that was to be expected.

The week since he'd proposed to Miss Pearson in the greenhouse had felt like a whirlwind, throwing him around and leaving him quite disorientated as he grappled not only with the work required to plan a wedding, but with all the difficult conversations his hasty, unplanned proposal had provoked. Their marriage announcement had been greeted with shock by his mother, who'd quickly convinced herself that the only possible explanation for his behaviour was that he was acting upon that damned threat he'd made.

His sister, meanwhile, had been incandescent with fury, accusing him of stealing her friend.

Neither response would be forgotten in a hurry. Nor would that of his friend Ross, who had met the news of their betrothal with utter disbelief. Worse still, when Ted informed him that he'd secured a licence from the bishop and that they would be married in a private ceremony at St Oswald's next Tuesday, Ross had assumed that the reason for the swift wedding was because Miss Pearson was with child! Ted had protested his innocence, of course, although he was perturbed to realise that the way his blood had heated as he did so had less to do with indignation and more to do with the thoughts which had crept unbidden into his mind. The sight of her in that wet dress, clinging to every curve. The feeling of her waist beneath his fingers as he held on to her, however briefly, in the greenhouse that night.

The realisation that, for a brief moment, he'd hesitated to let her go.

Ted reached the village and slowed his horse to a trot as he made his way along the muddy lane. Miss Pearson's home was at the other side of the village, in a secluded spot just before the small cluster of dwellings which comprised Kelda gave way to rolling fields and thick woodland once more. He breathed in deeply, appreciating the crisp country air—so much cleaner than that which he'd become accustomed to in Edinburgh. He had to admit, sometimes rural Northumberland did have its advantages.

Curiously, he found himself wondering what Miss Pearson would think of Edinburgh—found himself entertaining the idea of taking her there. Perhaps he would, for a little while. He did still have a few matters to attend to concerning his old life, not least an outstanding commitment to deliver some lectures which circumstances, in the form of his brother's death, had forced him to postpone. A commitment which he'd always intended to fulfil in secret, since he knew that his mother would not approve.

Nor would your bride, especially if she knew the particular subject of those lectures...

The thought made him bristle. It was probably best if Miss Pearson was never made aware of either the lectures or their subject matter. But he had no doubt that he could fulfil his commitment discreetly, and that they could spend the rest of the time settling into married life. And doubtless being so many miles away from her mother would suit Miss Pearson very well. Another aspect of their arrangement which could suit them both, then. He supposed it would be a sort of honeymoon...

Honeymoons. Weddings. Unplanned proposals. What on earth has got into you, man?

Now, there was a question—one which, in truth, he

was still grappling with. Just what had come over him in that greenhouse that evening? Despite his mother's repeated assertion to the contrary, he was sure it had nothing to do with that ridiculous threat he'd made to marry the next eligible lady to walk through his door, or the mortifying moment when Miss Pearson had been the one to walk in. However, he could not deny that the moment in question had brought Miss Pearson firmly to his notice. Nor could he deny just how much he'd continued to notice her, and continued to think about her, ever since that day he'd encountered her near the stream…

He also could not deny that his behaviour in the greenhouse had been impulsive and reckless—two things which neither Edward Scott the physician nor Edward Scott the Duke had ever been. And whilst he had tried to make his proposal sound rational afterwards—to Miss Pearson, to himself and to his family and friends—he had to admit that in the heat of the moment he'd been driven by emotion, not reason.

He'd seen the look in Miss Pearson's eyes and he'd recognised it as clearly as if he'd been looking at himself in a mirror. A swirling tide of emotions over which she fought to maintain control—sadness, anger, perhaps even despair. And as for those words she'd said to him, stoic yet heartfelt words about life dealing you a difficult hand of cards and leaving you no choice but to play them—those words had struck him at his core. How well he understood that. How well he knew how that felt. An overwhelming feeling had washed over him then, one which made him want to rescue her. One which made him want to take her away from it all and offer her something better.

Perhaps you wanted to mend her, too, Ted. Perhaps you wanted to fix what was broken, just like you always do.

Ted heaved a sigh as Miss Pearson's cottage came into view. Perhaps it had been his physician's instincts which had overtaken once again. He didn't know. Nor did he know quite how his visit this afternoon would proceed. There were formalities to conclude, of course, and arrangements to finalise with her mother, but beyond that… Was it too much to hope that they might manage a little time alone, since they were about to be husband and wife?

He dismounted from his horse, securing the creature to a nearby tree before striding towards the cottage door, trying to think only of the duties he must perform and the preparations which must be made. Trying not to think about just how much the idea of being alone with Miss Pearson, of walking with her and holding her arm in his as they talked, suddenly seemed like the most appealing idea on earth.

Charlotte hurried to answer the Duke's knock, remembering to remove her apron just in time. These past few days, she'd spent more time at home than she had in weeks, her work at the school necessarily reduced as she prepared for her wedding. If her mother had got her way, that work would have been brought to an end altogether. She'd made it plain that, in her opinion, it was not appropriate for a duchess to be teaching sewing at the local school. Charlotte had stubbornly clung on, however, reminding her mother that she was not yet a duchess and insisting that whilst she could attend the school less, she wished to help the girls finish a project before her wedding. She'd been surprised to win that battle, but was swiftly reminded that she would never win the war. The time she spent at home had been far from restful, filled not only with wedding preparations but also household duties as she was instructed to assist their maid and, frankly, to wait on her mother and Aunt Maud hand and foot. Teaching might not be suitable work for a future duchess, but apparently drudgery was absolutely fine.

'You know we cannot afford more than one servant, not on our limited means. You must make yourself useful, whilst you are still here with us,' her mother had lectured, giving Charlotte the sourest of looks. 'Although I do hope His Grace will see fit to improve our circumstances. You must speak to him about that, the moment you are wed.'

The knot which resided permanently in Charlotte's

stomach had tightened at that. Once again, her mother was determined to milk this marriage for all it was worth. She also suspected that her sudden confinement to the house and full itinerary of chores was her final penance. Her mother saw clearly that her daughter had made the ultimate bid for freedom and was determined to punish her for the sins of the past, one last time.

What did you expect? You have secured yourself a far better future than you deserve...

Marrying the Duke of Falstone was certainly far more than she deserved. In the days since her betrothal, that guilt which usually she managed to keep locked away had sprung free with alarming regularity. Guilt that she was escaping. Guilt that she'd somehow cheated the fate which her past mistakes had long since condemned her to. Guilt that she was marrying a decent, upstanding nobleman who really knew nothing at all about her, or her foolish actions in the past.

And what would be the point in telling him about that? The scandal is dead and gone, Charlotte. You know that. It can do no more harm than has been done already—unless you let it...

'Good day, Miss Pearson.'

It took several awkward moments before Charlotte brought her mind back to the present and realised that she had, in fact, opened the door. She looked up, blinking several times at the sight of the Duke, who stood just across the threshold, his hands clasped behind his back. A familiar posture, and one she increasingly suspected that he adopted when he was nervous. The thought was endearing, and brought a smile to her face.

The Duke smiled back, briefly. 'May I…may I come in?'

Charlotte grew suddenly and painfully aware that she was still standing there, grinning like a ninny instead of greeting him properly. 'Oh…um, of course, Your Grace,' she stuttered, the heat of an embarrassed flush creeping on to her cheeks. 'My mother and aunt are waiting in the parlour.'

Another long moment passed, and yet Charlotte still had not the presence of mind to move aside and welcome him in. It was as though her legs were frozen to the spot. What on earth had got into her? Perhaps it was nerves at the prospect of the Duke being in her home for the first time. Perhaps it was the thought of him walking inside and seeing their ramshackle parlour, sparsely furnished, its walls in dire need of a coat of paint. Perhaps it was the thought of him being confronted by how simply they lived, and just how reduced their circumstances were.

Perhaps it was the sheer dread she felt at bringing him into her mother's territory…

'Come in, Your Grace!' Mrs Pearson's shrill voice

called out from the confines of her armchair, clearly growing impatient. 'You are most welcome!'

Speak of the devil.

Whether it was her mother's interjection or her deeply uncharitable thought which startled her, Charlotte did not know, but before she could stop herself, she flinched. Worse still, she knew that the Duke had seen it. She watched as he narrowed his eyes slightly, although there was no judgement lingering in those brown depths, only careful reflection, as though he was weighing up the situation. As though he was working out how best to proceed.

If you've any sense, Your Grace, you will run for your life.

'Actually,' the Duke called out in reply, 'I think I must quickly go and…'

Oh, no! I didn't mean it! Don't run away—she will never let me hear the end of it...

'…attend to my horse. He seems restless and I've left him tethered rather loosely.' Charlotte's stomach flipped as the Duke gave her a small, knowing smile. 'Miss Pearson can assist me, I'm sure.'

'Oh! But really, Your Grace, we must…'

Charlotte shut the door behind her, leaving the remainder of her mother's sentence unheard. Before she could stop herself, she let out a small chuckle, enjoying their brief collusion to evade her mother's clutches, at least for a little while. The Duke laughed too, those brown eyes of his seeming to light up with amusement as he offered her his arm.

'Thank you,' she said as they walked together towards the nearby tree where the Duke's horse was waiting.

He inclined his head in acknowledgement. 'I thought that perhaps you might need some air,' he said, giving her another of those knowing looks.

'Indeed. The past few days have been rather…trying.'

'I can imagine. They have not been particularly easy for me, either.' He drew a deep breath. 'The news of our betrothal has caused quite a stir, Miss Pearson.'

'It's Charlotte, Your Grace,' she replied quietly. 'If we are to be married, I think you should start calling me Charlotte.'

He nodded briskly, as though taken aback. As though the idea of being on more familiar terms hadn't occurred to him. 'Oh, right—yes, of course. All right—well, in that case, please call me Ted.' He paused, before shaking his head and chuckling wryly. 'I'm sure most people use each other's first names before agreeing to get married. We rather put the cart before the horse, didn't we, Charlotte?'

The sound of her name rolling off his tongue did strange things to her insides. 'We did, Your… I mean, Ted. Yes, we did.' She watched for a moment as he adjusted the tether on his horse, making a show of attending to the animal, no doubt in case her mother was watching from the window. 'So, why Ted and not Edward?'

He shrugged. 'My mother always shortened our names as children. My brother was Perry and I was always Ted. Elspeth was Elsie, although she refuses to let anyone call her that now.' He rolled his eyes in mock exasperation at his strong-willed younger sister.

'I can imagine,' Charlotte chuckled. 'Although, if I recall correctly, Lady Elspeth calls you Teddy?'

Ted groaned. 'Oh, don't remind me. I cannot believe she told you that!'

'So I may not call you Teddy, then?' Charlotte grinned, unable to resist teasing him.

He smiled back. 'No, you may not.'

A jovial silence fell between them and for several moments they simply stood there, next to Ted's horse, smiling at each other. Charlotte felt her breath hitch as those brown eyes seemed to heat as they held hers, and her heart fluttered wildly as she saw his smile fade and his gaze flit briefly towards her lips. Did he mean to kiss her? Surely not…

Before Charlotte could consider what she was doing, she'd taken a step closer to him, still meeting his smouldering, dark stare with her own as she sensed that wayward, impetuous side of herself break free. That side of herself which wondered what Ted's lips pressed against hers would feel like. That side of herself which dared to contemplate the feeling of his hands coming to rest upon her hips, before moving to encircle her waist and pulling her close to him…

You mean, the side of yourself best known as Charlotte the Harlot? That's what Crowgarth called you, didn't he? Or have you forgotten already?

The intrusion of that thought—of that awful, mocking name, the one she'd locked away in the deepest, darkest corner of her mind—made Charlotte gasp aloud, and the spell was broken. Ted stepped away and cleared his throat, although for once he did not clasp his hands behind his back. Instead, he seemed to collect himself, then took hold of one of her hands and lifted it to his lips, placing the gentlest of kisses upon it. It was a simple, tender gesture, and it shook Charlotte to her core. Here was a man who'd offered her an escape, who'd been nothing but honourable and gentlemanly and thoroughly decent towards her. A man who'd proposed marriage and wanted to make her his Duchess. And all she could think about was kissing him.

She saw Ted's brow furrow with concern. 'Is everything all right, Charlotte?' he asked, and it was clear he'd read something in her expression.

'Of course, I… I was just thinking about the school,' she said hurriedly. 'About how I shall have to give up my work there, after our wedding.'

His frown deepened. 'You will? Why?'

'Because I will have a new set of duties, won't I? My mother says...'

Ted shook his head gently, reaching for her hand once more. 'You do not have to give up your involvement with the school—not if you do not wish to. If anything, you might like to become more involved as a patroness, like my mother and Elspeth.'

Charlotte felt an enormous smile spread across her face—one of relief, and of excitement. If there was anything in her life which she had not wished to leave behind, it was the school. 'That would be wonderful, Ted. Thank you.'

'I would never wish for this arrangement between us to make you unhappy,' he replied. 'And there is perhaps no greater source of unhappiness than losing something you love.'

Even as he returned her smile, Charlotte could not mistake the heavy look which lingered in his dark eyes. Before she could query either his expression or the meaning of his words, however, he turned back towards the cottage and offered her his arm once more.

'I suppose we ought to go inside,' he continued. 'I need to speak with your mother and finalise the arrangements for Tuesday. I also... Forgive me, but could I ask you to do something for me?'

Charlotte nodded, wrenching her thoughts back

to the present. To Tuesday. To the wedding. To the future, and away from the darkest parts of her past. 'Of course.'

Ted regarded her sheepishly. 'Would you pay a visit to Elspeth before the wedding? I'm aware that in the days since our betrothal the pair of you have had little opportunity to really talk, and I'm afraid she is rather angry with me for asking you to marry me. Perhaps if you were to reassure her, somehow…'

Charlotte murmured her agreement, trying not to think about how she might achieve the impossible as they walked back towards the cottage. Lies about love would not do—Lady Elspeth would see right through those. It would have to be the truth, or a version of it, at least. A guarded, carefully curated version—much like the version of herself that she needed to embody if she was going to fulfil her side of their arrangement and successfully inhabit the role of a duchess. The sort of role which she'd spent her life preparing for, she reminded herself. A role which Ted had entrusted to her, and a role which she was determined to fulfil, from the moment they made their vows next Tuesday.

Chapter Eight

Charlotte drew a deep breath as she stood before the altar, trying to steady her nerves as the curate began to speak. This morning, the small village church seemed unusually bright, the sunlight streaming in through its old lattice windows and illuminating everything from the dark wood of the pews to the cold grey stones below her feet. As she'd walked up the aisle the brightness had made her feel dazed, as though she might be dreaming. As though none of this was real.

She'd tried hard to focus on putting one foot in front of the other, to get herself swiftly to the altar where her groom, immaculately dressed with his hands clasped behind his back, had waited. As she'd drawn closer, she'd managed to meet his eye—just briefly. She might have even smiled, but in truth she wasn't sure. This morning, it seemed, she was not sure of anything. She couldn't be sure what was real or imagined, and certainly, she was not sure whether getting married to the Duke of Falstone was the right thing to do at all.

Days ago in the greenhouse, Ted's offer of escape had been all but irresistible, and her confidence in their arrangement had not faltered since. If anything, those final, unbearable days at home with her mother had only served to strengthen her resolve. Yet now, as she stood in church and listened to the curate speak of God, of holy matrimony, of it being an honourable estate, she felt the full weight of reality begin to dawn. They were on the cusp of making vows to each other, of becoming husband and wife. Of entering into a lifelong commitment—all so that she could be free of her mother, and Ted could tick another ducal duty off his list.

Charlotte sucked in a sharp breath as she heard the curate begin to speak about the purposes of marriage, feeling her cheeks begin to flush at his words about having children. Good Lord. In making their hasty arrangement, neither of them had said anything about that particular aspect of marriage…

Of course Ted will expect you to produce his heir! Why else would he need a wife? Besides, you know how much you would like to have children.

That was true—if anything, it was a feeling which had intensified during her time at the school. The thought of having her own little brood of daughters, of telling them stories, of teaching them to sew. Followed, usually, by the painful reminder that motherhood was not likely to feature in her future—a future which had seemed destined to be spent unwed and at her mother's side. But now she was getting married. Now everything had changed.

Hadn't it?

Next to her, she sensed Ted shift a little, flexing his hand so that his fingers brushed briefly against hers. She felt his touch all the way down to her toes, and found herself longing for him to take hold of her hand. To lace his fingers through hers and give them a gentle, reassuring squeeze.

Don't be a ninny. This isn't that sort of marriage, remember?

No, it certainly wasn't. It was a marriage of logic, opportunity and convenience between two people who believed they could be contented with one another. That was enough, wasn't it? Indeed, Charlotte reminded herself, it was more than she ought to expect and absolutely more than she deserved. She pressed her lips together, trying to keep her attention focused on the curate and thinking neither about Ted standing at her side, nor about the small congregation gathered behind her. In keeping with their plans for a quick private wedding, only their families were in attendance, save for a friend of Ted—Mr Deane, the surgeon apothecary. Charlotte had little doubt that the presence of the village's medical man would have particularly delighted her mother.

Lady Elspeth had acted as Charlotte's single bridesmaid, a duty she'd carried out in an uncharacteristically sombre fashion. Charlotte suspected that despite her attempts to reassure her friend about this unexpected marriage, Lady Elspeth remained unconvinced. But then, Charlotte knew, her explanation had sounded woolly, littered with half-truths about getting along well and their mutual need to wed for more worldly reasons. She'd shied away from spelling out the misery of her current existence and had been too ashamed to confess her desire to evade her mother's clutches. Unfortunately, by neglecting these important details, she feared she'd rather sounded like a cynical title-hunter.

'I will.'

The deep timbre of Ted's voice as he made his vow breached Charlotte's thoughts, and she realised that the curate was now speaking to her—words about love, honour, sickness, health. Charlotte nodded along, trying not to deliberate too much upon their meaning. Trying not to take it all too much to heart. This was just another part of their arrangement, she told herself. Just another means to an end.

'I will,' she said.

At the curate's behest, Charlotte turned to face Ted, placing her hand in his. Although she knew it was only a requirement of the ceremony, nevertheless she found herself feeling comforted by his touch. A tangible reminder, perhaps, that they were in this together—for better or for worse. She looked up at him, struck again by how perfectly he'd risen to the occasion—freshly shaven, his dark hair trimmed and tamed into order, his dark tailcoat exquisitely tailored and emphasising his broad shoulders and trim physique. There was no doubt that Edward Scott, Duke of Falstone, was a very handsome man.

By contrast, Charlotte felt rather plain in her pale blue gown. In recent times, her wardrobe had diminished to match her circumstances, and with only a few days' notice, trimming an old dress and a matching cap with some fresh lace had been the best she could do. And as for having a trousseau of new clothes to take with her into married life—well, that was simply far beyond her means, even if there had been sufficient time for it.

She watched as Ted slipped a ring upon the fourth finger of her left hand—a plain gold band which fitted well enough. Where had that come from? How had he managed to organise a ring, as well as everything else, in a matter of days? He continued his vows then, pledging himself to her, promising to worship her with his body...

After that, Charlotte didn't hear the rest. She was too busy trying to instruct her heart to stop pounding and her cheeks to cease glowing scarlet. Trying to tell herself that they were just words, that the ceremony required Ted to say such things to her. That he didn't mean it—that he couldn't mean it, because words like that had no place in an arrangement which delivered an escape, which fulfilled a duty, which promised contentment and, at most, companionship. That she didn't want him to mean it.

Did she?

No. The Charlotte who might have wanted such intimacies was consigned to the past now. That Charlotte had flirted and teased, she'd allowed her wicked mind and wayward mouth to rule her, and she knew where such behaviour led. She knew the dangers, and she knew the cost.

But surely this is different. You are his wife...

Yes, she was. His wife so that she could flee from a wretched life spent under her mother's critical eye. His wife so that Ted had a duchess to manage his household, to play the hostess at his parties, to accompany him at social gatherings and to London, when his duties required it, and...

To bear his heir, Charlotte. That is the duty which, above all, a duchess is meant to fulfil.

Charlotte felt Ted glance at her as the curate pronounced them husband and wife and the blessing and psalms began, but she did not trust herself to look back. Did not trust that her eyes would not betray the turmoil which she could feel churning in the pit of her stomach. Turmoil at having leapt so quickly into the unknown, and turmoil at the dawning realisation that, having made her hasty arrangement with Ted, she'd left far too many of the details of their convenient marriage unaddressed.

Ted tucked into the plate of hot rolls, meats and eggs in front of him with as much refinement as he could muster. In truth, he was famished; he'd not had the time to eat anything before departing for St Oswald's earlier that morning, and even if he had, he suspected that his nerves would have put paid to his appetite in any case. As soon as the service had ended, the wedding party had returned to Chatton, gathering around the dining table for the customary breakfast, followed by wedding cake to mark the occasion.

As he ate and listened to the chatter of his family and guests, he found himself beginning to relax a little, his nerves abating now that the formal part of the day had concluded. It was done now. Their arrangement had been formalised by the curate's blessing, and now he had a wife and a Duchess. He had fulfilled another of those duties Perry had bequeathed to him, and had given Charlotte the escape she desired. That was reason enough to celebrate.

Wasn't it?

He glanced briefly at Charlotte, who sat to his side, sipping her tea. He had to admit, making those vows to her had been more difficult than he could have anticipated. Not because he'd been having any last-minute doubts—he'd made an agreement with her and he was a man of his word—but because the sentiments he was required to express had struck him with the full force of their solemnity and intensity. Being an honourable and faithful husband was something he knew he would do, and well, but loving and cherishing? Those things were very much not a part of their agreement. It still surprised him how smoothly he'd managed to make those pledges. He'd been taken aback, too, by the warmth which had surged through him as he'd watched Charlotte walk down the aisle dressed in a pretty pale blue, those red curls of hers as striking as ever. Indeed, throughout the service he'd been unable to stop himself from stealing glances at her. Theirs might be a convenient marriage but he was still a man, and she was an indisputably beautiful young lady.

All in all, he'd found the entire ceremony discomfiting, and he suspected he wasn't the only one. The blush which had stained Charlotte's cheeks when he'd spoken the part about worshipping her body had been something to behold! It was clear the idea had alarmed her, and he prayed she hadn't sensed his heart beating faster when the curate had prompted him to make that particular vow. Her reaction served as absolute confirmation that there were aspects of their arrangement which they still needed to discuss, and reassurances which he needed to give her. The reassurance that he'd no expectation of being invited into her bedchamber that very night. The reassurance that they could take their time and get to know each other better before fulfilling that particular duty.

You mean your duty to produce an heir to secure the Dukedom and the security of your family? A duty which cannot wait for ever...

Ted swallowed down a mouthful of bread, quashing that niggling inner voice. That duty could wait for now, at least. The Dukedom and its ceaseless demands had had quite enough from him for one day.

'My mother has arranged for your trousseau to be collected from your aunt's cottage,' Ted said, leaning towards Charlotte so that he might speak to her quietly. 'And later, she will show you which rooms are yours.'

Charlotte's eyes widened as she regarded him. 'Rooms?' she repeated.

He nodded, unable to suppress his smile. 'Of course. You are the Duchess now, remember? You will have your own private rooms—and your own bedchamber, naturally,' he added.

Charlotte took another long sip of her tea. Ted

glanced at her plate, noticing that she'd barely eaten anything. He frowned. 'Are you not hungry?'

She shook her head. 'No, not particularly.' She pressed her lips together for a moment, those bright blue eyes regarding him carefully, and Ted sensed she wanted to say something but wasn't sure how to proceed.

'What is it, Charlotte?' he prompted.

She shook her head again, giving him a smile which did not reach her eyes. 'Nothing. It is kind of the Dowager Duchess to arrange for my belongings to be collected. Although I'm afraid there was not time for a trousseau to be prepared, as such.'

Ted felt the furrow between his brows deepen. The way Charlotte had begun to blush made him suspect that time had not been the only obstacle. 'I see. In that case, is there anything you need?'

Another smile, more genuine this time. 'No, thank you. I have plenty of gowns. They just need a little brightening up, is all. Nothing I cannot do myself.'

Ted grinned. 'Of that I have no doubt, given your reputation with a needle and thread.' He felt his smile fade as an idea returned to him, one he'd first entertained just a few days ago. One he had yet to suggest to her. 'However, if you did desire some new gowns, then I know of somewhere where there are dressmakers aplenty.'

Charlotte's blue eyes widened. 'You do?'

'Yes—Edinburgh. In fact, Charlotte, I was thinking…'

'What are the newlyweds whispering about, I wonder?'

The shrill voice of Mrs Pearson intruded, bringing a swift end to their conversation. The older woman's keen stare flitted from Ted to her daughter and back again, and it was clear she would not be satisfied until she received an answer.

'We were just discussing the arrangements for the Duchess's trousseau to be brought here,' Ted replied drily, hoping she would make no further enquiries and would leave them to finish their conversation.

Alas, Mrs Pearson was not to be discouraged. 'Trousseau?' she repeated, giving Ted a tight smile. 'I'm afraid we had so little time to prepare, Your Grace, that my dear Charlotte has very little to call a wardrobe at all. Indeed, I do believe she will require a good number of new gowns…'

Beside him, Ted felt Charlotte flinch. Without thinking, he placed his hand over hers. 'Do not concern yourself, Mrs Pearson. The Duchess will have everything she needs.'

'That is good of you, Your Grace, but these are not matters to trouble yourself with,' Mrs Pearson replied, her voice sickly sweet. 'It is women's work, surely.'

'In that case, I am sure my mother and sister will be happy to advise the Duchess on a suitable wardrobe,' Ted replied, glancing at his mother and Elspeth in turn.

'Of course,' the Dowager Duchess interjected enthusiastically, giving Charlotte a warm smile. 'It would be my pleasure.'

'Then I am sure that myself and the Dowager Duchess will work well together,' Mrs Pearson continued, undeterred. 'It is fortunate indeed that I am only a short distance away in the village. I'll be able to visit my daughter regularly and assist the new Duchess with all manner of things. It will bring me great comfort, since I will miss my dear Charlotte so much.' She paused, dabbing her eyes with her napkin before grasping the hand of Miss Fenwick, who sat beside her. 'Although the future for my sister and myself is far from certain, reliant as we are upon our brother's kindness. And that little cottage in Kelda is far from comfortable for a delicate creature such as I. Poor Mr Deane has been forced to increase my tinctures with growing frequency of late, haven't you, Mr Deane?'

Ted watched as Ross shifted uncomfortably in his seat. 'Well, yes, Mrs Pearson, but…'

'You see, Your Grace,' Mrs Pearson continued, addressing Ted again now. 'It is a terrible thing for a widow and a spinster to be forced to live in such a manner. And with only one servant, too. One servant! But now I do believe that the Lord smiles upon us once more. Perhaps there might be some way that I—we—could be more conveniently situated so that we might be even closer at hand. A cottage on the estate perhaps, or…'

'No!'

Charlotte's loud and emphatic refusal of her mother's request cut across the conversation. Immediately, Mrs Pearson fell into a stunned silence, looking much like she'd just swallowed a wasp. Beneath his hand, Ted felt Charlotte's fingers grow tense. He turned to look at her and saw for a brief moment a look of absolute determination writ across her face—her jaw clenched, her normally bright blue eyes stormy and challenging as she regarded her mother. Then, almost as soon as the look appeared, it faded, and he saw Charlotte's resolve begin to waver, the realisation of what she'd said and how she'd said it clearly beginning to dawn on her.

She dropped her gaze towards the table. 'What I mean to say, Mama, is…no, but you see…'

Mrs Pearson glared at her daughter. 'Come now, Charlotte, spit it out. Surely you would wish to see that your poor, suffering mother and aunt are well cared for,' she said, clearly sensing her daughter's faltering confidence and seeking to exploit it, as no doubt she'd done many times before.

As no doubt she has done throughout poor Charlotte's life. Enough of this, Ted. You promised Charlotte an escape, remember? You know exactly where the two of you can go. Indeed, you'd been about to suggest it...

Ted gave Charlotte's hand a reassuring squeeze. 'I believe what my wife wishes to say, Mrs Pearson, is that dress fittings, frequent visits and more conveniently located accommodation won't be necessary, I'm afraid.'

Mrs Pearson turned her challenging birdlike gaze towards her new son-in-law. 'Oh, Your Grace,' she said, her tone honeyed even as she curled her lip at him. 'And why is that?'

Ted looked at Charlotte, answering the wide-eyed, quizzical look she gave him with a broad smile. A smile which asked her to trust him. A smile which sought to tell her that everything was going to be all right.

'Because we are going on our honeymoon,' he replied. 'We leave tomorrow for my house in Edinburgh, and I cannot say exactly when we will be back.'

Chapter Nine

'Charlotte? Charlotte, wake up. We're here.'

Wearily, Charlotte opened her eyes, squinting at the brightness which flooded in through the open carriage door. She groaned, feeling disorientated, her head beginning to pound and her mouth feeling horribly dry. Two clear signs, if she ever needed them, that she had slept for far longer than she should have. Across from her sat Ted, that dark gaze of his observing her carefully, a small furrow of concern etched upon his brow. Two very clear and definitely unwelcome signs that she looked truly dreadful. Carefully, she pulled herself upright, shaking off her sleepiness as she attempted to straighten her bonnet and quietly prayed that she hadn't been snoring all the way up the Great North Road.

'I am sorry to have to wake you. You looked so peaceful,' Ted remarked.

'How long have I been asleep?' she asked groggily.

'Since we left Berwick. You didn't even stir when we stopped to change the horses. You must have been very tired.'

Charlotte nodded, licking her lips. She was tired—exhausted, in fact. Last night she had barely slept, tossing and turning in that big, unfamiliar bed, hearing every unsettling creak and spying every strange shadow in that enormous bedchamber which now belonged to her. At first, she'd told herself that she was restless because it was her first night in her new home, and her wedding night no less—even though the chaste way Ted had bid her goodnight, stressing that he would be retiring shortly to his own room too, had made it plain that he'd no intention of fulfilling certain vows he'd made earlier that day. Vows which they still needed to discuss…

However, as dawn had approached and sleep had continued to evade her, she'd forced herself to acknowledge that it was the enormity of it all which kept her awake. The enormity of getting married, of becoming a wife and a duchess and all the duties which would come with it. The enormity of trying to suppress the guilt which had bubbled up in recent days—guilt about her past mistakes, and guilt about having made her escape. A niggling guilt that she'd somehow secured a position in life which she did not truly deserve.

As the sun had risen, however, she'd made a silent

vow to herself. She would not allow herself to be consumed by her doubts, nor would she allow herself to be led astray by that impetuous, wayward side of her character which regrettably still reared its head from time to time. Instead, she would rise above it all and fulfil the role which her husband had entrusted to her. She would be sensible, responsible and, above all, determined. She owed Ted that much.

Pity that making your vow didn't help you to sleep. You must look frightful...

'Are you all right, Charlotte?' Ted asked, and she could see that the furrow in his brow had deepened. 'Forgive me—I fear now that I was not thinking, taking you away from Chatton so soon.'

In her sleepy state, she forced a smile. 'I am quite well, Ted, and I am looking forward to seeing Edinburgh.'

Despite her assurance, Ted continued to frown, and she could see that he wasn't convinced. 'If you are worried about your mother, please be assured I have left instructions to ensure that both she and your aunt are well cared for while we are away.'

'I'm not worried about my mother.'

'Is it the school, then? Because you know it is in capable hands, and I promise that we can sit down with my mother and the curate and discuss your involvement once we return...'

She nodded. 'I know, and I am not concerned about the school.'

He regarded her carefully. 'All right, but if it is Elspeth who vexes you, then I must tell you that she did not decline to accompany us to Edinburgh because she bears us any ill will. She was insistent that we should have some time to ourselves, given, well, how quickly we were wed.'

Charlotte nodded her agreement. Elspeth had said much the same to her, just before she had retired to bed last night. She'd also confessed that she still did not really understand her friend and her brother's mad dash down the aisle, but that she was determined to make her peace with it. That was the thing with Elspeth; she was as fiercely pragmatic as she was intelligent.

'I'm not worried about Elspeth, although I must confess that I will miss her company.'

Ted fiddled with his collar. 'I know it is customary for a lady to have a female companion during the early days of marriage,' he continued. 'But given how quickly matters…um, developed, my sister does perhaps have a point.' Charlotte watched as a pained look swept across his face and he regarded her once more. 'Is it the lack of a lady's maid? My mother cautioned me against whisking you away so quickly without taking the time to appoint a suitable attendant…'

Despite her weariness, Charlotte laughed. 'I can

manage perfectly well by myself, Ted,' she assured him. That much was true—the solitary maid who'd attended them in the cottage had seldom helped her with much more than lacing her stays. It did strike her as odd that they were travelling without a single servant, and stranger still that Ted did not appear to feel the need for any such assistance. But then, she supposed the journey was not so very long, and she supposed, too, that there must be a full household awaiting them in Edinburgh.

Ted nodded. 'All right. But you have my word that you will be well attended once we get to Edinburgh. I will ask my housekeeper to make the arrangements.' He placed his hand reassuringly over hers. 'We will have a pleasant time in Edinburgh, Charlotte. You will see. It will provide some welcome distance from your cares back in Northumberland.'

'I'm sure it will,' she replied, trying to focus on their conversation rather than the way that her skin tingled beneath his touch. 'It is fortunate indeed that you still have your old house and staff in Edinburgh. That you had not yet given them up.'

'Yes… I suppose it is.' The look he gave her then was odd, unreadable. Charlotte watched as he got up from his seat and climbed out of the carriage door before turning back to offer her his hand. 'Shall we go, then?'

'Where are we?' Charlotte asked, realising then that she did not know.

'We are at a coaching inn, not far from a village called Cockburnspath. The afternoon grows late, so we shall stay here for tonight.'

Before she could say another word, Ted led her across a bustling courtyard, weaving their way around coaches, carriages and clusters of weary travellers. The clatter of luggage being loaded and unloaded and the ceaseless clopping of hooves as stableboys came and went with horses reached a painful crescendo in Charlotte's pounding head. Suddenly the lure of a quiet room and a soft bed adorned with crisp white linen sheets felt irresistible. She could only hope that she would manage to sleep better tonight.

'This is one of my favourite inns on the Great North Road,' Ted explained as they hurried towards a neat white building, punctuated with little windows. 'I have often stopped here on my way to and from Edinburgh. The innkeeper knows me well.'

They walked through a low door and into a very orderly parlour where several small groups of well-dressed ladies and gentlemen sat, enjoying glasses of wine and some hearty fare. Charlotte felt immediately self-conscious as she felt all the eyes in the room wander simultaneously towards her. Judging, assessing, scrutinising. She huddled into her travelling cloak and bowed her head, allowing the brim of her bonnet to shield her from view. The Charlotte she used to be might have basked in such attention, but the Charlotte she'd become after London shied away from it. That was not about to change now that she was a duchess. If anything, she was determined to be more guarded and more reserved than ever.

Aloof dignity, Charlotte. That is what being a duchess requires of you. Remember that.

'Dr Scott!' A short, stocky man who Charlotte presumed must be the innkeeper stepped forward, greeting Ted with open arms. 'It is a pleasure to have you with us once again, sir. It has been a while, has it not?'

Charlotte glanced at Ted, waiting for him to correct the man, to invite him to use his proper title. To her surprise, however, he did not. 'It has indeed been a while,' he said smoothly, tipping his hat in greeting. 'Two of your best rooms please, for myself and Mrs Scott.'

Mrs Scott! Not the Duchess of Falstone, but Mrs Scott! Why was Ted concealing their true identities? It was very perplexing.

'Two rooms?' the innkeeper repeated, raising his eyebrows briefly. 'That won't be possible, I'm afraid, sir. I have only one room left, you see. The inn is very busy tonight.'

Oh, Lord.

'Ah… I see. Well…um…' Ted looked at Charlotte,

and she could see a flush of embarrassment creeping up from beneath his collar. 'Are you certain you've nothing else?'

'I'm sorry, sir. But the room I have, it is the very best, and I will arrange for some supper to be brought up to you, as I always do. And for Mrs Scott too, of course.'

Around them, Charlotte sensed every pair of ears in the room attuning themselves to the discussion. Doubtless entertained by what was unfolding. Doubtless wondering exactly why Dr and Mrs Scott, a married couple, seemed quite so reluctant to share a room for the night.

'Dr Scott and I will take the room,' she interjected. 'I am sure it will do perfectly well.'

Looking visibly relieved, the innkeeper led them away from the parlour and up a set of stairs which presumably led to the inn's rooms. As they followed him, Charlotte glanced over her shoulder, giving Ted a quizzical look. Dr and Mrs Scott, indeed! He would be explaining that to her, just as soon as they'd worked out how on earth they were going to wash, change and sleep in a single room with only one bed between them. She could only hope and pray that, at the very least, there was a dressing screen.

Ted surveyed the room with his hands on his hips, his mind racing through the practicalities of how the two of them could share this space and keep their dignity intact. It was, at least, a reasonable size, furnished with not only a large bed but a sofa, chairs and a small table where they could sit and enjoy some supper. However, there was little opportunity for privacy; he'd already noted that there was no dressing screen, which made changing their clothes a problem, particularly for Charlotte.

Inwardly, Ted groaned. He knew it was inevitable that complications would arise, that their arrangement, such as it was, meant they would sometimes have to confront the challenges presented by living as husband and wife. But really, on the second day of matrimonial bliss? It seemed unfair.

'I think we will manage,' he said in the end. 'I can sleep on the sofa, and I will leave the room when you want to wash and change.'

Charlotte nodded, pressing her lips together tightly for a moment. She'd been very quiet since the innkeeper had left them, hovering near the door as though she didn't know quite what to do with herself. 'Would it not make more sense for me to sleep on the sofa, since I am smaller than you?' she asked. 'And what about when you want to change? I can leave the room, although perhaps you will need to change first since I cannot leave the room in my nightclothes...' He watched as she began to blush, before falling silent.

'What sort of a gentleman, or indeed what sort of a husband, would I be if I allowed you to sleep on the sofa?' he asked, smiling despite the absurdity of the situation. 'And as for when I change—there is no need for you to leave. Just…avert your eyes.'

Charlotte's cheeks turned a vibrant shade of scarlet, and Ted realised he'd been too blunt. It was all right for him, wasn't it? His choice of profession meant he was well acquainted with the human form—both the female and the male. Little fazed him in that regard. Charlotte, however, was doubtless an innocent. She would never have been in such close proximity to a man, much less spent the night sleeping in the same room as one.

'Forgive me,' he began, shaking his head at himself. 'What I mean is…'

'It's fine,' she interrupted crisply. 'As you say, we will manage.'

Charlotte took several steps towards him, finally moving away from the door and removing her travelling cloak and bonnet before draping them over a nearby chair. Ted found himself casting an approving eye over her pale green dress—the way it contrasted with her bright red hair and alabaster skin and the way it skimmed over the delightful curve of her waist. He gave himself a mental shake, hoping Charlotte had not noticed his roaming gaze.

Not helpful, Ted. Not when you've got to spend the night together.

'Ted, why did you not correct the innkeeper when he referred to you as "Dr Scott"?'

Ted drew a deep breath. He'd wondered how long it would be before Charlotte asked him about that. 'I've been stopping at this inn for years, before I became a duke and when I was still Dr Scott. I didn't like to contradict the man, that's all,' he replied, feigning nonchalance, as though it had not mattered to him at all. As though the way that the innkeeper had addressed him had not caused him to feel a profound sense of longing for the name and the life which he had once called his own.

'But every man whose inheritance is a dukedom must have to contradict others upon becoming a duke, surely?' Charlotte countered. 'In my experience, most noblemen are not quiet about their rank.'

She was right, of course, and yet the observation felt like a knife being driven into his heart. A painful reminder that he was not most noblemen, and that the Dukedom was never meant to be his inheritance.

'To be frank, I doubt the innkeeper cares very much if I am a nobleman or a physician,' he huffed, fiddling irritably with his collar. 'Or whether you are Mrs Scott or the Duchess of Falstone.'

The colour rose again in Charlotte's cheeks, and immediately he regretted his stern tone. What was the matter with him? She had merely made an innocent observation, one which merited a proper explanation from him about why he was so content to be called a doctor rather than a duke. The problem was that he had no idea where to begin, and a strong suspicion that if he attempted to talk about it he might never stop. Besides, he reminded himself, he was taking Charlotte to Edinburgh to give her a reprieve from her cares, not so that she could be burdened by his sorrows on their first day alone as husband and wife.

She pressed her lips together for a long moment, watching him warily. 'Of course,' she said in the end, clasping her hands together. 'I dare say you are right.'

The cautious note in her voice caused his heart to lurch painfully in his chest. 'Forgive me, Charlotte, what I mean is…'

'I'd quite like to freshen up now,' she interrupted him, turning away and busying herself with her portmanteau. 'Perhaps you could go and see about that supper the innkeeper promised.'

Well done, Ted. Day two of your matrimonial arrangement and you've managed to upset your bride already. Carry on like that and she'll wish she'd stayed with her mother.

He hovered for several moments, considering making a further attempt at an apology. Charlotte continued to rummage through her portmanteau, however, making it clear that she was not going to turn to look at him, much less listen to his feeble attempts to excuse his behaviour. And indeed, why should she? He'd asked for her hand in marriage and offered her an escape, only to let all of that pain and grief he felt rear its ugly head at the first opportunity. All Charlotte had done was point out the obvious—that no duke in his right mind would wish to be known by anything other than his title.

Apparently, he was not in his right mind. And apparently, his desire to reject who he was now ran deeper than he'd thought.

'Right—yes, supper,' he said after a long moment.

Without another word, he hurried downstairs to find the innkeeper, hoping the man would be able to offer them something warming and hearty, accompanied by some wine. He could only hope that sharing a nice supper might thaw the chilly air which had crept into that bedchamber. Otherwise, it was going to be a long night.

Chapter Ten

'I don't think I've ever managed to render my mother speechless before,' Ted said, laughing as he recounted the Dowager Duchess's reaction to his greenhouse proposal. 'That was always Perry's gift rather than mine. I'm still not sure she's recovered from the shock of it.'

Sitting across the table from him, Charlotte found herself laughing too. Something she'd done a great deal this evening. She felt much better now, her earlier headache having apparently been cured by a hearty supper and prevented from returning by the numbing effects of that potent claret which Ted had sourced from the innkeeper downstairs. A claret she'd consumed with enthusiasm as they dined together and spoke quite frankly about the whirlwind of the past few days. A claret which had left her feeling very relaxed and more than a little dizzy.

What would your mother say, Charlotte, if she saw you in this condition?

It didn't matter what her mother would say—she was a married woman now. A married woman who was spending what had turned out to be a very lovely evening with her new husband. That was a pleasant surprise, especially considering the way the evening had begun. As a maid had appeared at their door with their supper, Charlotte had still been chastising herself for the way she'd clumsily questioned Ted about his choice to inhabit the role of Dr Scott. It was clear that she'd upset him and, worse still, she'd ended the conversation abruptly, choosing rudeness rather than risk allowing the discussion to continue and saying something even more tactless.

Nevertheless, his behaviour had intrigued her. He'd been evasive in his answers but there had been no disguising the hurt which had flickered briefly in his brown eyes. A look which suggested there was far more to his willingness to be addressed as Dr Scott than he was prepared to say. A look which he'd successfully suppressed and which had not returned. Indeed, as Charlotte met his eye across the table, she saw only merriment in that dark gaze. Doubtless Ted was feeling the effects of the wine, too.

'But do you think your mother approves of our marriage?' Charlotte asked, returning her thoughts to their conversation and daring to ask a question which had been on her mind. The Dowager Duchess had been kind and friendly enough, but their interactions following the greenhouse proposal had been so brief and limited that it was impossible to read anything into them. 'I hope she was not angry, like Elspeth was.'

'Oh—no, not angry,' Ted insisted. 'She'd have a nerve if she was, given how relentlessly she has urged me to marry over these past months. No, I believe that whilst it has come as a surprise, my mother is actually relieved, although that has not prevented her from…' He shook his head at himself and sipped his wine, as though thinking better of what he'd been about to say.

'From what?' Charlotte couldn't resist asking.

Ted cleared his throat. 'From reminding me what marriage is for,' he said, and even in the dim candlelight Charlotte caught the pained expression flicker across his face.

'Oh.'

'I'm just glad you'd retired already last night and did not hear how blunt she was in reminding me of my duty,' he added, grimacing. 'Of our duty, as Duke and Duchess, to secure our lineage.'

Charlotte sipped her wine, hiding her growing blush behind her glass. That aspect of marriage had been on her mind ever since they'd made their vows yesterday. Perhaps now was the time to discuss it, she thought—while they were alone, sharing a candlelit dinner, emboldened by sufficient quantities of claret...

'I don't believe we ever talked of that, when making our arrangement,' she began. 'But I know that you need an heir, Ted, and so—'

'Charlotte,' he interrupted. He reached across the table and gave her hand the gentlest, briefest squeeze—a gesture which she felt all over. 'I do not want you to worry about that—at least, not yet. I think it would be wise to give ourselves some time to become friends first before we concern ourselves too much with...certain duties. Don't you agree?'

'Friends—yes, of course,' Charlotte replied, mustering a smile and trying to ignore the way his words seemed to sting her in a way which felt suspiciously like rejection. It was ridiculous to react that way, she told herself. Ted was just being honourable and decent, just as he always was. Theirs was not a passionate love match, after all, but a pragmatic arrangement. He was absolutely right to suggest that they should take their time and get to know each other better first.

Be sensible, Charlotte. At least now you know where you stand, and what to expect.

'It is getting late,' Ted said, his deep voice cutting through her thoughts. 'We ought to retire soon.' He finished the last of his wine, then gestured towards the jugs of water and washbowls which a maid had set out for them earlier. 'If you wish to wash and change now, I will go outside.'

Charlotte shook her head, pointing at her glass, which was still half full. 'You go first. I will sit here and finish this.'

She made a point of turning to look at the wall. She heard Ted murmur his agreement as he rose from his chair and strode across the room, then sat frozen as she listened to the rustle of linen and the burble of water being poured. She felt her cheeks grow hot as a potent sense of awareness curdled in her stomach. She'd never been in such close confines with a man before. Never been present while a man readied himself for bed. Never slept in the same room as a man. She'd abandoned her attempt to elope with Lord Crowgarth on the first day, long before darkness fell and the intimacies of a night at a coaching inn could commence. Thank God! Thank God she'd seen sense and fled. She nursed her wine, struck by the realisation that whilst the thought of being in a situation like this with Crowgarth horrified her, with Ted she felt comfortable, and safe, and…

Intolerably curious.

Before she could stop herself, Charlotte felt her gaze creep away from the wall and over to where Ted stood. He had his back turned to her, which was just as well since from that angle he could not possibly see the way her mouth had fallen open as her gaze swept over his magnificent physique, from the broadness of his shoulders to the hint of muscles beneath his taut skin as he ran a washcloth over his arms. He twisted slightly, and she caught sight of a large scar running down the side of his slender waist, ending just above the fawn-coloured pantaloons which, mercifully for her pounding heart, he still wore.

That will serve you right for looking. Now you are more curious than ever.

She was. No doubt emboldened by the wine, she'd allowed wayward, impulsive Charlotte to break free once again, and now she was curious about the rest of Ted, about the parts which she had not seen, and curious about that scar. There was a story behind that—she felt sure of it.

She whipped her gaze away just in time as Ted turned round to grab his nightshirt. She drew several deep breaths, trying to slow her racing pulse and willing her burning cheeks to cool down. If he saw the flustered state of her now, he'd surely know that she'd been looking at him—a realisation which would hardly bode well for their agreement to be friends...

'Your turn, Charlotte,' he called. 'I will wait outside.'

Charlotte glanced up just as Ted hurried out of the door. She drew another long, calming breath as she rose from her seat and set about removing her gown, petticoat and stockings, her thoughts still unashamedly fixed upon the sight of him, gloriously unclothed. No doubt that image would be imprinted upon her brain for all eternity now. She fiddled absently with the laces of her stays, trying to loosen them enough to remove the undergarment—no easy task without a maid to assist her.

She thought again about their earlier conversation about friendship, and Ted's apparent lack of urgency over their duty to produce an heir. She could not help but wonder at it; he was well aware, after all, of the pressure he was under—not least from his mother. And as a man who'd inherited the Dukedom precisely because of his own brother's untimely demise, he was surely aware of the imperative of securing his lineage. In the cold light of day, his attitude, as gentlemanly as it was, made no sense…

Perhaps he simply does not desire you. Or perhaps you are not the only one with secrets…

Staring at herself now in the mirror and still struggling to unlace her stays, Charlotte found her thoughts taking a darker turn. What if there were other, murkier reasons lurking in the shadows? What if making her his Duchess was about more than fulfilling his duty and nobly giving her the escape she'd craved? What if their arrangement was designed to shield other, less savoury aspects of his life from view? What if the reason he'd been so keen on having a practical, loveless marriage was because his heart was already committed elsewhere? To someone he could never have as his wife?

Charlotte's heart began to race and her head spun ever faster as all the awful possibilities dawned on her. Ted was a man who'd had a life before the Dukedom had fallen unexpectedly into his lap. A life she knew next to nothing about. A life he'd had to leave behind. Was this why he was taking her to Edinburgh, not to give her some welcome distance from her cares, but to reunite him with the woman he loved, the woman from whom duty had parted him? Or perhaps, even worse, to allow him to indulge in his pleasures with a favourite mistress one last time?

Frustrated, Charlotte yanked at her laces, forcing them into a tighter knot than ever. 'Argh! Drat it!' she cried out, angry with herself. Angry that she could not get her stays undone. Angry that she'd lacked the self-control to resist peeking at Ted. Angry that his offer of friendship had felt like rejection. Angry that it had taken a good deal of claret for her suspicions about his true reasons for marrying her to ferment.

Angry that she was angry, when really, she had no right to be. Ted had offered her an escape, and given her a better life. Why was that not enough?

Before she could attempt to answer any of her own questions, she heard the doorknob squeak and the door creak open. She spun around, just in time to see Ted rush in.

'Charlotte?' he said, his brown eyes filled with concern. 'Is everything all right? Only, I thought I heard you scream.'

The sight of Charlotte in nothing but her stays and chemise, her red hair loose and tumbling over her shoulders, was something to behold. Gripped by his instincts, Ted hurried towards her, trying to ignore the lump which had risen in his throat, and how fast his heart had begun to race. Trying not to acknowledge the disconcerting feelings which conspired with the wine he'd drunk to make him feel extremely off-kilter—feelings of searing lust, tinged with the sting of regret that he'd been so quick to promise a purely platonic start to their marriage.

Serves you right. Marrying a flame-haired goddess only to solemnly pledge your undying friendship is probably the most Ted-like thing you've ever done.

Not that he could have done anything else, could he? The look of alarm which had swept across her face at the merest mention of his mother's lecture on *the true purpose of marriage* had told him so, in no uncertain terms. Everything about their union had been done in haste, from the proposal to the wedding day and the honeymoon. Now he had to give Charlotte time—to adjust to her new life, with him. They would get to know each other better, and then, eventually…

Eventually would be far easier to bear if you could take your eyes off her.

That was a problem he was increasingly grappling with; it was no use pretending otherwise. That particularly discomfiting fact had really hit him with its full, significant force on that day outside her aunt's cottage, when their eyes had locked and for one brief, mad moment he'd contemplated kissing her. An idea which, he knew, was occurring to him again as he drew close enough to detect that tantalising lavender scent she wore, and to spy the heated, distressed look which shone in her sky-blue eyes.

'Is everything all right, Charlotte?' he asked, repeating his earlier question as he tried and failed to put thoughts of kisses out of his mind.

She shook her head furiously. 'I was trying to loosen my stays,' she replied, tugging at her back. 'The laces are all knotted and I can't quite reach—oh, drat it!'

Ted swallowed hard, his gaze wandering to the offending item, which remained steadfast over her tempting curves. 'Can I...er...be of any assistance with the...er...laces?' he asked.

God help him.

Charlotte's cheeks glowed a wicked shade of scarlet and she huffed a breath. 'I suppose I am going to have to say yes,' she said, not meeting his eye. 'It's either that or sleep in the dratted thing tonight.'

Without another word, Charlotte turned around, pulling that mass of fiery curls over one shoulder so that Ted could see the back of her stays and the tangled laces. He got to work quickly, his physician's fingers as precise as ever as he teased the knots apart. He tried to apply his mind wholly to the task in front of him, to concentrate solely on the laces and to not allow his thoughts, or his eyes, to be distracted by who he was unlacing. The intimacy implied by helping a woman out of her undergarments was bad enough, but to let his mind linger on the way her pale skin glowed in the candlelight, or the way that moving her hair aside had exposed the curve of her shoulder and nape of her neck, was downright dangerous. And as for considering how easy it would be just to lean forward and place a tender kiss upon the soft skin of her back…

The mere thought was a clear breach of their agreement.

'There,' he said at last, triumphing over the final knot. 'All done.'

He wasn't certain at what point he took leave of his senses. Perhaps it was when Charlotte glanced over that perfect shoulder, murmuring her thanks as she slipped out of the troublesome item. Or perhaps it was when she turned back to face him, entirely unbound now and wearing only a loose white chemise which skimmed over her pert form and inflamed his imagination. He should have stepped away—he knew that. He should have returned to wait outside until she'd finished changing. Certainly, he should not have cupped her cheek with his hand and leaned towards her, allowing his lips to softly and tentatively meet with hers.

Except that was exactly what he did. And it might, just might, have ended there, if he had not heard Charlotte sigh against his mouth. If he had not seen her eyes flutter closed as he gathered her into his arms. If she had not responded in kind, pressing that petite, alluring form against him and inviting him to deepen the kiss—an invitation he welcomed as every last ounce of his yearning attraction was translated into potent, burning desire.

It might have ended there, if he had remembered sooner, much sooner, just how much wine they'd both consumed. If he had remembered sooner that he'd made a promise to her—a promise which on his honour as a gentleman it was imperative that he keep. A promise to be her friend first, and not to ravish her at the first opportunity when she was under the influence of a little too much claret...

'I am so sorry,' Ted said, forcing himself to relinquish her. 'I really should not have done that.'

For a long moment, Charlotte stared at him, lips still parted, her expression impossible to read. She did not appear angry, but stunned, perhaps? He could hardly blame her—he was reeling from what had just happened, too, and he was the one who'd initiated the kiss. Then, before he could say anything else, she gave a rapid shake of her head—one which made those loose red curls lick at her shoulders like flames.

'No—of course,' she replied, stepping away from him now and towards the bed. 'It is getting late, and we ought to get some sleep. Let's just forget that anything happened.'

Ted nodded dumbly, wondering how on earth such a thing might even be possible. He glanced forlornly at the sofa which was to be his bed for the night. It looked about as inviting as a wooden board, but then, he supposed it did not matter. The night ahead promised to be long and sleepless as he grappled with the memory of that kiss and the fact that the object of his clearly rampant desire would be slumbering in the bed mere feet away. At least it was only for tonight. Tomorrow they would reach their destination, where separate bedchambers at a safe distance awaited them both.

'Yes—sleep,' he agreed, grabbing a blanket and suppressing a groan. Their arrival in Edinburgh could not come soon enough.

Ted wasn't sure if he'd been asleep or not. He felt as though he'd been in a restless state for some hours, hovering somewhere between waking and sleeping as a myriad of images and memories raced unabated through his mind. What he saw swirled and melded together, so that one moment he was a boy again, climbing a tree, and the next he was falling, but instead of hitting the ground, he landed at the altar of St Oswald's, right at Charlotte's feet. He could see her looking down at him, wearing that same fetching blue dress she'd made her vows in, but the expression on her face was disapproving, even hostile.

'You're not Perry,' she said to him, arms folded, her foot tapping impatiently. 'I was waiting for Perry.'

'Perry?' he repeated, shaking his head in disbelief. 'But he's...'

Dead.

That word echoed around Ted's mind, accompanied by music which sounded distinctly off-key, like a piano in need of tuning. No, wait—not a piano, more like a voice. A fraught voice, calling out.

Charlotte.

Ted's eyes flew open. Immediately he bolted off the sofa, not bothering to light a candle and instead allowing the sliver of moonlight which shone through the thin curtains to illuminate his way. He hurried towards the bed; he could see the outline of her, could hear the rustling of sheets as she moved and whimpered.

'Charlotte?' he said, bending down at her side. He

placed a gentle hand on her arm, trying to rouse her. 'Charlotte? Are you all right?'

'Couldn't help him…' she murmured. 'My fault, and I couldn't…'

'It's all right,' Ted said softly, trying to soothe her, not sure if she was yet awake. 'You are safe. I am here, and…'

'Ted? Where am I?' Her limbs stilled. Her words, though lucid now, were tinged with panic. 'What happened?'

'Shh, my darling, you were dreaming, that is all,' he whispered softly, placing a tender kiss on top of her head.

Charlotte didn't answer. Instead, she reached for him, wrapping her arms around his neck and pulling him close to her. Instinct overtook him as he complied, climbing on to the bed beside her and holding her tightly in his embrace. Instinct to comfort her, to protect her. That was what this was, wasn't it? He heard her sigh, sensed her body relax against him and her breathing resume a steady rhythm as she fell asleep once more.

He'd meant to leave her then. He'd meant to return to the sofa and continue his own restless night upon his wooden board. Instead, as the dawn of a new day crept lethargically through the curtains some hours later, he awoke to realise that not only had he fallen into a deep, dreamless sleep, but he'd done so with

Charlotte still cuddled against his chest and with one of his own traitorous hands still planted, possessively and damningly, upon her waist.

Chapter Eleven

Let's just forget that anything happened.

Charlotte stared out of the window as their carriage rattled along, those words echoing in her mind. They'd arrived in Edinburgh some time earlier, the gentle countryside gradually giving way first to narrow roads lined with ancient buildings and bustling with people, carts and carriages, and subsequently to wider, newer boulevards, filled with the palatial homes of the city's wealthiest inhabitants. Now they found themselves on the grandest square of them all, one which was capable of competing with the finest areas of London. A scene which she would have been in awe of, were it not for the fact that her thoughts were hopelessly preoccupied by everything that had happened last night.

Everything that she had said they should forget.

As if she could ever forget about that kiss! As if she could forget the way Ted had held her, his warm lips pressed against hers, and how right it had felt. How perfect. But she also could not forget the abrupt way he'd ended it, and that apology he'd issued, thick with panic. Thick with regret. That had stung her, and all those suspicions which had begun to ferment in her mind had come racing to the fore. Suspicions which felt increasingly well-founded. Their kiss had perturbed him because he wished he'd been kissing someone else. Someone in this city. Someone with whom he intended to be reunited.

'This is Charlotte Square,' Ted announced from his seat opposite her, breaking the tense silence which had lingered between them for much of the journey. 'Named after the late Queen, of course.'

Charlotte glanced up at him, just long enough to acknowledge what he'd said. Long enough, too, to see a pained look flicker across his face as he regarded her. A look which spoke of his discomfort—over that kiss, yes, but no doubt over the way they'd awoken together in the bed this morning, too. The way she'd been tucked against him, his strong arms still wrapped around her, with one hand resting upon her side. She could only vaguely recall how they'd ended up like that. She knew that she'd been dreaming, lost in that nightmare which her memories always forced her to endure in the darkest hours of the night—about Crowgarth, and about her father. She must have called out because she remembered

Ted coming to comfort her, remembered his tender touch, and remembered how she'd reached for him, reassured by knowing that he was there. Then…nothing. Just deep and dreamless sleep. Until the morning light had woken her, and forced her to confront the fact that she'd slumbered contentedly in the arms of a man who had likely spent the night wishing she was someone else.

Let's just forget that anything happened.

If only she could, then she might be released from the effect that last night was having upon her. At least, she assumed that was the reason why her face heated every time Ted's leg brushed against her skirts, and why her heart raced every time her eyes wandered towards his lips. Why their mere proximity in this stifling carriage provoked foolish, futile feelings which Ted had made abundantly clear he did not share.

'We're almost there,' Ted continued. He pointed out of the carriage window, to a pale grey stone townhouse with a blue door on the north side of the square. 'That house is mine. Or rather, it is ours, now,' he added with a strained sort of smile.

Moments later, Charlotte felt the carriage draw to a halt. Ted climbed out first, then turned back to offer Charlotte his hand. She felt her breath catch in her throat as she accepted it, his touch making her cheeks burn afresh as she stepped out. They were greeted by an older lady, her face ruddy and her breathing laboured, as though she'd had to hurry outside.

'My apologies, Doctor,' she began. 'I mean… Your Grace. My apologies, Your Grace, but we only received word of your arrival this morning. Your bedchamber is ready for you, and as you requested, a bedchamber is being prepared for Mrs… I mean, the Duchess.' Her speech was rapid, delivered in a Scottish accent, and Charlotte found she had trouble keeping up.

Ted smiled. 'That all sounds very agreeable, Mrs McGowan, thank you. Allow me to introduce my wife, the Duchess of Falstone. Charlotte, this is Mrs McGowan, my housekeeper.'

Mrs McGowan smiled and gave a small curtsey. 'It's a pleasure to meet you, Your Grace. The whole household was so delighted to hear that the good doctor has married.' She paused, her rosy cheeks reddening further. 'Not that he's the doctor any more, of course. My apologies, Your Grace.'

Charlotte looked up at Ted, reminded at once of the hurt she'd seen in his eyes when she'd challenged him over his willingness to allow that innkeeper to call him Dr Scott. If Ted's housekeeper's words troubled him, however, then he didn't show it.

'No need to apologise, Mrs McGowan,' he replied. 'Much has changed. We all have a lot to get used to. Now, would you be so good as to have some tea brought to the parlour? I'm sure the Duchess is in need of refreshment after our journey.'

Mrs McGowan nodded obligingly, and Ted led Charlotte through a wide entrance and up the stairs to a well-appointed parlour at the rear of the house. Once they'd made themselves comfortable, Mrs McGowan returned with some tea, and a suggestion that she present the remainder of the household to Charlotte, once she had rested awhile.

'That reminds me, Mrs McGowan,' Ted interjected. 'The Duchess is going to require a lady's maid. Perhaps you could see about getting two or three suitable candidates for the Duchess to choose from?'

Charlotte watched as the housekeeper's wrinkled brow knitted together in a frown. 'I can, Your Grace. However, we are going to need more than a lady's maid now that you have returned. A few members of the household have left us recently. I did write to inform you,' she added pointedly.

Charlotte could not help but notice how Ted shifted ever so slightly in his seat at the reminder. 'You did, Mrs McGowan. All right—leave the matter with me and the Duchess, and we will consider what other positions might need to be filled.'

'Very good, sir. Now, if there is nothing else? Only, I've left young Becky preparing Her Grace's bedchamber alone, and she's ever such a slight wee thing.'

'There's nothing else, Mrs McGowan. I will leave you to your duties.'

'Thank you, Your Grace,' Mrs McGowan replied, before turning again to Charlotte. 'If there is anything you require, Your Grace, please do let me know. We are all very excited that you are here. It is nice to have a mistress in the house at last.'

Charlotte watched as the housekeeper bustled purposefully towards the door, leaving them to resume the uncomfortable silence which had persisted between them during the journey. Charlotte sipped her tea, taking in her tastefully decorated surroundings, from the pale green walls to the mahogany furniture and the large Persian rug adorning the wooden floor. It was a very fine house and, as Mrs McGowan had said, she was its mistress now. The realisation made her stomach flip with nervous anticipation and something like excitement. Ted might not have room in his heart for her, but he had made room in his life, and in giving her an escape he had also given her a title and duties which she was determined to fulfil. She'd made an agreement with him, and she would keep her promise. She would perform the domestic duties of a wife and a duchess, she thought, even if the intimacies of her role were reserved for someone else…

'Mrs McGowan is quite a force of nature,' Ted said, interrupting her thoughts. 'But she is the very best.

I've no doubt she will ensure that you have a lady's maid in no time at all.'

'From what Mrs McGowan said, I got the impression that there are a number of vacancies to fill in the house,' she replied pointedly. 'Why has there been such an exodus of servants?'

She saw Ted flinch. 'I would not say it was an exodus, exactly, but a number of staff have left. Chief among them was my butler, Lamont, and also several maids.' He rubbed his jaw thoughtfully. 'I suppose the sudden nature of my departure will have been the cause of it. An absent master hardly inspires confidence, and… I had not told them what I planned to do about the house,' he said in the end.

'Why not?'

'Because I had not decided,' he confessed. 'It was all quite a shock—Perry dying, becoming the Duke. I left all this behind in rather a hurry. I knew that common sense dictated that I should sell this house, or at least have a tenant living in it, and yet I think I wanted to keep everything here as it always was, just in case.'

'In case what?' Charlotte asked.

She watched him hesitate again, a pained look flickering briefly across his face.

'In case I was ever able to come back, I suppose.'

Charlotte gave a brittle nod then sipped her tea, resisting the temptation to press him further, or to interrogate that wistful look which she'd spied in his deep brown eyes. A look which contained the answer to a question, an answer which she knew she did not have the stomach to hear—about why Ted had wanted to come back to Edinburgh now and, more to the point, for whom.

Coming back to his Edinburgh home had been more difficult than Ted had imagined. It had inspired a feeling of nostalgia, a longing for his former life, and he'd expected that. What he hadn't expected, however, was to feel so provoked by just how much had changed in his absence. It had been almost a year since he'd last returned, on a brief springtime trip to collect belongings and to tie up the loose ends of his former professional life once the chaos caused by Perry's sudden death had somewhat abated.

A mere year, and yet Edinburgh had not waited patiently for him—that much had been obvious from the window of his carriage today. On Princes Street, sumptuous new gardens were being fashioned where the last remnants of the Nor Loch had once been, and on the south side of Charlotte Square those final houses, their building delayed by the years of uncertainty caused by the war with France, were almost complete. And in his own home, many of the faces of those who'd loyally served Dr Edward Scott were notably absent. Edinburgh had moved on. Life had moved on, and all without him.

And to add to that discomfiting realisation, he was thoroughly unsettled by what had happened at the coaching inn on the previous night. Not only had he kissed Charlotte, he'd climbed into bed beside her and remained there all night. Waking with her in his arms, feeling the warmth of her body pressed against his, breathing in her lavender scent—all of it had been intoxicating, and about as far from friendship as it was possible to be. Indeed, he'd spent most of that interminable carriage journey trying to dampen his lust—no mean feat when the object of it had been seated opposite, steadfastly avoiding his gaze and looking both breathtakingly beautiful and devastatingly uncomfortable.

He could hardly blame her; earlier last night he'd spoken of his honourable intentions, promising to give her time for them to become friends first, only to allow his actions to send a very different message. Seeing her discomfort had dissuaded him from raising the matter directly, but it had also strengthened his resolve to honour that promise through his actions. He would be a considerate and attentive husband, and he would ensure Charlotte felt at ease in his company. They would get to know each other better and, until they did, everything else could wait.

Including his rampant desire for her.

* * *

'Did you ever hold balls in here?' Charlotte asked as they stood together in the red drawing room. As part of his mission to ensure she felt at home, Ted had spent the evening giving her a tour of the house. As they'd wandered from room to room, she'd seemed to relax, their earlier tense silences mercifully giving way to a little conversation.

'Balls? No. The occasional dinner party, yes. But the company I kept was not particularly inclined towards dancing. We were a small group of gentlemen, physicians mostly, and I believe ladies are usually required if there is to be any dancing.'

'So there were never any ladies present?'

He shrugged, feeling suddenly conscious of the quiet life he'd lived, focused almost entirely upon his work. 'In all honesty, I hardly ever entertained here. Usually, I would go out to a tavern in the old part of the city, and a group of us would spend the evening deliberating on matters of professional interest over a bottle of claret. Rather like a convivial club, I suppose,' he added, wincing at the wistful note in his own voice.

'It sounds very different to the life of a duke,' Charlotte observed, and he wondered if she'd detected his nostalgia.

'It was,' he said, suppressing the urge to sigh. 'Peers are meant to prefer their exclusive London clubs, aren't they? But for me, there was always something about the informality of a tavern. They are much like the inn we stayed at last night, really,' he added briskly. 'Except for the lack of bedrooms, of course.'

The way her eyes widened at the words *inn* and *bedrooms* made him immediately regret raising the subject. But then, he supposed, was it really wise to avoid it for ever? Last night he'd apologised for kissing her, but today he'd steadfastly avoided discussing the fact that he'd ended up in bed beside her. He realised now that he should have addressed the matter, at least to reassure her that his intentions had been honourable, that he'd sought only to comfort her.

He cleared his throat. 'Last night,' he began. 'When you called out in your sleep, and I came to you…'

'Ted, please do not worry. I had a bad dream,' she interrupted. 'That was all. Please, let us just forget it—all of it.'

He frowned, recalling that she'd said much the same in the aftermath of that earth-shattering kiss. Clearly, she did not wish to discuss any of it, and clearly, if he was intent upon being a decent and considerate husband, he would respect that. Even if he was now desperate to gain some insight into how she felt, not to mention increasingly curious about why she'd called out in her sleep like that.

'Of course,' he replied. 'Although, if it's any comfort, I also had a bad dream last night.'

'You did? What about?'

Ted hesitated, recalling now some of the particulars of that dream. Of the vision of Charlotte, standing at the altar, his brother's name on her lips. He collected his thoughts, resolving to tell her some of it. If he confided in her, he reasoned, might she then feel encouraged to do the same?

'It was about something which happened to me as a boy,' he said. 'An accident. I was climbing a tree with my friend, Ross—the surgeon apothecary, as he is now. I fell from the tree and was injured quite badly. A sharp branch tore through my shirt, wounding me.'

Charlotte's eyes widened. 'That scar you have on your side,' she breathed. 'That is…' She pressed her fingers against her lips, her cheeks reddening so much that she matched the shade of the wallpaper.

Ted frowned. 'How do you know about my scar?' he asked. 'Surely Elspeth did not…'

'No—it wasn't Elspeth,' Charlotte replied, glowing an almost impossible shade of crimson. 'It was me. I saw it—last night, when you were changing for bed. I did not mean to look, obviously, it was quite by accident…' she insisted.

'It really does not matter. Best forgotten,' he replied, repeating her favourite sentiment as he tried not to dwell upon exactly how accidental her stealing a peek at his shirtless form had been, and whether that daring act might suggest that his attraction to her was in any way reciprocated.

Don't be a fool. This isn't that sort of marriage, remember? She was probably just curious.

'That scar has a lot of significance,' he continued, pushing his errant thoughts aside once more. 'What happened that day has a lot to do with why I became a physician. After I fell from the tree, Ross ran to fetch his father, Mr Deane, who was also a surgeon apothecary. I was eleven years old, frightened and in pain, but the way he treated me, with such kindness and expertise—it made a lasting impression, I suppose.'

Charlotte regarded him thoughtfully. 'I can understand that. You were so badly hurt that day, and yet, because of the impression the elder Mr Deane made on you, it proved to be such a turning point in your life.'

'A turning point,' he repeated. 'Yes, I suppose it was.'

Ted could only muster a tight smile as they walked out of the drawing room, ready to retire for the night. He was not about to confess to the other memories his recollection had provoked. The way his father had glared at his wayward younger son as he refused for the umpteenth time to become a clergyman. The way his mother had pleaded with him to choose a more *respectable* career. The fact that they had not relented out of goodwill to their second born son, but because they were simply worn out with worry about the behaviour of the Dukedom's heir. The fact that he'd not only become a physician, but an expert in midwifery—a field which his mother found so unsavoury and shameful that he was forbidden ever to speak of it.

A field which he planned to return to, albeit briefly, when he delivered his lectures. He was not about to tell Charlotte about those, either. As proud as he was of his own achievements, he was acutely aware of the dim view others took, of just how distasteful they found it. Charlotte seemed content to regard his profession as a part of his past, but he did not wish to imagine her reaction if she was made aware of the finer details of it, or that he—a duke now—continued to associate himself with it.

Not that it mattered. Once the lectures were over, he would draw a line under his career for good. He would confirm, as if confirmation were needed, that all those years of fighting, of studying, of practising his profession, were little more than a collection of futile acts undertaken by a man whose ambitions had ultimately been ground into dust.

Chapter Twelve

Charlotte gave herself a final, cursory glance in the mirror, satisfied with the fit of her new emerald-green gown and, if she was honest with herself, feeling every inch the Duchess. It was a feeling which had struck her more than once during that first, busy week in Edinburgh. She'd assumed her new role and responsibilities with a confidence which had surprised her, overseeing Mrs McGowan's efforts to secure new staff and directing all manner of domestic matters, from their menus to which rooms should have fires lit, and when.

She tried to remind herself that she'd been raised for a role such as this, and that was why she inhabited it so comfortably. She tried not to reflect too frequently on just how free she felt, running a household on her own terms, far away from her mother and the criticism she'd had to endure. Far away from constant reminders of the past. Thinking about that only reminded her that she ought to feel guilty, not liberated, and she did not want to feel guilty any more. She wanted to move forward, and to embrace her new life.

Whilst her domestic life was decidedly full, however, her social life was not. So far there had been no diary of engagements for her to manage, but then, honeymooning couples were generally expected to keep to themselves and enjoy their early days of married life. An expectation which would be all well and good, except that most days her husband was notably absent from their home. It was not that his absences were prolonged, but they were frequent and unexplained. Several times she'd tried to gently question him about his whereabouts, but all he would say was that he had business to attend to.

Yes, and you know exactly what sort of business.

She did know, and that knowledge gnawed at her. Perhaps that was why she'd thrown herself so wholeheartedly into managing their home; the busier she was, the less she could think about where Ted was and what he was doing. The less she could imagine him in the arms of another woman—a woman he'd met years ago, perhaps during one of those many evenings he'd spent in Edinburgh's taverns. A woman whose devastating beauty had captured his heart, but whose situation in life meant that she could not be a doctor's wife, never mind a duchess. A woman who tempted him away from his home and into her bed every afternoon. Charlotte fiddled absentmindedly with a stray curl, trying not to conjure the image of Ted's hands wrapped possessively around the woman's waist as he honoured her with the kisses he denied to his wife.

Apart from that one kiss, of course. The one she could not stop thinking about.

She drew a deep breath, determined not to dwell on it and to put on a pleasant face for the evening ahead. Not only was Ted remaining at home this evening, but they had a guest coming for dinner—an old friend and colleague of Ted named Mr Henry Tarbolton. As she heard Ted knock at the door, ready to escort her down to dinner, she reminded herself of the importance of being a warm and gracious hostess. Of giving no hint of the turmoil which simmered beneath the surface.

She opened the door to see Ted standing there, immaculately dressed for dinner in a dark coat which emphasised his broad shoulders. She bit her lip, trying not to recall the sight of those same shoulders that night at the inn, gloriously bare in the candlelight. She stepped towards him, ready to take his arm, noticing how different he smelled tonight. Not his usual citrus scent but stronger and sweeter, like sandalwood. Perhaps he had wanted a change.

Or perhaps that is the scent that his other woman prefers.

'You look lovely,' he murmured, although his gaze barely moved from her face. 'Is that one of your new gowns?'

She nodded. 'Thank you. Yes, it is.'

Ted might have been absent a good deal this past week, but he was attentive in other ways. Despite her protestation that her extant wardrobe would suffice, he had insisted that she should have some new gowns and a dressmaker was duly sent for. She appreciated the gesture, although she sensed the underlying necessity of it, too. As talented as she was with a needle and thread, even she had to admit that it was a tall order, making those well-worn gowns she'd brought with her into suitable attire for a duchess.

Ted leaned closer. 'You have a...'

He raised his hand, reaching for that loose curl she'd been fiddling with. As he did so, his hand came to rest upon her cheek, just as it had done that night at the inn.

Charlotte lifted her gaze, allowing her eyes to meet his. Allowing herself to become lost in his dark stare. She watched as his eyes dipped and he leaned closer still, his hand moving from her cheek to caress her arm, the skin which remained bare beneath her short sleeves inflamed by his touch. Barely an inch separated them now, his lips tantalisingly close to hers as her eyes fluttered closed, and...

Ted kissed her. A chaste and swift kiss upon the cheek. She opened her eyes, feeling every bit the fool for having been swept up in the moment so easily. At having responded so eagerly to the merest touch. Although she was sure she had not imagined it, that he had been about to kiss her—to properly kiss her. Hadn't he?

'Becky is still learning exactly how to style my hair,' she said, trying hard to recover herself whilst trying to fix the offending strand. 'She is doing well, however. She is young but keen to learn and will make an excellent lady's maid, I'm sure.' She pressed her lips together then, conscious that she was beginning to ramble, and that her emotions were scattered all over the place. She had to compose herself.

Ted offered her his arm and together they made their way down the stairs to dinner. Once or twice she glanced at him, trying to discern any hint of emotion or awareness about what had just occurred between them. Any hint of whether he had been about to kiss her, or if she'd misread the situation entirely. His face, however, gave nothing away and in the end she concluded that it had been her imagination, that he'd intended all along to compliment her and to kiss her cheek and nothing more.

Because, she reminded herself, there was nothing more to their marriage than this. A duke and a duchess bound together for convenience so that she could be free of her mother, and so that Ted could indulge his passions elsewhere.

He'd kissed her. Again. Ted sat at the dining table, trying to keep his attention fixed on his guest and not allow his eyes to wander to the stunning woman sitting near to him, looking thoroughly tempting and every inch the resplendent duchess. The sight of her standing in her doorway wearing that striking green gown had taken his breath away and made him think thoughts which had been entirely inappropriate, considering Henry was awaiting them downstairs. It had taken every ounce of self-discipline he had to keep his gaze gentlemanly, to not allow it to linger upon the daring cut of that sweeping neckline and all the alabaster skin which seemed to call to him to be caressed. Then there was that loose fiery curl—he'd only meant to point it out, but then somehow his hand had brushed against her cheek and, before he knew it, he'd lost himself in that bright blue gaze and was leaning towards her lips.

He'd stopped himself just in time, and hopefully he'd salvaged the situation with that brief, respectful kiss on the cheek. Although even that had felt far too sensual and downright dangerous. He picked at his food, cursing himself for his weakness. Was it really so hard for him to fulfil a promise, to give Charlotte time and to be her friend first before seeking affection and intimacy? What on earth was the matter with him?

At least during this past week he'd had much to occupy him, from calling upon friends to visiting former colleagues and places of work, and making the arrangements for finally delivering his lectures. Being out of the house had given him a welcome reprieve from his desire, because when he was within its walls he felt Charlotte's presence everywhere. The sight of her sewing box and exquisite embroidery work, sitting neatly on the table in the parlour. The sound of her humming a tune as she made her way down the stairs. The scent of her floral perfume lingering in every room. The thought of her lying in bed at night, with mere doors separating them. It was torture.

His gaze slid briefly towards his wife. She was smiling, her blue eyes shining with merriment as Henry regaled her with one of his many amusing anecdotes about growing up in the tenements of Edinburgh's Old Town. Of all the friends who Ted could have invited to dinner, Henry Tarbolton was perhaps not the wisest choice, not least because of his roving eye, love of beautiful women and penchant for saying a little more than he ought to when well-greased by a bottle of port. Henry was a good man—a reliable friend, a hardworking physician and a kind soul, but he was not particularly well-behaved.

However, Henry had more or less invited himself to dine, and Ted had reluctantly agreed on the condition that Henry solemnly swore to say nothing about lectures or indeed any of the other business which had detained Ted this week. His friend had taken the oath, although he had not understood it, even when Ted had pointed out that Charlotte was hardly likely to look kindly upon her husband—a peer of the realm—revisiting aspects of his old profession which many people found distasteful. But then, Henry was hardly a man who cared much what others thought. If he did, he'd be more restrained this evening, instead of being thoroughly charming and flirtatious with his hostess, who he gazed at with undisguised admiration. An admiration which left Ted feeling decidedly provoked. Perhaps even downright jealous.

'You must tell me how the two of you met,' Henry said to Charlotte. 'Edward has told me nothing about it, and I must confess to being enormously curious. I always thought him wedded to his work.' He paused, sipping his wine thoughtfully. 'Although times do change, I suppose, as do circumstances.' He grinned at her from behind the rim of his glass. 'Let me guess—a match made in a ballroom in Mayfair?'

Ted watched Charlotte shake her head, those red curls distracting him yet again. 'We met in Northumberland, actually. I lived with my mother and aunt in Kelda, the village near to Chatton House, and we met through my acquaintance with Lady Elspeth.'

'Ah!' Henry began to laugh, glancing at Ted. 'So it's your sister's doing, is it, Edward?' He turned back to Charlotte, gesturing animatedly as he began to explain. 'Edward always used to believe it would be his mother who'd scheme her way into marrying him off one day. Lived in mortal fear of it, as I recall. I reckon that's why he hid up here for so many years. Out of sight, out of mind and all that.'

Henry's candour made Ted wince. The man really wasn't safe to be around strong drink of any kind. Ted looked at Charlotte, trying to read her expression, but it was frustratingly impassive. Perhaps, given what she knew already of Ted's aversion to the marriage mart, the cringeworthy little anecdote Henry had just shared hadn't come as much of a surprise.

'My sister had nothing to do with the matter,' he said firmly, giving his friend a warning look. 'It was our decision to marry. Ours, and ours alone.'

'Oh—oh, I see. A love match, then,' Henry said, raising his glass. 'Well, we should drink to that. I am all in favour of love matches. I've made one or two of those for myself over the years, although I dare say those are not stories for polite company.'

The lusty way that Henry looked at Charlotte as he spoke about *love matches* made Ted curl his fists. Quite frankly, if he'd had less self-control and less regard for his friend he'd have risen from his chair and flung the man out of the room there and then! As it was, he permitted himself a grimace, pressing his eyes shut and willing Henry to stop talking before he could make any more mischief. No doubt Charlotte would be mortified.

He opened his eyes, stealing a glance at her, but was surprised to see that there was no horrified expression etched on her face. Instead, as she met his eye, he was astonished to see something else in her gaze. A flash of something hotter, like indignation or, dare he think it—jealousy? Henry's remark was tactless, shocking even, but why should it make her jealous? He blinked, and when he looked again, her expression had become indecipherable once more as she lifted her wine glass and took a long sip.

Perhaps he had misread her. Perhaps she'd simply been offended by Henry's remark. Or perhaps she'd also spied the hungry look Henry had given her and was similarly affronted by it. She was a genteel young lady, after all, unused to the sort of talk and behaviour which, frankly, was better suited to the tavern than the dining table.

'However, I do have a good story for polite company,' Henry continued, clearly sensing the need to move on. 'My grandfather was acquainted with the poet Allan Ramsay. Indeed, he used to visit his shop in the Luckenbooths…'

Ted half listened as Henry rambled on, his thoughts still fixed on that look in her eyes. Whatever it had signified, it had been unguarded, hinting momentarily at unspoken feelings bubbling beneath the surface. Feelings she usually managed to repress—except, perhaps, when they caused her to call out in her sleep, as she had done that night at the inn. Feelings which, if he was honest with himself, made him intolerably curious.

'I'm all in favour of love matches. I've made one or two of those for myself, over the years...'

Charlotte tossed and turned in bed, those words circling in her mind. The hour was late, their guest having left only a short while earlier, swaying all the way to the front door after enjoying several generous glasses of port in the drawing room. Charlotte had retired immediately afterwards, insisting she was tired. In truth, her head was spinning, and not only because of the wine she'd consumed at dinner. Every time she closed her eyes, she saw the pained expression on Ted's face as his friend spelt out some very revealing truths—about his mortal fear of his mother marrying him off, of how he'd sought refuge from her machinations in Edinburgh. And as for Mr Tarbolton's talk of *love matches*…

The look on Ted's face had been excruciating, seeming to confirm everything Charlotte had suspected.

Just how many *love matches* had Ted enjoyed? Or had there only ever been one—a deep and abiding love which moved him to stay far away from his mother's efforts to find him a suitable bride? Was that the singular love he clung to now, the one which explained his frequent absences as well as his desire to foster friendship with his wife rather than take her to his bed? She had to find out, somehow. She had to know, because all the wondering and imagining she was currently doing was driving her mad.

Until now, direct questions about how Ted had spent his day had proven fruitless, and she'd been too willing to let the matter go. If she was going to discover the truth and tease out the details of Ted's secret life, she would have to be more persistent, and cleverer about it, too. She turned over once more, squeezing her eyes shut. First, she would sleep, and then tomorrow she'd set about getting the answers she sought.

Chapter Thirteen

The next morning Charlotte rose late, expecting to discover that Ted had already gone out. Instead, as she sauntered down the stairs and past his study, she was surprised to see that the door was ajar and that he was sitting at his desk, intent upon some papers in front of him. She paused, taking in the sight of him as he rubbed his chin, deep in thought. He hadn't shaved yet, his dark stubble looking as becoming as his mussed hair which likewise had not yet been tamed to order. She noticed, too, that he wore neither a coat nor a cravat, and that his simple shirt was loose at the collar, with his sleeves rolled up. In short, he looked overwhelmingly handsome—and clearly preoccupied with something. She decided she would not disturb him then. The conversation she wished to have could wait until luncheon.

'Did you sleep well?' Ted called as she turned her

back, letting her know that he had seen her hovering outside.

She returned to the door of the study, pushing it open a little wider. 'I did, thank you,' she lied. In truth, she'd slept fitfully, her mind still churning over the matter of Ted's *love match*. She peered at the sheet of paper beneath his hand, noting the untidy scrawl and the many parts which had been scored out. 'A tricky piece of correspondence?' she ventured, inclining her head towards it.

'Something like that,' Ted replied, and she could not help but notice how he shuffled the page away, out of sight. 'Did you enjoy our dinner last night? I hope you did not find Henry too…wild.'

'Wild?' she repeated. 'No. Indeed, I found some of what he had to say very interesting.'

Ted nodded. 'Well, he does know how to spin a good yarn. Although I must caution you not to believe everything he says.'

She raised an eyebrow at him. 'Oh, really?' she replied. 'And which parts would you caution me not to believe?'

He gave a helpless shrug. 'Well, now—all that talk about Allan Ramsay and about the time he met Walter Scott. I am not sure that any of it is true. He does get rather carried away after a few glasses of wine.'

'Hmm,' she mused, skimming a finger over the edge of Ted's desk. 'I suppose he did say some rather outlandish things. And as for all that talk about love matches—I hardly knew what to make of that,' she added, giving Ted a pointed look.

She watched as Ted bristled. 'Ah—yes. Well, I'm afraid such bawdiness comes with the territory with Henry. He does enjoy…female company. I hope that he did not vex you with his remarks.'

'I was not vexed. Merely intrigued.'

Ted regarded her carefully. 'Are you sure? Only, I thought you looked a little provoked.'

Had she? Now that she thought about it, she did recall Ted giving her some odd, inquisitive looks. Clearly, he'd seen something in her eyes—something she hadn't managed to entirely disguise.

'I wasn't provoked,' she replied.

Ted smiled then, although she noticed the smile did not reach his eyes. 'I am glad to hear it.'

Charlotte nodded slowly, wondering how far she dared to push this conversation. How she could interrogate whether Ted, like his friend, also enjoyed *female company*. Whether it was such company which lured him out of the house, day after day. She decided it might be safest to change tack. If she sailed any closer to the wind, she'd end up making an accusation and she had not gathered sufficient evidence for that. Not yet.

Besides, if he thinks you're asking about his past

entanglements, he might start to enquire about yours...

That was the very last subject she wanted to see raising its ugly head. And, after all, it was not the women in Ted's past who concerned her, only the question of whether there were any in his life now.

'You've a lot of papers on your desk. Is there anything I can be of help with?' she asked. 'That tricky piece of correspondence, perhaps?'

Ted shook his head. 'Thank you, but no. It is a trifling matter of business, is all. But it is almost concluded now.'

'I see. And what about all the other business that has detained you this week? Have you been able to bring that to a conclusion?'

Another bristle. 'Yes—well, almost.'

'What sort of business is it? Only, you've never really said.'

Ted looked up at her, his gaze searching hers, and she sensed that he was trying to gauge if there was anything beyond mere curiosity lurking behind her questions. She resisted the temptation to look away, forcing herself instead to meet his eye, to keep her face from betraying the maelstrom of emotions currently churning away in her gut. Frustration—yes, but something else, too. Something she'd felt at dinner last night. Something like hurt, only tinged with something sharper, like envy. Envy of the faceless, nameless woman who held Ted's heart in the palm of her hand.

'It is really nothing to concern yourself about, Charlotte,' Ted said, rising now from his desk and walking towards her. 'Just one or two things I have had to deal with. As I've said to you before, I had to leave Edinburgh very quickly after Perry's death.'

He had to leave her quickly—is that what he means?

Charlotte rubbed her temple, feeling her head begin to pound as a hot fury grew within her chest. This arrangement they'd made, the one which had seemed so perfect and so simple on that cold night in the greenhouse, was turning out to be infinitely more complicated than she could have imagined. Why was that? What had changed since that evening, when all she'd been able to think about was making her escape?

Her next words spilled forth before she could stop them. 'I am not concerned,' she protested, the lie tasting sour in her mouth. 'In fact, it occurs to me that it is fortunate that this is neither a real honeymoon nor a real marriage. If it was, I suspect I'd be feeling sorely neglected by a husband who has quite so much *business* to attend to!'

Ted stepped behind Charlotte with as much calm as he could muster, and gently shut the door. The very last thing they needed was for the servants to overhear this conversation. A conversation which had grown heated, and that was largely his fault. He was being evasive with her, but what else could he do? Confess that when she'd spied him at his desk, he'd been grappling not with estate business but with his notes for the lecture he was due to deliver that evening? That he'd been sitting there, feeling apprehensive, as he forced himself to confront the risk he was taking by wading back into what society would regard as the most unseemly aspects of his old profession? That he'd been feverishly imagining the reports of the London scandal sheets if they caught wind of the story?

Our very own accoucheur of the realm, the Duke of F, has given a lecture on man midwifery...

His mother would never forgive him for bringing the family name into such disrepute, and his wife would look at him in horror and disgust. Fortunately, they were a long way from London and the chances of his lecture becoming fodder for the gossips of the *ton* were remote, but imagining Charlotte's reaction to such headlines had only strengthened his resolve to ensure she knew nothing about it. He would fulfil this final commitment he'd made and then he would leave it all behind—for good. Even if the thought of doing so made his heart ache.

'I'm sure that Mrs McGowan would be alarmed to hear that you're not my real wife,' he said once they were safely out of earshot. 'As am I, since I can very clearly recall us making our vows to each other before the altar of St Oswald's.'

She crossed her arms defensively in front of her chest. 'I think you understand very well what I mean, Ted. It can hardly be called a honeymoon when you are so often out of the house, attending to your business. And it is not a marriage—at least, not in the full sense of the word. Believe me, that is something that the servants will already be well aware of, and when we return to Chatton it will not take long for your mother to realise it, too.'

He had to admit that she was right there—no doubt their nocturnal activities, or lack of them, would have already been observed here, just as they'd be noted at Chatton by the eagle-eyed Dowager Duchess.

'The way we conduct our marriage is no one's concern but ours, Charlotte. We agreed that we would take our time and get to know each other better before we worry about the intimacies between husband and wife.'

Even saying the words made his blood heat with longing. He went to sleep every night and woke every morning with the image of Charlotte there beside him etched upon his brain. He imagined her, breathless and naked beneath his sheets, her bright red hair spread across the pillow as he took her in his arms again and trailed kisses down her neck, her shoulder, her breasts. Yet as heady and consuming as his lust for her had become, he would not rush this—not after the way they'd rushed into marriage. It simply was not right. They would foster a deeper bond first, and that would take time. He wanted Charlotte to want him just as he wanted her, not to go to his bed because she felt duty-bound to provide him with an heir, or worried about what the servants or his mother would say if she did not.

'Getting to know each other better would be far easier if you were at home more often,' Charlotte replied, folding those arms ever tighter.

Another point which he had to concede. He had been absent a good deal of late and whilst organising the lectures had been relatively time-consuming, undoubtedly, he had allowed himself to be swept up in his nostalgia for his old life. If he was honest with himself, he owed Charlotte an apology for that. But to apologise might prompt her to ask further questions about his whereabouts—questions which he could not answer.

'Yes, you are right,' he replied. 'But as I said, there have been matters which required my attention.'

'Oh, I give up!' She threw her arms up in exasperation and moved to grab the doorknob. Moved to leave the room and get away from him. 'We are going round in circles, and…'

Before Ted could think about what he was doing, he caught her around the waist, pulling her back towards him and pressing his lips against hers. This kiss was nothing like the one they'd shared at the inn—that kiss had been gentle and searching, but this one was fierce and urgent. He expected her to push him away, to rebuke him, but instead she pulled him closer, melting against him as she groaned and poured all of her frustration and fury into the embrace. Ted responded in kind, allowing the kiss to speak where he could not, allowing it to convey all the desire which he did not yet dare to express to her in words. But as the kiss deepened and his hands wandered first to the curve of her waist, then over her skirts to caress her bottom, he forced himself back from the brink. He tore his lips away from hers, knowing that if he did not stop it right then, he would end up ravishing her in his study and breaking his promise to them both.

'I'm sorry,' he breathed. 'Again.'

Charlotte's blue gaze searched his. 'Why?' she asked. 'Why are you sorry?'

'Because it was a mistake… It would not be right…' He faltered, at a sudden loss how to explain that he spent each and every day wrestling with his passion for her, trying to be honourable, trying to be a gentleman. He glanced back towards the lecture notes, half written and abandoned on his desk. 'Perhaps we could discuss this later,' he said. 'There are a number of matters I must attend to this afternoon.'

Charlotte followed his gaze towards the messy piles of paperwork which were scattered across his desk. She pressed her lips together for a moment, as though composing herself. 'Of course, I understand,' she said finally. 'We can talk tonight, after dinner.'

Tonight. The lecture. Damn.

'I won't be at home tonight,' he said, sighing heavily. 'I have some pressing...'

'Business?'

'Yes.'

Those bright blue eyes flashed angrily. 'Of course you do,' she replied, shaking her head in disbelief before she opened the door and marched back into the hallway.

'Charlotte, wait,' Ted called after her. 'You don't understand, I...'

His words died in his throat as Charlotte spun around to face him once more. 'I understand perfectly, Ted,' she said quietly, her expression grave. 'I understand what sort of marriage this is, and there is no need to talk about it. You are right—it was a mistake. I can assure you it won't happen again.'

Chapter Fourteen

Ted stared absently at the crowd which had begun to gather in the Physicians' Hall and tried to force his mind to focus on the lecture he was about to deliver. His mind, however, clearly had other ideas, returning repeatedly to that morning's encounter with Charlotte. To their heated conversation. To that kiss. He was fairly certain he could spend an eternity trying to analyse the feelings which flooded through him each and every time he'd kissed her and he would still fail to find adequate words for them. Lust—yes. Desire—absolutely. But something else, too. Something he could not quite name. A sense of rightness, of it all making sense, as though embracing Charlotte was the answer to a question he had not even posed.

Ironic, really, since it was his unwillingness to answer Charlotte's questions which had been his downfall. He was beginning to wonder if he should have just told her about the lectures, and about the other business he'd conducted in town during the past week. If he should have risked provoking her disgust and disappointment—if that would have been preferable to the anger which had greeted his evasiveness. He could hardly blame her for being angry; he would be, too, if he knew, as she clearly knew, that he was being kept in the dark. Perhaps it would be best just to tell her about his past life—about all of it. Perhaps, as his wife, she did deserve to know.

And you did insist that you ought to get to know each other better, Ted. Warts and all.

That was true. Certainly, he wanted to understand Charlotte better, to find his way beneath all the layers of reserve and impassivity which she wore like a mask. To dig deeper into all those emotions he'd seen in her eyes that night in the greenhouse—emotions which he suspected were as potent as they were painful. And then there was the way she'd called out in her sleep at the inn—words of desperation and distress.

Couldn't help him... My fault...

Words which might mean nothing but could mean everything. Words which might have nothing to do with her reasons for desiring an escape, but which could be at the centre of it all. Words which she'd dismissed as merely a bad dream and asked him to forget. That was another promise he'd struggled to honour, since he had not been able to forget them at all. Instead, he replayed them and interrogated them, just as he was now, searching for any hint of their context and their meaning. Wishing he could be direct and simply ask her about them, and whether they had anything to do with why she'd been so desperate to escape and so willing to accept his proposal. There were other questions he longed to ask her, too—about the difficulties with her mother, and the precise nature of what she'd had to endure.

Quite the list of questions for a lady who has not said a word to you since she marched out of your study this morning. You should probably begin with a few confessions of your own, if you want her to trust you.

Probably, but which ones? The fact that he was a duke who couldn't help but stray into the disreputable waters of his former profession? The reasons why his family had come to regard that profession as quite so distasteful? Or should he tell her about the impulse he felt to hold her, to touch her, to run his fingers through her fiery red curls every time she walked into a room? Or the fact that he was fairly certain he'd felt the heavens move each time they'd kissed?

Inwardly Ted groaned, his thoughts fixed yet again upon the way he'd kissed her earlier that day. How he wished now that he hadn't been so quick to apologise, or so woeful in his effort to explain exactly why he was sorry. Hearing Charlotte echo his sentiment about the kiss having been a mistake had been bad enough, but hearing her speak about their marriage as though it was a mere performance had been utterly bruising.

But as painful as it was to acknowledge it, the fault for that rested entirely with him. He'd sought to be honourable and gentlemanly, to give their marriage time to blossom with what he hoped would be true affection before they rushed headlong into intimacy. Instead, he realised now that he'd inadvertently driven a wedge between them—a wedge made larger no doubt by his frequent absences and evasiveness. Charlotte was right; he had not behaved as though they were on their honeymoon at all. That needed to change, and he needed to make amends to her. Somehow.

'It's good to see you back where you belong, my friend.'

Henry's words, delivered with a smile, startled Ted from his thoughts. He returned the smile tightly, shaking his head. 'To be frank, I'm not sure this is where I belong any more.'

'Oh, nonsense,' Henry replied, pointing over his shoulder. 'I do believe this lot have rather missed your pearls of wisdom.' He peered at the notes which Ted clutched in his hand. 'I am certain you will have plenty for them to chew over tonight.'

Ted shrugged. 'Hopefully, I will not disappoint.'

Henry glanced about him. 'The attendance is impressive. I had thought the College might have cancelled the event, given everything that has been happening of late.'

'What do you mean?' Ted asked.

'All this talk of unrest, of workers in the west banding together in the name of insurrection.' Henry shook his head. 'Mind you, when isn't there such talk? It's all there seems to be these days. The threat of revolution is never far away.'

Ted nodded. He was aware of the reports of crowds clashing with the yeomanry and workers setting fire to mills in recent weeks, although with everything else he'd had on his mind, he'd perhaps paid them less attention than he should.

'Perhaps if those with the power to do so were to seek to remedy the causes of unrest, then it might not continually rear its head,' he mused. 'It strikes me that a decent wage and affordable bread would quell the enthusiasm of most men for revolution.'

'Spoken like a true peer of the realm,' Henry replied sardonically.

Ted sighed. 'I know, and I'm sure there are many who'd call me a Radical for such a remark. Unfortunately, I'm fairly certain that the peerage is somewhere I don't belong, either.' He looked over Henry's shoulder towards the crowd. 'Why am I here, Henry? Who wants to listen to a ridiculous nobleman wading into debates about medical training or practice, reliving an old life that he is so thoroughly out of touch with now?'

'You're not ridiculous, old friend, and I very much doubt you are out of touch.' He gave Ted a sympathetic smile. 'Fate has not dealt you an easy hand, I'm afraid, although it is a good deal easier than those poor souls choosing between starvation and insurrection, is it not?'

'Point taken. I'm a privileged fool—I am well aware of that.'

'A very lucky privileged fool, when it comes to your lovely wife.' Henry gave him a pointed look. 'I presume that lovely wife doesn't know that you're here tonight?'

'No, she does not.' He sighed again. 'However, I'm beginning to think that is a mistake I need to rectify.'

Henry grinned. 'A wise conclusion. You see, I was right—you are not a ridiculous nobleman, after all.' He tipped his hat. 'Good luck with the lecture, Edward, and remember—the answer to the question of where you belong is an easy and an obvious one.'

Ted frowned. 'It is?'

'Of course it is,' Henry said, laughing. 'I dare not spell it out in polite company, except to say that it involves a certain comely redhead to whom you are wed.'

Ted shook his head at his friend's wicked sense of humour. 'You're fortunate that I need these notes, otherwise I'd be flinging them in your direction,' he growled, waving his papers about. 'Now, be off with you. I've a lecture to deliver.'

He watched as Henry gave a theatrical bow, then sauntered past the row of grey-haired men seated at the front, who gave him identical looks of disapproval. Henry's reputation for the borderline scandalous certainly preceded him in Edinburgh and its environs, and the man often only had one thing on his mind.

Nonetheless, as the room fell silent and a colleague rose to introduce him, Ted could not help but reflect upon his friend's remark about belonging with Charlotte. In one sense, of course, it was true—if his place was anywhere, it was at her side. In the eyes of God and the eyes of the law, that was an absolute certainty. But the sort of *belonging together* implied by Henry's comment—so far, that was uncharted territory for them both.

Territory which you'd very much like to explore.

That was a certainty, and one which grew more irresistible by the day, if the way he'd struggled to tear himself away from their earlier embrace was anything to go by. But it was territory they were not ready to wander into yet, not when there was a wall between them which he needed to dismantle. A wall erected by his own secretive, evasive and distant behaviour. Instead of fostering closeness with Charlotte and encouraging her to trust him, he'd made her unhappy. He had to remedy that. First, however, he had to deliver his speech.

'Good evening, gentlemen,' he began. 'It is a pleasure to be invited to speak to you tonight on a subject which has occupied a great deal of my practice as a physician, that of midwifery…'

Charlotte stood beneath the grand colonnade of St Andrew's Church as the rain began to fall, determined not to surrender to the tears which she could feel prickling in her eyes. Tears of frustration, and tears of shame at having let that wayward and reckless side of herself rule her once again. That version of Charlotte had well and truly broken free today, summoned no doubt by her determination to confirm once and for all that Ted's affections lay elsewhere.

She winced to remember how bluntly and how angrily she had spoken to him earlier in his study. She'd meant to remain calm and clear-headed, to be sensible and subtle in her efforts to interrogate the matter. She had not intended for her tongue to become so loose or her words so heated. All that talk about theirs not being a real marriage, and her implications about the lack of intimacy between them—what on earth had she been thinking? She might as well have simply asked Ted whether he had a mistress and had done with it!

Then there was that kiss. It had been as fierce as it had been passionate, lighting a fire deep within her—a fire which burned ever hotter as Ted's hands had explored her waist, her hips, her bottom. A fire which had wanted desperately for him to continue, to see where their embrace would lead. But instead, Ted had ended it; he'd broken the spell, his hasty retreat and fumbled apology conspiring to shatter the illusion that he desired her at all.

I'm sorry...it was a mistake... It would not be right...

Words which had spelt out his regret in no uncertain terms. She'd hardly needed his confession that he had yet more pressing business to attend to that evening to remind her of the reason for his regret. That suspicion she harboured about a mistress or a lover, the one which had been niggling at her since that night in the inn near Cockburnspath, had been all but realised. That was why it had suited Ted to bring her to Edinburgh, and that was the reason he'd disappeared so often and without proper explanation since they'd been in town. It had to be. Their marriage was a shroud for Ted's secrets, and she was a convenient duchess in every respect. All that remained now was to prove it.

That proof was exactly what she'd sought when she'd followed Ted out of the house a little while earlier. It had been an impulsive decision, and one which had proved futile, since she'd quickly lost sight of him in the early evening crowd. Now she stood at the east end of George Street, watching the rain fall and the horses and carriages making their way along the increasingly muddy road, and wondering what on earth she was going to do. Frankly, she'd no idea where Ted was. She couldn't even be sure if he was inside one of George Street's grand buildings, or if he'd ventured to St Andrew's Square and beyond.

Now she was stuck, sheltering from what was fast becoming a torrential downpour, sensible enough to know that wandering around town unaccompanied as darkness fell was unwise, but not willing to return home just yet. She reasoned that if she waited a while longer, she might see him return this way. Better yet, she might see him emerge from one of the surrounding addresses where her fevered imagination had already decided that he was currently ensconced in sumptuous surroundings with his mistress. Then at least she could confront him. Then at least she would know…

But why do you want to know?

Perhaps because she wanted to understand the price of this arrangement, the price of her escape. Perhaps because she knew that the sense of liberation she'd felt since arriving in Edinburgh, the distance it had afforded her from the past, could not last. There had to be a comeuppance—there always was.

She could not cheat fate so easily, and she was a fool for ever believing that she could. She had not traded lonely spinsterhood and misery at her mother's side for a companionable marriage. Instead, this was a painful masquerade, one in which she wore a duchess's disguise while pretending not to notice that her husband's affections were engaged elsewhere.

But why is it painful? You agreed to marry him so that you could flee from your mother, and the past. Perhaps Ted asked you to marry him to protect his secrets. You both had your reasons...

Charlotte swiped angrily at the solitary tear which slipped down her cheek. She had had her reasons, and it had all seemed so much simpler then. Now, after living in close proximity as husband and wife, and after those kisses, she'd allowed her confused feelings to get the better of her, and she'd allowed that impetuous side of her personality to break free. She would need to take care, to keep herself in check, and to remember the hard lessons she'd learned. She knew all too well the harm that recklessness could cause.

The sight of a crowd of gentlemen exiting the grand building across the street caught Charlotte's attention. She dabbed her eyes with her handkerchief, watching the top-hatted procession huddling into coats and capes before making their way along the street under an ever-darkening sky. Doubtless they were going home after some sort of event in whatever that building was. If she was wise, and God only knew she was trying hard to be, then she would go home, too. Society might make no objection to a duke staying out to all hours entertaining his mistress, but a duchess lingering on the street alone after dark would cause a scandal. She'd had enough brushes with those to last her a lifetime.

Tentatively, Charlotte stepped out from under the portico, grimacing beneath her bonnet at the heavy droplets of rain which greeted her. She huddled into her pelisse and hurried across the street, blinking as the rain flew into her eyes, making it difficult to avoid both the growing puddles and the danger of ending up in the path of one of the many grand carriages passing up and down. Halfway across, she heard a horse whinny and a driver shouted angrily. Startled, she felt a wave of panic wash over her. What on earth had she been thinking, standing out here so long? It was almost dark now, and here she was, a woman, a duchess—alone in the street, in a city she barely knew. She could get run over, or worse. Had she taken leave of her senses?

Her vision still obscured by the rain, she rushed to reach the pavement and to be out of harm's way. In her haste, she found herself colliding with a gentleman, knocking him sideways and causing his top hat to fall from his head.

'Oh! I am so sorry, sir, please forgive me…'

'Charlotte?'

She looked up to see that familiar pair of brown eyes regarding her with concern, accompanied by a deep frown which was etched upon his face. She swiped a careless hand over her bonnet, trying to straighten it, although goodness knew why—it was sodden now, just like the rest of her.

'Charlotte…' Ted repeated, bending down to pick up his hat. 'What on earth are you doing out here?' In one swift action, he pulled her close to him, wrapping part of his long cape around her shoulders. 'You're drenched. Let's get you home.'

The feeling of his cloak covering her wet clothes reminded her of that day by the stream, mere weeks ago, when he'd nobly placed his coat over her shoulders. When they'd walked together and talked at length for the first time. When he'd invited her to dine at Chatton. When all of this began.

'No,' she said, recoiling from him and pushing those pleasant but nonetheless unwanted memories aside. She'd followed him tonight; she'd sought him out, and now she'd found him. There were things she needed to say. Questions which required an answer. 'I came to find you, Ted. I was looking for you. I know where you've been, and I know what you've been doing. I know… I know that you have someone else. A mistress, a lover. A woman in this city who you had to leave behind. Who you've come back for.'

'What? No, Charlotte. No—that's not what…' She watched as he stared at her, his face turning noticeably pale, his eyes wide, his lips parted in a look of astonishment. 'I think we need to get home and out of this rain,' he said, pointing up at the sky. 'Then we can talk—properly.'

'About how you've made a fool of me?' The words were out before she could prevent them.

He nodded grimly. 'Yes, about that, but not in the way that you think. Come,' he continued, offering her sanctuary beneath his cape once more. 'The weather is appalling, and the streets may not be safe tonight. There is much talk of unrest. I believe that trouble may be brewing.'

Alarmed by his warning and soaked to the skin now, Charlotte relented. She accepted his offer, sheltering beneath his cape as they made the short walk back to Charlotte Square. Once or twice she glanced up at him, spying his grave expression even in the dim lamplight, and she could not help but consider just how apt his cautionary words had been, albeit not in the way he had intended. Trouble was certainly brewing—the sort of trouble which might yet have grave consequences for a convenient marriage and cause unpalatable truths and secrets to be laid bare at last.

Chapter Fifteen

'I do not have a mistress, Charlotte.'

Ted leaned forward in his chair, regarding Charlotte carefully as they warmed themselves by the fire in the parlour. They'd both arrived home soaking wet, thanks to the deluge which continued to fall ceaselessly outside. Mrs McGowan had fussed over the state of them both, and had made known her worry over her mistress having disappeared without her maid and without explanation. However, his ever-perceptive housekeeper seemed to quickly detect that something was amiss between them and made herself scarce, making no further enquiries except to ask if they both wanted tea once they were dry and had changed their clothes. Ted had nodded, although given the nature of what he and Charlotte needed to discuss, he suspected that something stronger might have been more appropriate.

Charlotte wrinkled her nose, staring down into her

teacup. Despite the awkward, painful situation, Ted could not help but allow his gaze to sweep over the sight of her, sitting across from him in the firelight. Even in her nightdress and a thick shawl, with her red curls hanging loose about her shoulders, she was positively arresting.

'A lover, then,' she said after a long moment. 'Or a lady you intended to marry but had to leave behind when you inherited the Dukedom. Someone you knew your family would not approve of.'

He raised his eyebrows. Clearly, she'd given this theory of hers a lot of thought.

'I have no mistress, no lover, and no would-be bride in Edinburgh. I can assure you, when I lived and worked here as Dr Scott I was unattached.' He shifted uncomfortably. 'Sometimes there were women, of course—I am neither a saint nor a monk. But I was not in love with anyone, Charlotte.'

She looked up at him then, those bright blue eyes searching his. 'Then I do not understand,' she said quietly. 'The hurry to come here, the moment we were wed. The unexplained *business* which has kept you so preoccupied since we arrived…'

'I decided we would come to Edinburgh when I witnessed your mother's behaviour on our wedding day,' he replied. 'I could see that you desperately needed to put some distance between yourself and her, and besides, we had just got married—it was only right that we should have a honeymoon.' He drew a deep breath, dragging a hand wearily down his face. 'However, I confess that the thought of coming back here—with you—had occurred to me before our wedding. I must also confess that the idea was not entirely selfless. I do have some matters here which I must attend to. But they are not at all what you have imagined them to be, Charlotte, I promise you that.'

'So, what are these matters?' she prompted him. 'Where were you tonight, Ted?'

Another deep breath. 'I was at the Physicians' Hall—that large, grand building near to where you collided with me. I was there to deliver a lecture.'

'A lecture?' she repeated. He watched a look of dawning realisation creep over her face. 'All those gentlemen I saw leaving,' she mused, shaking her head. 'They were there for you. But what was this lecture about? And why didn't you just tell me about it?'

'Because I...' Ted paused, searching for the right words.

Tell her the truth, Ted. She deserves that much.

'Before Perry died, I'd committed to deliver several lectures to members of the Royal College of Physicians, about aspects of my work,' he began to explain, choosing his words carefully. 'But when my brother died and I was recalled to Chatton, they were postponed. As well as coming to town for our honeymoon, I thought I could finally fulfil that particular promise, and fortunately the College were happy to oblige me, even at such short notice.'

Charlotte's brow furrowed, and it was clear she was not satisfied by his explanation. 'I do not understand why you would feel the need to hide this from me, Ted. Unless, of course, you think me too stupid to understand.' Her jaw hardened, her blue eyes blazing with a myriad of unspoken feelings, just as they had that night in the greenhouse. 'Perhaps that is it—you think me an empty-headed ninny, easily fooled. I suppose I should not blame you for that, since my own mother was at pains to stress to you just how incapable I am of even teaching the village girls to read.'

The hurt note in her voice was almost more than Ted could bear, and he was forced to grip the arm of the chair to prevent himself from leaping up and gathering her into his arms. 'You are not stupid, Charlotte, and I have never thought so—not for a moment. Please, please understand, the way I have behaved, it is not about my regard for you.'

'Then, what is it about?' she challenged him.

'It is about...'

The truth, Ted. The truth.

'I thought you'd be horrified, if you knew,' he said, emitting a heavy sigh and slumping back in his chair. 'I thought you'd be disgusted, even ashamed of me.'

Charlotte frowned. 'I do not understand. Why did you think that?'

'Because you married the Duke of Falstone, not Dr Edward Scott. You were perturbed enough at the inn near Cockburnspath, when I used my old name instead of my title, and when I introduced you as Mrs Scott. I didn't wish to contemplate what you'd think if you knew I'd been venturing into my former profession.'

'The way I questioned you at the inn was clumsy, and I am sorry for it,' Charlotte replied. 'I understand that you were discomfited by the idea of correcting the innkeeper. I am sure I would have understood about the lectures, too, if you had told me about them. I am well aware that you were a physician before you inherited the Dukedom. How could it possibly horrify me?'

'Because there are aspects of my work which my own family find distasteful,' he blurted out. 'Aspects which made them so ashamed, they forbade me to ever speak of them.'

'Such as?' Charlotte asked quietly.

You must tell her.

Ted dropped his gaze, staring into his teacup. 'Such as my work as an accoucheur,' he said quietly. 'And my work at Edinburgh's lying-in hospital. My work in the field of midwifery is the subject of my lectures.'

He glanced up to see Charlotte's eyes had widened, but there was no look of horror evident on her face.

Instead, she merely looked surprised. 'That is not at all what I expected you to say.'

'What did you expect me to say?'

She narrowed her eyes briefly. 'I'm not sure—that you were an anatomist, perhaps? Since I know that is controversial.'

He gave her a grim look. 'As is being a man involved in the business of childbirth. Or at the very least, it provokes strong opinions.'

'How did you come to be interested in midwifery?' she asked.

'For that, I think the blame lies squarely with Henry.' He let out a heavy sigh, feeling a wry smile creep on to his lips. 'We were both studying medicine at the university, and Henry cajoled me into accompanying him to the classes on midwifery. It was not a compulsory subject for graduation—still isn't, in fact—but it became apparent to me fairly quickly that this was a field I wanted to be involved in. And so, after completing my studies, I began to practise as an accoucheur, attending mostly wealthy women privately in their homes. Later I became involved with the lying-in hospital, which offers care to a greater number of the city's women,' he concluded, not wishing to spell out the circumstances of some of those women, or indeed the poverty and peril they often faced. A conversation for another time, perhaps.

He watched as Charlotte nodded slowly, absorbing

every word he'd said. 'But why?' she asked, then immediately hesitated. 'Forgive me, but given that you knew you'd encounter the strong opinions of others, there must have been something in particular which drove you to choose this path.'

He laughed, shaking his head. 'You have no idea how many times in my life I have asked myself that question. Why would I risk incurring society's disapproval, not to mention scandalising my entire family? I suppose it was because I found a sort of hope in midwifery which I did not find elsewhere in my studies. So much of medicine is about sickness and injury, but this is different. Bearing children is fraught with danger, of course, but it is also inherently hopeful because it is about bringing new life into the world. I suppose I wanted to contribute to that.'

Charlotte smiled at him. 'Oh, Ted. That is very admirable.'

'Yes, well, my family did not think so. You ought to have seen my mother's face, the night my damnable brother told her I was a man midwife. I'd returned to Chatton for Christmas and somehow—God only knows how—Perry had learned of the reputation I was building in that particular field. He capitalised upon it, of course. He could never resist the opportunity for a little public humiliation.' He gulped down the last of his tea, then set his cup aside. 'At least my father never knew, since he was dead by then. His opposition to me becoming a physician in the first place had been strong enough.'

'That must have been dreadful.' Charlotte looked at him sympathetically. 'What about Elspeth? She spoke to me quite openly about you having been a physician. She did also acknowledge it was not discussed at Chatton, although she said she did not understand why that was.'

'Elspeth doesn't know about those parts of my work. She had retired for the evening when Perry made that particular announcement. Indeed, as I recall, Mother had sent her to bed because Perry was making a drunken spectacle of himself, as usual. Anyway, Mother forbade any discussion of man midwifery in front of her, insisting it would scandalise her impressionable mind.' Despite himself, Ted could not resist rolling his eyes. 'Sometimes I think my mother does not understand who my sister is at all.'

'Perhaps she doesn't. I don't believe my mother understands me. I don't think she's ever had any inclination to understand me.'

The bitter note in her voice caught Ted off-guard, and when he looked at her he saw that her expression had darkened and that her eyes brimmed with emotion once again. It occurred to him that none of this—the heartfelt discussion, the sharing of secrets—had formed part of their arrangement, and yet something about doing so felt so natural. So right.

'What happened that made you want to get away from your mother so badly, Charlotte?' he asked.

The moment she'd said those words, Charlotte knew that she'd allowed her feelings to bubble to the surface and made them plain for Ted to see. Why had she even mentioned her experience with her mother, when the conversation had been fixed so firmly upon Ted? Why, when he'd finally begun to shed light on his evasive behaviour since their arrival in Edinburgh, had she turned his attention to her? Why could she not be satisfied with letting him explain himself, especially since what he'd had to say had come as something of a relief? There was no mistress, no thwarted bride lurking in some murky corner of this city. There was, however, a good deal of fear—fear of allowing her to know about his past, lest he lose her good opinion. That was abundantly clear. It was also something she could relate to.

Can you imagine what he would think if he knew all about your past?

The thought made Charlotte shudder. Raking up the most lurid details of her past, the parts which were quite literally dead and buried, could do no good. But he had not asked about that, had he? He'd asked only about her mother, and as she looked up and met his eye, she realised that she wanted to tell him. She wanted him to know.

She drew an uneven breath. 'There was not one particular reason that I wanted to escape from that cottage in Kelda,' she said. 'Rather, there were a lifetime's worth of reasons, each one like a stone placed upon my chest and weighing me down. That evening at Chatton, when my mother belittled me in front of you, and in front of Elspeth and your mother, the weight finally felt unbearable. It was as though I could not breathe. It felt like the culmination of the years I've spent enduring her scorn for failing to live up to her expectations.'

'By expectations, I presume you mean marriage,' Ted said quietly. 'Only, I could not fail to observe her less than subtle hints in that regard during that dinner at Chatton. Not to mention the way she insisted that I must have seduced you in the greenhouse, and that we would have to marry.'

Hearing Ted talk about seduction made Charlotte's cheeks grow warm. 'You're right,' she replied. 'The fact that I'd managed to reach the grand old age of three-and-twenty without duping a suitably titled man into marrying me was a great source of irritation and disappointment to her.'

'I can't imagine you'd need to dupe anyone, Charlotte,' Ted countered. 'Any man, titled or otherwise, would be fortunate to have you as his wife.' He cleared his throat, shifting slightly in his chair. 'Indeed, I am very fortunate in that regard.'

'Thank you,' Charlotte replied, trying to accept his compliment gracefully rather than dwelling upon how untrue it was. She'd risked everything in her attempt to secure Crowgarth, only to discover that she was nothing more than a woman worth ruining to him. 'I will admit, until you proposed marriage to me, I'd quite given up on becoming anyone's wife.'

Oh, no, Charlotte, what did you say that for?

Ted frowned, his attention clearly and regrettably captured by those fateful words she'd just uttered. 'What happened to make you feel like that?' he asked.

Charlotte drew a deep breath. She knew she had to tell him something. Indeed, she realised, she wanted to tell him something.

'I spent the summer of eighteen with my parents in Lowhaven, on the Cumberland coast. While we were there, the younger son of a local prominent family seemed to take an interest in me. However, my mother utterly objected to him, and tried instead to thrust me upon his older, titled brother, despite the fact that the older brother was clearly interested in another young lady, with whom I'd become friends. The whole thing was horribly humiliating and deeply regrettable.'

'This younger son, did you care for him?'

The question took Charlotte aback, and as she met Ted's deep brown stare she saw something surprising lingering there. Something which looked rather like jealousy. Surely not?

'I liked him a great deal and I was flattered by the attention he paid to me,' she began carefully. 'But it was too short-lived a thing to really speak of any deep affection on either of our parts. I was just a silly girl, then. Young and naïve.' She bit her lip, forcing herself to stop speaking. She'd answered Ted's question. That was quite enough.

Ted smiled kindly. 'You speak as though it was a lifetime ago, and not barely two years.'

'Yes, well, much has happened in barely two years,' Charlotte answered. 'Much has changed. I have changed. That summer in Lowhaven might as well be a lifetime ago.'

The uncomfortable truth of those words seemed to sit heavily upon her chest. Painful experience had changed her, but the nature of that experience was something Ted could never know.

'I can understand that…' Ted mused. 'In the summer of eighteen I was here, working as a physician, with no intimation that my brother's death was mere months away and that I would inherit everything. No intimation that my entire life was about to be turned upside down. Those stones you spoke about, pressing down on your chest. I feel them, too. Every damned day.'

The sorrow on Ted's face was palpable and before

Charlotte could truly consider what she was doing, she'd moved to perch on the arm of his chair. She draped her arm around his shoulder, pulling him close, telling herself that she merely meant to offer him comfort, even as her heart began to tell her something else. Even as her heart whispered that perhaps she'd begun to care for him, in a way that a wife might care for her husband. A way which went beyond the friendship which they'd both promised to foster.

Perhaps Ted glimpsed something of this in her eyes, because as he gazed up at her his expression seemed to change, a sort of smouldering desire replacing the sadness which had lingered in his dark stare just moments ago. Before she could say another word, he sat bolt upright, looped his arms around her waist and pulled her straight on to his lap.

Their lips met so quickly that it was impossible to say which of them had initiated the kiss. Charlotte heard herself murmur as Ted cupped her face with his hand, before allowing his fingers to trace the outline of her collarbone, her arm, before coming to rest upon her hip. Impatiently she shrugged off her shawl, suddenly desperate to remove unnecessary barriers between them as her hand wandered between the gap in his long robe and sought out the hint of bare skin at the open collar of his nightshirt. Her touch seemed to inflame him and against her mouth he growled, holding her closer to him before allowing his lips to trail kisses across her cheek then down her neck…

'We should stop,' he murmured against her skin, sending a shiver down her spine. 'If Mrs McGowan walked in now…'

The thought of the housekeeper spying their liaison was a sobering one.

'Yes, of course,' Charlotte replied, shuffling breathlessly off his lap and retrieving the shawl which she'd tossed to the ground mere moments earlier. 'It is getting late. I think I should retire.'

'Charlotte?' Ted stood up quickly, as though poised to say something else. As though he might wish to kiss her again.

'What is it, Ted?' Charlotte whispered.

He took one of her hands in his and gave it a gentle squeeze. 'I am glad we talked tonight, like this. Thank you for telling me about your mother, and for listening to me.'

She nodded, a thought occurring to her as she searched his gaze and saw that the sadness in it had returned. 'All this time I thought you were longing for a woman you loved, when in fact it was your old life that you were yearning for,' she said. 'That is why you wanted to come back to Edinburgh, isn't it?'

He relinquished her hand. 'Perhaps—but there is no going back to that time. I realised tonight when I was delivering my lecture that I am no longer a part of that world, and I am no longer that man. Duty has altered me, and I must spend the rest of my life bearing my dead brother's burdens and fulfilling his responsibilities to my family, to the Dukedom and to the estate. Duties I never wanted, but which are mine now, nonetheless.'

Charlotte was taken aback by his candour, and hurt by all that it implied. 'And what am I, then? Another burden?' she asked, her heart lurching painfully in the chest. 'Another duty you didn't want?'

'No, Charlotte, that's not what I meant…'

'Of course it is what you meant, Ted. As the Duke, it was your duty to marry—you told me so yourself. I was just the easiest, most willing means to that end.' Angrily, she swiped away the tears which had begun to fall from her eyes. 'I suppose that is no more than I deserve.'

'What do you mean by that?'

Charlotte shook her head. 'Nothing,' she said, marching towards the door. 'Goodnight, Ted.'

She did not wait to hear his answer. Instead, she hurried up the stairs towards her bedchamber, utterly overwrought and this time entirely unable to prevent the torrent of tears which flooded down her cheeks.

Chapter Sixteen

The next few days passed in an almost perpetual state of uncomfortable silence. Circumstances beyond Charlotte Square kept Ted and Charlotte largely confined to the house, as the rumours of impending insurrection proved true. Across the towns of western Scotland, workers had joined a general strike, and the army had been mobilised, ready to meet the Radicals' cries of 'Liberty or Death!' which could be heard openly on many a street.

Although there appeared to be no immediate danger in Edinburgh, the situation was clearly volatile, and Ted felt it was wise to remain close to home. As a physician he'd worked among those who lived in the increasingly crowded and sometimes squalid tenements which dominated the ancient part of the city, but that counted for nothing now. To any Radical on the streets he was an aristocrat, and therefore an adversary. The Revolution in France was not a distant enough memory for anyone to have forgotten where the drawing of those particular battle lines might lead.

The unrest across Scotland dominated their mealtime conversations, largely because it seemed to be the only matter which Charlotte was willing to discuss. For this Ted could hardly blame her; his behaviour that night in the parlour had been unforgivable. One moment he'd been caught up in the heat of passion, which had nearly overtaken him. The next moment he'd implied that she was a burden, and that their marriage was just another duty he did not want.

He'd spoken clumsily, his heady feelings of desire mixing potently with his earlier melancholy and loosening his tongue. He hadn't meant to suggest that there was anything about her, or their marriage, which was unwanted. But he had, and in doing so he'd hurt her.

Yet now he was at a loss as to how to make amends to her. Every time he tried to broach the subject Charlotte would thwart him, either by changing it or, in extreme cases, by simply walking away. In the end, there was nothing he could do but abide by her evident wish to limit their conversations to current events and, if he were really desperate, observations about the weather outside. It was clear that, as far as Charlotte was concerned, heartfelt discussions were now firmly off the table. As were passionate embraces—which was a damned shame, since he could not stop thinking about that last one.

'There is news from the west,' Ted announced as he wandered into the parlour that Thursday morning, to find Charlotte sitting in what had clearly become her favourite chair, embroidering.

'Oh? Good news, I hope?'

He noticed that she did not look up, but kept her eyes firmly on her work. 'It says here that the majority of Glasgow's weavers have returned to work,' he replied, holding up the newspaper which he clutched in his hand. 'There are reports also of a skirmish between some of the Hussars and a group of Radicals, but that this was put down and a number of prisoners have been taken to Stirling Castle. It sounds as though the army has matters under its control.'

She glanced up at him. 'Good news, then.'

'For the British Government, certainly.' He sat down opposite her, emitting a sigh. 'Not such good news for the disaffected workers, though.'

Charlotte looked up again, frowning. 'You sound almost as though you sympathise with them,' she observed. 'Well, I do not mind saying that I do not. Not after the worry of these past days. I would never have agreed to come to Edinburgh if I'd had any inclination that…' She paused, shaking her head at herself. 'But then, I suppose I have many reasons to question my decisions of late,' she added, murmuring the words just loud enough for Ted to hear them.

That latter cutting remark made Ted wince. 'I am not sympathetic to insurrection, to rioting or to violence,' he said gently. 'But it is undeniable that the voices favouring reform grow louder in every part of these isles. I have to wonder what lies ahead of us if the King and his government continue to meet those voices with repression.'

Charlotte shuddered. 'It almost makes me want to return to Kelda,' she said. 'Even if that means a reunion with my mother.'

Ted's heart lurched to note that she'd spoken of returning to Kelda, and not Chatton. It was clear that her hurt had been allowed to fester in the silence which had lingered between them on the subject of what he'd said in the parlour that night. It was clear, too, that he needed to redouble his efforts to make amends to her. Starting now.

'I think the worst of the trouble has now passed,' he said, offering her what he hoped would be a reassuring smile. 'And if ever proof was needed of that,' he continued, holding up his newspaper, 'it says here that there is to be a ball tonight, at the Assembly Rooms on George Street. Clearly, Edinburgh society believes it has nothing to fear from Radicals.'

Charlotte's bright blue eyes widened. 'Really?'

'Yes, really. And what's more, I think we should

attend. We have not been out in society here since our arrival.'

'I thought you did not care for society,' Charlotte remarked, raising her eyebrows.

'I do not care for London society,' Ted replied with a wry smile. 'Edinburgh society is tolerable. Besides, it would be unforgivable for the Duke and Duchess of Falstone to leave town without venturing into the fray at least once.'

Charlotte nodded briskly. 'As you wish,' she replied, returning her attention to her sewing. 'If it is safe to leave the house, I may ask Becky to join me for a walk this afternoon. I would benefit from some air after being cooped up these past days.'

'I would be happy to accompany you.'

'I am sure you have more important matters to attend to,' she answered him, not looking up. 'Besides, I wouldn't wish to be any more of a burden.'

Another cutting remark, this one driving a dagger straight into his heart. 'You are not a burden, Charlotte,' Ted said. 'I never meant to suggest that you were…'

'And yet you did.'

She rose from her seat, ready to make her escape, as she'd done so many times over the past few days. This time, Ted rose too, following her as she stepped towards the door and opened it. He was determined not to let the conversation end there.

'You're right—I did, and I am so very sorry for it,' he replied. 'I should not have spoken like that to you. You didn't marry me so that you could be subjected to my self-pity. But please, please know that when I spoke of my burdens, I did not mean you. Quite the opposite, in fact. If anything, having you by my side has made being the Duke of Falstone feel far more bearable of late.'

As he said those words, it struck him just how true that was. Just how accustomed to having Charlotte in his life he'd become. Just how content he was with the idea of having her at his side for the rest of his days.

Bearable? Content? Such insipid words, Ted. Why don't you tell her how those kisses you've shared make you burn for her? Why don't you ask her if you can kiss her again? That ought to liven things up.

He ordered that annoying inner voice to be silent. Livening things up was absolutely not what was needed right now. More kisses, however...

His candour, insipid though it was, must have given her pause for thought, as Charlotte closed the parlour door again and leaned against it.

'I cannot deny that marrying you has made my life more bearable in almost every respect,' she replied. 'But I also cannot deny that you hurt me, Ted. I did not expect you to be so secretive and so distant. The way you would disappear, and the way you evaded my questions—is it any wonder that I thought you regarded me as yet another obstacle you had to overcome?'

Ted nodded gravely. 'You're right,' he said, taking her by the hand. 'Of course, you are absolutely right. I promise you, things will change from now on.'

She raised her eyebrows, apparently unconvinced. 'Will they?'

'Yes,' he replied, the seed of an idea sowing itself in his mind. An idea which he hoped would demonstrate to Charlotte just how much he meant it, when he said that keeping secrets was a thing of the past. 'Starting this afternoon.'

'Why? What is happening this afternoon?'

He smiled, giving her fingers a gentle squeeze. 'We are going out. I will ask the servants to have the carriage brought round after luncheon. There is somewhere I'd like you to see.'

'Where are we?'

Charlotte took hold of Ted's hand, stepping warily out of the carriage and into the bright sunshine of a glorious spring day. Their journey had taken them into the heart of the ancient city and beyond, making their way slowly along rough, winding streets, densely packed with people and flanked by endless rows of tall buildings which appeared to have stood for centuries. She'd glimpsed some of this part of the city on the day that they'd first arrived, and now, as then, the contrast with the clean, orderly streets of the new part of Edinburgh struck her as stark.

Several times Charlotte had been forced to cover her nose with her handkerchief, her delicate senses troubled by a crescendo of smells emanating from the shops, the markets and, no doubt, the gutters. The surrounding crowds made Charlotte feel nervous and, despite Ted's assurances that nothing seemed to be amiss, she'd found herself gripping the cushion of her seat throughout the journey. Again, she found herself hankering after the sedate isolation of Kelda, miles from anywhere in the Northumbrian countryside. Although, of course, she knew that in truth her fear of imminent rebellion was not the only reason she'd entertained thoughts of going home of late.

Go home to your mother? Don't be a ninny. Ted told you that he was sorry, that his talk of burdens had not been about you...

He had said that, but that didn't mean that his remarks hurt any less. The fact that he'd made those remarks after she'd confided in him about her mother, and immediately after that earth-shattering kiss, made it all the worse. She'd opened up to him, at least a little, and she'd allowed him to glimpse some of her past pain and humiliation. She'd permitted his embrace, she'd allowed him to kiss her and to hold her, and for a few perfect moments she'd felt completely wanted. His words, even if they had not been about her, had managed to shatter that illusion, to remind her of what she was. An arrangement. A convenience. A necessary adornment for a titled man who had not wished to marry at all.

'This is the lying-in hospital I mentioned. This is where I worked last, when I was a physician.'

Ted's answer dragged Charlotte's thoughts back to the present, forcing her to focus on the fine building in front of her. It didn't look like a hospital, although admittedly she wasn't at all sure what a hospital should look like. Instead, it had the appearance of a mansion, brick built and with neat rows of large windows, indicating that it had two storeys. Unlike many of the buildings in the old parts of town, huddled together without even a hair's breadth to separate them, the hospital was set in small but attractive gardens, giving the place a pleasant and peaceful air.

'The house was originally a residence before being converted into a hospital at the end of the last century,' Ted continued, meeting her silence with further explanation. 'It is a charitable foundation for poor women, but also provides the opportunity to teach students of medicine, and midwives.'

Charlotte glanced up at him, noting the wistful expression etched on his dark features. 'It is a beautiful building. Did you spend a lot of time here?'

Ted smiled. 'As much as I could. I believed—indeed, I still believe that institutions like this can make an enormous difference. The women who come here are impoverished…some are unmarried. Many have nowhere else to turn.'

Charlotte's eyes widened. 'Unmarried?' she repeated.

He nodded. 'I can see that I have shocked you.'

'No,' she protested. 'Surprised, perhaps, but not shocked. Does your mother know about the lying-in hospital?'

'She does. Oddly, I think that philanthropic side of her meant that her attitude to my man midwifery softened somewhat, although she remained resolute in her decree that we should not discuss my work. But I did discover that she has made several donations to the hospital, which is interesting.'

'I wonder if that is her way of making amends to you,' Charlotte pondered. 'For the way she reacted to your work.'

'Perhaps.' He shook his head. 'Anyway, as my wife, you ought to know that I continue to support the lying-in hospital financially. It relies on public subscriptions, but these are regularly insufficient to sustain it. Since becoming a duke, I have increased the donations I give. I might no longer be able to offer them my time and my expertise, but money is something I have no shortage of.' He glanced at her. 'I hope you do not disapprove.'

'Disapprove?' She stared at him in astonishment.

'No, of course not. Besides, it is hardly my business how you choose to spend your money.'

'On the contrary, I believe it is absolutely your business,' he insisted. 'I am not one of those men who would hide his financial dealings from his wife. Our fortunes are bound together now. I would not keep you in the dark about them.'

'I appreciate that,' she replied. 'My father…he…'

Do not utter another word, Charlotte. There is no need to tell him about any of that.

When Ted turned to face her, however, she saw in his expression that he'd already grasped something of what she'd been about to say. 'Your father left you and your mother in a difficult position, I think. Living with your aunt, and reliant upon your uncle's kindness.'

She sighed. 'You don't know the half of it.'

'Then tell me.'

She closed her eyes briefly, steeling herself.

'When he died, my mother and I were left with almost nothing. Everything was sold to pay his debts, accumulated from years of gambling and terrible investments. If it had not been for my mother's marriage settlement, which was thankfully placed in trust, and the kindness of her family…well, we'd be destitute.'

Ted nodded, his dark gaze heavy with understanding. 'I know all too well what it is like to see a loved one wandering down that dark path,' he murmured. 'Perry's gambling was as unrestrained as his drinking, although he died before he could run through our family's fortune. My mother tried so hard to reform him, to make him see sense, but nothing ever worked.'

Charlotte gave him a watery smile. 'At least she tried. I don't know if my mother ever did. I know that she hid the perilous state of our finances from me until it was almost too late, and then…' She paused, questioning the wisdom of saying anything more. Questioning where it might lead.

'Then what?' Ted prompted.

'Then she heaped the responsibility for solving the problem on to me,' she said in the end, her voice barely a whisper. 'She told me I had to find a husband—an extremely wealthy, titled husband—who would clear my father's debts and save us.'

He nodded slowly. 'I presume that is why she objected to the young man in Lowhaven?'

'Yes. And obviously, I did not succeed in securing any such husband before my father died,' she continued quickly, desperate now to end this conversation before any more details of this sorry episode in her life could pour forth. 'My mother was never remiss in reminding me just how badly I'd let my family down,' she added.

Ted brushed her cheek with his fingers, sending a

tingling feeling of awareness through every part of her. 'It strikes me that if anyone was let down, Charlotte, then it was you. You have nothing to reproach yourself for.'

'Thank you,' Charlotte replied, offering him a small smile and trying not to consider how untrue that was. She had so much to reproach herself for, but she could not bring herself to share any of that with Ted, no matter how ardently she wished she could.

She glanced back towards the hospital. 'Were you planning to go inside?' she asked.

He drew a sharp breath. 'No, not today. Taking you to see the exterior of the place is one thing, but the sights and sounds of its interior are another matter. It might put you off from ever wishing to…'

She watched as he pressed his lips together, clearly thinking better of what he'd been about to say.

'From wishing to have children?'

Ted cleared his throat. 'Yes, exactly. Forgive me, that was a clumsy remark.'

She smiled. 'I do wish to have children, Ted. One day, of course. Just as we agreed,' she added quickly.

She could not fail to notice the odd look in his eyes as he returned her smile. 'Good—yes, just as we agreed,' he said in a way which suggested he wanted to say something more. Perhaps even something else entirely.

Before Charlotte could interrogate his response any

further, Ted offered her his hand and helped her back into their carriage before climbing in to sit opposite her. Almost immediately they set off for home, the carriage juddering along that unfamiliar web of winding, narrow streets which comprised old Edinburgh.

Charlotte sat back in her seat, her mind running over their conversation outside the lying-in hospital. Little by little, she kept giving Ted insights into her past as she seemed unwilling or unable to resist confiding in him. Why was that? And why had she started to wish that she could tell him everything, even the worst parts, about Crowgarth, and about the grave consequences of her reckless actions?

Before she could attempt to find answers to those questions, Ted leaned towards her and reached for her hand. 'I want you to know that I am determined to start afresh, Charlotte. No more secrets, and no more unexplained absences from the house. You were right when you said I have been yearning for my old life. Today I wanted to share something of that life with you, and to tell you that I am consigning it to the past, along with Dr Edward Scott. It is true that I have found it hard to reconcile myself to what fate has bequeathed to me, but I do not include our marriage in that. If anything, I count that as one of the best things to have happened to me since inheriting that damnable title,' he added, a smile spreading across his face. 'Dr Edward Scott was a committed bachelor, but honestly I believe the fool did not know what he was missing.'

His sincerity was touching and, yet again, Charlotte wished that she could be as honest with him. That she could lay bare her past and her feelings in the same way as he had.

'I think it's a shame that you've consigned the good doctor to the past,' she replied, pushing that thought away. 'Perhaps you might ask him to stay awhile? Only, I believe the Duke might find a use for his expertise from time to time.'

Ted raised his eyebrows. 'You do?'

She nodded. 'Of course. You have choices, Ted, and not only about how you spend your fortune. You might not be able to practise as a physician any more, but that does not mean you must cut your ties with your profession entirely. You have wealth and influence, something that none of those poor women you cared for ever had. In fact, something which most women do not have—myself included. You know about my mother, about what was expected of me. I was never free to make my own decisions, or to steer my own course, but you can.'

'You made the decision to marry me,' he observed.

'That is true,' she conceded. 'Although, given my mother was convinced you'd ruined me, I think we'd have been forced to marry in any case.'

He laughed. 'Point taken.' He squeezed her hand,

that dark gaze intent upon her own. 'I promise you, Charlotte, that you will always be able to steer your own course with me.'

Charlotte gave him a brief smile, then looked out of the window before he could spy the melancholy which she knew he'd see lingering in her eyes. Ted was so kind, so decent, and so determined to make her happy. If only she could embrace that without being plagued by a growing suspicion that she wanted more than the steady companionship Ted had offered her.

Because as she sat there, gazing out of the carriage window as they crossed the bridge which separated the old from the new part of town, she knew that she wanted him to be her husband in each and every sense of the word.

She wanted everything. She wanted so much more than she deserved. She wanted so much more than she could ever have.

Chapter Seventeen

Ted surveyed the bustling candlelit ballroom, conscious of the contented smile which appeared to have taken up permanent residence on his usually serious face and wondering what on earth had happened to his usual reticence and nerves. In the past he'd dreaded busy social events, enduring them if he had to and avoiding them if he could, and yet tonight he felt ready to embrace it all. To take the stares and whispers of onlookers in his stride. To make polite conversation. Even to dance. Dressed in his finest evening attire, his coat tailored to perfection, his shirt and cravat pristine, he felt almost as if he was…well, the nobleman he wasn't meant to be. For the first time since learning of his unwanted inheritance he felt he might actually be the Duke of Falstone. As if he was beginning to walk in his own shoes, and not those handed to him following Perry's untimely demise.

None of that had anything to do with his clothes, however, and everything to do with the breathtakingly beautiful red-haired woman who stood at his side, looking heavenly in a bold green gown. Their conversation outside the lying-in hospital earlier had come as something of a revelation, in more ways than one. Not only had Charlotte seemed to understand and accept those aspects of his old life which his family had considered unmentionable, she had encouraged him to think twice about whether it was necessary to leave all of it behind. She had confided in him about her father, too, and Ted's heart had warmed at the realisation that her trust in him was growing.

Your heart warms simply from being next to her, Ted. Don't you think it's time you told her so?

Perhaps it was time. If he could find the right moment, and the right words, to express himself...

'Do you know many people here?' Charlotte whispered to him. 'Other than those you've already introduced me to, of course.'

'I do recognise a few more faces.'

He took two glasses of punch from a nearby table, handing one to Charlotte and taking a considered sip from the other.

There were indeed a handful of familiar faces—a good number whom he knew from Edinburgh society, as well as several he recognised as former associates of his brother. Perry's characteristic indiscretion meant that he knew rather more about some of those gentlemen than he should, and knew that they were the Home Secretary's men. Given the recent trouble in the west, their presence in Edinburgh should perhaps not have surprised him. It was well known that Lord Sidmouth was keen to root out Radicals and revolutionaries, wherever they might be found. Although, given what Ted knew of the rakish characters of the gentlemen in question, he also knew that their presence at the Assembly Rooms that night was likely nothing to do with duty and everything to do with pleasure. In any case, he would not be introducing Charlotte to those particular gentlemen.

'Is Mr Tarbolton not attending?' Charlotte asked. 'Or any of your other acquaintances?'

'We may see one or two physicians I know during the course of the evening, although accoucheurs are not usually considered desirable company at George Street balls.' He shook his head, chuckling wryly. 'As for Henry, I'm afraid he managed to get himself barred from these events altogether.'

Her eyes widened. 'Barred? Why?'

Ted cleared his throat. 'Let's just say that he got on the wrong side of a prominent Edinburgh lawyer who has a great deal of influence over these matters, and who did not take kindly to an impertinent physician trying to seduce his daughter,' he whispered to her.

'Oh, no.' Charlotte's expression was grave. 'Given what you've told me about Mr Tarbolton, I do hope that he did not ruin her.'

'I believe he rather hoped to marry her,' Ted replied, sipping his punch. 'And I think she was keen on Henry, too. The exact nature of what passed between them, however, is something I cannot answer to. Indeed, Henry was unusually discreet about it.'

'He must have really cared for her,' Charlotte observed. 'What a pity that the courtship was not permitted.'

'In fairness to the young lady's father, I suspect his prejudice was against Henry's character as much as it was against his profession. That is the trouble with behaving like a libertine—no one knows if or when you're serious about becoming a husband.' He smiled at her before draining his glass and setting it aside. 'Anyway, as much as I enjoy Henry's company, I must confess I am content enough that he is not present tonight. I get to enjoy spending the evening with you, without spying him looking desirously at you at every opportunity.'

Charlotte's mouth fell open. 'He does not,' she protested.

'He most certainly does.' Ted turned to face her, that smile he'd worn all evening fading as his eyes met hers in earnest. 'The way he kept looking at you that night he dined with us made me want to burst. It made me feel like I...' He paused, shaking his head at himself, his mind warring with his heart over what he should say, and how he should say it.

'Ted, I am sure that you are being ridiculous.' She laughed, apparently oblivious to his turmoil. 'Mr Tarbolton was simply being friendly, that's all.'

'I doubt mere friendliness would have made me want to throw Henry out of the house,' he growled. 'But that thought did definitely cross my mind—especially when he started to talk about love matches, and gazed at you like a starving man.'

She laughed again. 'Now I know that you're being ridiculous!' she replied. 'He gave me no such look.'

Charlotte's denial was light-hearted, but even so it was enough to inflame him. Around them, Ted sensed the abrupt movement of a large group of people for whom one dance had ended and another was about to begin. He heard the music start again, the tune announcing the first waltz of the evening. It was strange; he'd never been a great enthusiast for dancing, and yet, as he stood before Charlotte, watching her finish the last of her punch and place the empty glass down, he found himself suddenly possessed by the urge to claim her in his arms and twirl her around the ballroom.

She raised an eyebrow at him. 'Well, now you're giving me an odd look,' she observed.

Ted growled again, catching her around the waist and pulling her towards him. 'I think we should dance,' he said, as though his actions had not already made that plain.

At first she regarded him with surprise, but quickly seemed to relax against him as they began to move together across the wooden floor. 'Yes, of course. I would like that very much,' she murmured.

Ted held her close to him, every sense he possessed thoroughly intoxicated by the floral scent she wore, by the enticing warmth of her waist beneath his hand, and by the heat which coursed through his veins every time their eyes met. He tried hard to tell himself that he needed to concentrate, to ensure that he performed the dance correctly, although he quickly realised this was not true. In fact, dancing with Charlotte like this felt like the most natural thing in the world. It was as instinctive and unconscious as breathing.

'Henry was looking at you,' he said softly, returning to their earlier conversation. 'Indeed, he could not tear his eyes away from you all evening.'

'I do not wish to talk about Mr Tarbolton,' she replied, bristling. 'In truth, I do not much like the idea of him regarding me in the way you describe.'

'And what about me?' He posed the question before he could stop himself. 'Do you mind the way I look at you?'

He watched as her lips parted slightly, her blue eyes meeting his gaze cautiously, as though she was trying to decide what lay behind the question. 'Most of the time, I cannot read the way you look at me,' she replied.

He nodded slowly, thinking that perhaps that was just as well. That if she had any insight into what he was thinking as he held her in his arms, and just how far those thoughts strayed from the terms of their convenient arrangement, then she'd likely be horrified. Wouldn't she?

If so, then God help him because, try as he might, he knew he could not hold those thoughts back much longer. Sooner or later, he would have to say something about how he felt about her. He would have to allow her to understand what all those looks she couldn't interpret had meant.

It was odd, really, but there was something about waltzing with Ted which felt so intimate. It was not as though they were a courting couple, seizing upon the opportunity for close contact which the dance provided. Indeed, on the few occasions when they'd transgressed the terms of their agreement and behaved in a way which was far beyond friendship, they'd enjoyed far greater physical contact than this. And yet there was something about the way Ted had tugged her into his arms, and something about the way his eyes met hers as they twirled, which heightened every sense she had. It made a strange, unfamiliar heat course through her, and made her skin tingle with awareness. It made her wish that those deep brown eyes were devoted only to her.

She tried hard to concentrate upon her footwork, to perform the dance properly and to keep her thoughts sensible. She hardly needed to remind herself just how dangerous a place the ballroom had been for her in the past. Just how easily that reckless, impetuous version of herself had been summoned by the sound of violins and the taste of punch. By the prospect of dancing with a handsome gentleman and the promise of a flirtation.

Although, of course, this was entirely different. Everything was different now, since the handsome gentleman in question was already Charlotte's husband, and what she felt for him went far beyond a superficial flirtation. Indeed, this was a man whom all of her, the sensible and the reckless parts, had very much begun to care for.

'Today has been unexpectedly enjoyable,' she said, finally breaking the silence which had settled between them. 'After the trials of the past few days, I must confess it has been a welcome change.'

A pained look crossed Ted's face. 'I know. I am so sorry that I upset you.'

She smiled. 'I was actually referring to the fear of insurrection in the city, but thank you—again.' She shook her head at herself. 'You were just being honest with me about how you feel, and I took what you said to heart. My mother always made me feel like such a burden, especially after my father's death. I could not bear the thought that you'd come to regard me in the same way.'

She felt him pull her closer. 'I could never think of you as a burden, Charlotte. Never.' His dark gaze was unwavering. 'And your mother should never have made you feel like that, either. Indeed, I dare say there are many things your mother should not have done.' He shook his head. 'When I think about the way she sat at my dining table and belittled you...'

Charlotte winced at the memory. 'She never did think my work at the school particularly worthwhile. Nor did she think me clever enough to undertake it.'

'Then she was entirely wrong, on both counts,' Ted insisted. 'You are both intelligent and perceptive, Charlotte. Today in the carriage you opened my eyes, you spoke to me about my choices in a way that no one else ever has. You made me realise that I do not have to sacrifice the man I was at the altar of the man I must be. For too long I have focused only on the responsibilities the Dukedom has brought me, and have neglected the possibilities afforded by my position. I am determined to see things differently now, and that is thanks to you.'

His candour was touching. 'That is kind of you, Ted.'

'I am not being kind.' The timbre of his voice was

low but insistent. 'I am being honest. Do you remember when I told you that I'd had a bad dream during that night at the coaching inn?'

Charlotte nodded, trying not to recall her own nightmare that night. Conjuring that particular horror would not help her right now. It could wait until she was alone in the darkness of her bedchamber, just as it always did.

'As well as dreaming about falling from that tree as a boy, I also dreamt about our wedding day. I could see you standing at the altar, but you were waiting for Perry, not me.' He shook his head at himself, apparently contemplating the memory of it. 'You were waiting for the real Duke of Falstone, not the second son who circumstance has forced to walk in his shoes.'

Charlotte frowned. 'From what you have told me about him, I don't think I would have been very happy with your brother, Ted.'

'No—certainly not. But I think the dream arose from this feeling I have had, ever since becoming the Duke. The feeling that I am an imposter, that this is all a terrible joke and should never have been mine. A feeling which I have noticed has begun to subside since marrying you. Since starting to build a life with you.' Those dark eyes of his smouldered as he leaned closer. 'I am no poet, Charlotte. I am not a man for grand gestures or declarations. But I want you to understand how I feel. I want you to know that I do care for you.'

She pressed her lips together, her heart racing and her cheeks growing flushed as her elation at hearing his words combined with the painful realisation that they could never be true. Not really. Not if he knew all about her and the reckless things she'd done.

Perhaps you've been too good at being sensible, after all. And now Ted thinks you're someone you're not.

'It has grown difficult to keep to the terms of our arrangement of late,' she whispered, her voice unfathomably hoarse all of a sudden. 'Instead of fostering friendship, we do seem to keep ending up in each other's arms.'

'I do wonder, though, if it is more than passion.' His breath tickled her ear, sending a shiver through her. 'Although I cannot deny that living under the same roof as you has been torment. I cannot tell you how many times I have cursed myself for proposing this arrangement between us.'

His words took her completely aback. 'But our arrangement has been good for both of us,' Charlotte protested. 'You do not regret it, surely?'

'No, of course not. What I mean to say is that if I could turn the clock back now, I would court you—properly. I would make sure you know how much I want you,' he murmured.

Charlotte stared over Ted's shoulder, unable to meet his gaze, lest her eyes betray her turmoil. Her feelings for Ted were powerful, visceral, and genuine. Perhaps the only part of the tangled web this convenient marriage had become which was not complicated. Everything else, she realised, was a mess—one which was entirely of her own making. These past weeks, she'd justified keeping the worst parts of her past hidden from him by telling herself that it was of no consequence to their companionable match, to the agreement they'd made. That digging up everything that was dead and buried was futile, since burdening Ted with the knowledge of it would not change a thing.

But now, having heard Ted confess what he felt for her, and knowing what she felt for him, she knew that those justifications no longer rang true. Could she really countenance allowing him to care for her, whilst still concealing the awful truth from him? Could she really bear to heap more guilt on top of that which she already kept buried within her? And if not, could she actually bring herself to tell him everything?

Time to decide how honest you can bear to be, Charlotte. Unless you are too much of a coward to risk losing affection you have not truly earned.

Charlotte swallowed hard. 'Ted…' she began. 'We need to talk. I must tell you something, but not here. I…'

Charlotte felt the words die in her throat as her gaze came to rest upon a man, standing among those gathered at the edge of the room, watching the dancing. A man whose shock of straw-coloured hair and piercing blue eyes were dreadfully familiar. A man who she'd believed she would never see again. She saw his gaze come to rest upon her, and felt her breath hitch as a sly smile spread itself slowly across his face. A smile which took her back to that fateful London Season. To all the candlelit balls during which she'd basked unashamedly in his hungry gaze. To all the times her ambition had rendered her deaf to the whispers about her conduct and his reputation.

To that day at the coaching inn when she'd teetered on the edge of ruin, oblivious to the devastating consequences her foolish and reckless behaviour had already wrought.

The violins ceased playing as the waltz ended, which was perhaps just as well as Charlotte realised she'd stopped dancing. Instead, she was rooted to the spot, staring at that man, even though every ounce of reason she possessed told her that he could not possibly be there. Then she blinked, and he was gone.

'Charlotte?' Ted's voice sounded oddly distant as he regarded her, a frown gathering between his eyes. 'What's the matter? You're as white as a ghost.'

A ghost—that is what he must be. A spectre, summoned by your guilty conscience. Unless...

'I… I'm sorry,' she stammered, her voice sounding strangled. 'I'm… I feel suddenly unwell. I need to go home, I think.'

Ted agreed and led her out of the ballroom, his tenderness and palpable concern making her feel even more wretched. That man she'd seen had not been a ghost—he'd been flesh and blood, just as he had been the last time she'd seen him, when the veil had finally fallen from her eyes and she'd leapt on the first stagecoach back to London.

She'd been able to run then, but this time she knew there would be no escape. That man was neither dead nor buried, but a very real, very living threat—to her and, worst of all, to Ted. The exposure of her awful secret promised not only to harm her, but the Falstone Dukedom, the Scott family, and her husband.

As Ted whisked her out of the Assembly Rooms, she felt that particular fear claw at her most painfully of all. The fear that the kind and decent man she'd married was about to learn that the agreement they'd forged that night in the greenhouse came at a far higher price than he could ever have imagined.

Chapter Eighteen

Ted fell back on to his pillow with a heavy sigh, listening to the ceaseless tapping of the rain against the window of his bedchamber as he tried and failed to quieten his racing thoughts. Recollections of that evening at the Assembly Rooms replayed over and over in his mind, forcing him to pick over the details and to realise that he had not the first idea what to make of what had occurred. Impulsively taking Charlotte into his arms and insisting upon a waltz. Losing control of his tongue, speaking to her about passion and torment, about caring for her and wanting her—all without either invitation or encouragement from the woman who'd agreed to be his duchess. Even thinking about the words he'd said was enough to set his teeth on edge. Words which he had never expected to hear himself utter. Words which were a clear breach of their arrangement.

Charlotte's reaction to those words told him everything he needed to know. A feeling of sheer horror and mortification had swept through him as he'd watched her face grow pale and felt her come to an abrupt halt in his arms, and he'd realised immediately just how serious his transgression had been. Not only were his feelings for her uninvited, they were thoroughly unwelcome and unreciprocated. He ought to have realised that, ought to have heeded the warning in her words about their arrangement, about how it had been good for both of them. Yet instead he'd continued, speaking so bluntly that the thought of it now made his toes curl. He'd been honest—too honest. He'd given her no choice but to grapple with his honesty, and he had not even had the courtesy to do so in private. Speaking to her like that in the middle of a ballroom was truly unforgivable. Little wonder she'd looked as if she was going to faint. Little wonder she'd wanted to go home.

You promised Charlotte an escape, you damned cork brain. You promised she would be able to steer her own course with you. Yet there you were, confessing your feelings and backing her into a corner...

Ted groaned as he buried his face in his pillow. Why had he not just kept his thoughts and his feelings to himself? Why had he not been able to content himself with nurturing friendship, as they'd both agreed? Why had he not permitted his head to continue to rule him, to remind him of why he'd made this arrangement with Charlotte in the first place? He'd married to fulfil his duty to the Dukedom, and to give Charlotte the escape she'd desired—two good and honourable reasons which ought to have satisfied him. Theirs was meant to be a companionable and steady marriage which, given time, would result in heirs for the Dukedom—that was the agreement they'd struck. Why was that not enough? Why did his heart have to get involved?

Your heart was involved from the beginning, Ted. Perhaps it's time to admit that to yourself...

Perhaps it was. Perhaps, for all his protestations that this was a sensible, rational match and the answer to their respective problems, that had never been the full story. Perhaps if he had not been so wedded to his former life as an unmarried physician and so averse to the mere idea of courting a young lady, he might have understood that at the time. Perhaps he did need to acknowledge that—but only to himself, and not to Charlotte. He'd said far too much to her already.

Given the absolute mess you've made of everything, it would seem your aversion to courtship and your pursuit of a convenient match was justified. It would appear that you'd never have managed to get a lady like Charlotte to marry you any other way...

How true that was. How devastatingly, heartbreakingly true. Charlotte did not care for him the way that he cared for her—he would have to find a way to set his hurt and his pride aside and accept that. He would also have to find a way to make amends to her, and to find a way back to the friendship they'd agreed to foster in the first place. He had to hope that such a thing was possible, that it was not too late. Ted covered his face with his hands, barely daring to contemplate the alternative. God help him if Charlotte now wished to separate…

A gentle tap at the door to his bedchamber interrupted this darker turn his thoughts had taken, causing Ted to sit bolt upright in his bed. He frowned. It had been some time since he'd retired and the hour was late, which meant it was unlikely to be his valet. Charlotte, meanwhile, had been whisked off into the care of Mrs McGowan and Becky as soon as they'd arrived home from the ball, and was surely sleeping soundly by now, wasn't she? Unless…

Another tap at the door, more urgent this time. Ted leapt out of bed and hurried towards the door, not troubling himself to either light a candle or to pull on a robe over his nightshirt and preserve his dignity. Instinctively he knew who stood on the other side of that door, and he knew there was not a moment to waste. If she was seeking him out in the middle of the night, then whatever she wanted to say to him was important—for better or for worse. He knew he would not sleep a wink if he did not discover, here and now, what it was.

He pulled the door open, peering into the gloom at the small, slender silhouette of a woman standing in his doorway. Even in the darkness he could make out the captivating vision of her dressed in her nightclothes, her long hair loose about her shoulders. Immediately his mind added the details and the colours which had etched themselves permanently in his memory. The alabaster skin. The tempting curve of her waist, hinted at beneath a loose nightgown. The smattering of freckles across her nose. The fiery colour of those tantalising curls.

'Charlotte,' he breathed. 'What is the matter? Are you still feeling unwell?'

He sensed her hesitate. 'I… We need to talk. I cannot sleep, not until…'

In the black of the night he heard what sounded like a sob and, before he could say another word, Charlotte ran into his arms. Instinct triumphed over thought as he held her close, running his fingers over the soft tendrils of her hair as she pressed her head against his chest and clung to him for dear life. It was clear that she was upset, and clear too that he was tired and overwrought but, even so, the sheer potency of the moment was not lost on him. Even as his head reminded him of her reaction to his heartfelt declaration earlier that night, he felt his foolish heart begin to hope. Hope that there might be something between them—something beyond their agreement. Beyond friendship.

'Charlotte...' He murmured her name as he pressed his lips against the top of her head. 'If I have upset you, then please forgive me, but I could not conceal my feelings any longer. I could not go another moment without telling you that I care for you.'

Agreements be damned. Friendship be damned. He was in danger of completely losing his heart to this woman, if he had not already. Whatever was wrong, he wanted to make it right. Whatever was causing her distress, he wanted to fix it. He wanted to rescue her now, just as he'd wanted to rescue her that night in the greenhouse when he'd first proposed.

'You cannot care for me, Ted,' she whispered, her voice hoarse and uneven as she stepped back from him. 'You will not care for me, when you know what I have done.'

He frowned. 'What do you mean?'

'I did something truly shameful,' she replied, her voice thick with tears as she closed the door behind them. 'I do not deserve to be your wife. I do not deserve to be your Duchess.'

Charlotte slumped down on the edge of Ted's bed and watched him light a candle, feeling the weight of every word which needed to be said. She knew now that this was her comeuppance, to have to endure the knowledge that she'd married a thoroughly decent and kind man who had come to care for a version of her which did not truly exist. This was her penance—shattering his illusions about her and watching his affection fade away, even while her own continued to burn brightly and unrequited for eternity.

Oddly, she found herself recalling a Greek story which Elspeth had told her once about Echo, the nymph who provoked the wrath of the Queen of the gods and was cursed to only ever be able to repeat another's words. When Echo fell in love, she was unable to express herself to the object of her desire, and so was rejected. Echo's past actions had damned her, and so too, Charlotte thought, had hers. Now she was condemned to have to repeat her tawdry tale, to reveal all that she was, and to bear the consequences.

And yet she had to tell Ted. She'd known that, even in those moments before her past had appeared, looking roguish and dangerous as ever, at the edge of the ballroom. Ted's words to her during that waltz had served to shatter an illusion of her own—the illusion that their marriage was a mere convenience in which deeper feelings did not feature. The illusion that there was no need to tell him about mistakes which were dead and gone, because she was Ted's wife and Duchess in name only.

Discovering that the man who'd partnered her in her dalliance with ruin still lived and breathed had only served to make her confession more urgent. She'd read that smile he'd given her, and knew only too well the destruction he was capable of. The sort of destruction which terrified her, since it would wreak havoc on Ted's life, too. The thought of seeing him dragged into this awful mess was unbearable.

Ted sat down at her side. Despite herself, the distance he left between them made Charlotte feel bereft. Doubtless she was already grieving what she knew she was about to lose.

She drew a deep, shuddery breath, keeping her eyes cast down and avoiding Ted's dark eyes, intent upon her. If she was going to muster the strength to tell him this story, she knew she could not do so while looking at him.

'About a year and a half ago, I went with my mother and father to London. My mother was determined that London was where I would find a husband who was wealthy enough to save us from financial ruin, and so she planned a Season for me. Of course, my mother's customary impatience meant that we arrived in town long before the start of the Season, but I didn't mind. After that humiliating summer I spent in Lowhaven, I admit I was desperate to get away. We stayed in London over Christmas and into the spring, during which time I attended a number of dinners, balls and soirées with my mother.' She gave an involuntary shudder. 'My father was seldom with us, preferring his club, of course. Preferring to gamble away the last of his fortune.'

Ted reached over, giving her hand a small squeeze. 'I am sorry, Charlotte.'

'Trust me, Ted, I do not deserve your sympathy.' She drew another deep breath. She'd begun now; she had to continue. 'It was at one of those balls that I met the eldest son of an earl, who seemed to take an interest in me. As you can imagine, my mother was delighted by this and was determined from the outset that I should secure him. She schemed endlessly, ensuring our paths crossed at every opportunity, and even orchestrating situations where we might find ourselves alone together. Even when whispers about his less than desirable character and conduct reached her ears, still she was not dissuaded. Nor was I—stupid, foolish me had been thoroughly taken in by his rakish, roguish charms.'

The pain of guilt clawed in her chest as she felt Ted shuffle uncomfortably before clasping his hands in his lap. He was her husband and he cared for her—this would be as hard for him to hear as it was for her to say.

'Did you love him?' he asked.

'I don't know—perhaps I thought I did, at the time. Certainly I loved the attention, the flirtation...' She paused, reluctant to spell out the depths of her own wantonness. The kisses she'd allowed him to steal, the liberties she'd allowed him to take with those insatiable, roaming hands. She swallowed hard, suppressing a shudder. 'And I loved my mother's approval,' she continued, shaking her head at herself. 'I'd never had that before. She was never so good to me as she was in London. I was so completely ridiculous. So focused on fulfilling my mother's ambitions for me and on preventing us from falling into penury. I think I convinced myself that if I could do that, it would somehow make up for...' Her words died in her throat as yet more unpleasant memories raced to the fore.

'For?' Ted prompted her.

She swallowed hard, fighting back the fresh tears which had begun to gather in her eyes. 'For my conduct in Lowhaven with the gentleman I told you about, the one my mother objected to. I had no choice but to put an end to our attachment, and I did so really badly. I hurt him, and he did not deserve that.'

'I'm sure you're not the first young lady to wound a man with a clumsy rejection, Charlotte,' Ted said gently.

'I'm sure I'm not. Indeed, I know I won't be the first lady to make any of the mistakes I've made. But that doesn't make them any more forgivable. After Lowhaven, I swore that I would only ever be led by my head, and never my heart. But I learned to my cost that my head can be just as reckless.'

'What happened?'

Charlotte shuddered again. She'd arrived now at the worst part of it all. 'I continued to enjoy the attentions of the earl's son, and my mother worked herself into feverish excitement, convinced that her conniving would lead to a proposal. But then the earl's son seemed to have a change of heart. He told me that his father would not consent to a marriage between us, that he had another young lady in mind for him. I was devastated, and as for my mother's reaction—well, I am sure you can imagine.' She paused, feeling the first of her tears fall as she pressed her eyes closed and collected herself. 'After that I panicked, and I did something really terrible.'

'What did you do, Charlotte?' Ted asked, his voice low with trepidation.

'I agreed to an elopement!' she sobbed, the tears flowing freely now. 'When he came to see me again, a few days later, I agreed to run away with him. He told me that it was the only way we could be together, and I believed him. I was so convinced of his affection for me, and so desperate to rescue my family from ruin, that I left with him for Scotland as soon as I could.'

She looked at Ted then, saw how tightly his lips were pressed together. Saw how white his face had grown. Was it shock, or fury, or both?

'Please, tell me you did not marry him,' he said

quietly. 'Tell me you are not already wed, because if you are, then our marriage is…'

'No!' Charlotte exclaimed, fresh panic surging through her at the mere thought of it. 'No, I did not marry him. We were at a coaching inn not far from London when I came to my senses and realised he had no intention of marrying me. That he had set out only to ruin me.'

She whispered that final part, ashamed of the words even as they fell from her lips. The rest of it she could not bring herself to describe—the way he'd tried to bed her at the coaching inn. The way he'd mocked her when she'd pushed him away. The way his eyes had danced with wicked amusement as he'd protested that he'd been certain that was what she'd wanted. The way his taunts had given way to his anger as he'd called her that dreadful name for the first and only time, shattering her belief that he cared for her at all.

'You're not fit to be my mistress, never mind my wife,' he'd spat, his eyes blazing. *'Do you know what my friends and I call you? We call you Charlotte the Harlot.'*

She watched as Ted balled his fists. 'If he hurt you, I will kill him,' he vowed.

Charlotte stared at him, taken aback by his words. She'd never heard Ted speak like that before. 'He did not hurt me, and I promise you, I did not lie with him.

I ran out of the inn and on to the first stagecoach bound for London.' Her bottom lip quivered as she struggled to maintain her composure. 'I was terrified of what was to come. Our flirtations at society balls and soirées had already given people cause to whisper. I knew that if the story of our failed elopement got out, my reputation would be in tatters. I know now that my behaviour came with far worse consequences than that. I arrived back in London to discover that my father had died. His heart had failed, because of me,' she wept. 'Because of what I'd done.'

'Surely you cannot hold yourself responsible for that,' Ted said softly. 'Your father was facing ruin and will have been under enormous strain.'

'My mother said it was my doing,' she protested. 'She said he died from his distress over me. Now perhaps you understand why she behaves as she does towards me. She blames me—for all of it.'

She sensed Ted grow tense. 'No,' he said quietly. 'I do not understand why any mother would behave in such a manner towards her daughter. Nor do I understand why scoundrels like that earl's son whisk young ladies off to coaching inns to ruin them.' He glanced at her, and Charlotte noted the apprehension in his dark eyes. 'Who is he, Charlotte?'

She sniffed, trying to prevent any more tears from falling. Trying to muster the courage to utter his name, as though afraid that doing so might summon him, just as her overwhelming guilt seemed to have summoned him to the Assembly Rooms tonight.

'His name is Lord Crowgarth,' she said after a long moment. 'And until today, I believed that he was dead.'

Chapter Nineteen

Ted drew a deep breath, suppressing a groan at hearing that name fall from Charlotte's lips. A name, and a man, with whom he was all too familiar. Crowgarth's exploits were infamous and, regrettably, Ted was better acquainted with their lurid details than most. The man was notorious—dangerously handsome and charming, he seduced society ladies for sport, although running away with them and tricking them into thinking they were going to elope was not his usual habit. Then again, Ted thought, he knew enough about the man to know that there was no limit to his wickedness.

'Crowgarth is a notorious rake and philanderer,' he said after a long moment. 'I cannot believe your mother was willing to consider him as a suitable husband for you—heir to an earldom or not. He is wicked, Charlotte. He indulges in every imaginable excess and exercises no control over his appetites. His father, the Earl of Malham, despairs of him. I cannot believe that you…' Ted bit his lip, forcing himself to hold back the words. It was clear that Charlotte was distressed enough by her association with the man; hearing his sheer disbelief that she'd ever wanted to wed that scoundrel would do no good.

In the flickering candlelight, he saw Charlotte's eyes widen. 'You know him?' she asked quietly.

'Unfortunately, yes,' he replied bitterly. 'He was a friend of my brother, Perry. The two of them were thick as thieves in the gambling hells, along with a handful of other rebellious, dissolute sons of noblemen, intent upon disgracing themselves.' He shook his head sadly, looking away from her. 'In Perry's case, of course, his behaviour did more than just that, in the end.'

Beside him, he sensed Charlotte shiver, and felt his hands itch with the temptation to pull her close. Something stopped him, however. Something which made him question whether his touch would be welcome. After all, he reminded himself, Charlotte plainly did not share his feelings—he knew that now. Acting upon his impulses and desires would make him no better a creature than Crowgarth, and he could not countenance that.

'I'm sorry, Ted,' she murmured. 'I had no idea of Lord Crowgarth's connection to your brother.'

Ted shrugged. 'Crowgarth isn't responsible for Perry's demise. My brother managed that all by himself.' He frowned, a fresh thought occurring to him. 'Why did you think Crowgarth was dead?'

'My mother told me.' She shook her head. 'The weeks after I returned home were a blur. Between burying my father and confronting the wreckage he'd bequeathed to us, and coming to terms with what I'd done...suffice to say, I barely left the house. I was terrified that word of my disgrace would get out, that I would have a ruined reputation to add to everything else. As time went by, however, it became clear that no one knew anything about my failed elopement. Then one day, my mother came home and told me that Lord Crowgarth had left England, that he'd sailed for the Continent but that it was believed he'd perished in a shipwreck.'

The furrow in Ted's brow deepened. 'Fleeing to the Continent certainly sounds about right—he'd done that before, to escape his creditors and his father's wrath. I never heard about any of this, but then last year we were all at Chatton, and my mother's friends in London were no doubt too conscious of her grief to relate such gossip to her in their letters, especially given Crowgarth's regrettable connection to my brother.'

He heard Charlotte draw a deep, uneven breath. 'Yes, well, as it turns out, the story my mother heard wasn't true.' She shivered again. 'Tonight, at the Assembly Rooms, I saw him and, worse still, he saw me. That was why I wanted to leave.'

Ted nodded slowly, the realisation dawning that the cause of her sudden illness had not been his heartfelt declaration, but Crowgarth's presence. Oddly, it made him feel worse, to know that he'd chosen such a dreadful moment. To know that he'd been professing his affection for her while she'd been in the grip of horror.

'I didn't see Crowgarth,' Ted said, swallowing down that discomfiting thought. 'However, I did notice a few of Perry's other wastrel friends there tonight. I suspect they're all in Scotland at Lord Sidmouth's behest.'

Charlotte frowned. 'What do you mean?'

'I happen to know that a number of Perry's associates are in the employment of the Home Secretary—Crowgarth included. Perry used to joke that it was the result of their respective fathers' attempts to correct their behaviour. And I suppose Sidmouth, for his part, must have his uses for such unpleasant characters,' he added. 'Anyway, I imagine their presence in Edinburgh is connected with the recent unrest. Sidmouth will have eyes and ears everywhere.'

He watched as Charlotte pressed her hands against her cheeks, shaking her head as though she was at war with herself. 'Perhaps that explains it,' she said, her voice wavering again. 'I've been lying awake, convinced that Crowgarth was coming for me, and imagining all the terrible things he might do. The triumphant way he stared at me, and the menacing way he smiled…it brought it all back.' She paused, letting out a sound which was somewhere between a sob and a groan. 'To my eternal shame, when my mother told me about the shipwreck, all I could feel was relief. If he was gone, then so too, it seemed, was the threat of scandal. The only other person who knew then what I'd done was my mother, and while she blamed me for what happened to my father, I knew she would never tell another soul about it. I thought my secret was safe, but now…'

'Now you've been forced to tell me.' Ted finished her sentence for her, every word like a knife in his heart as the truth dawned upon him. 'If Crowgarth really was dead and gone, would you ever have told me about him, Charlotte? Would you ever have trusted me with the knowledge of it?'

His stomach lurched painfully as he saw her hesitate.

'I wanted to, Ted, please believe that. These past weeks in Edinburgh, as we've grown closer, I found myself wishing that I could be entirely honest with you. And tonight, when you told me that you care for me, I realised that I could no longer countenance keeping the truth from you. But please, you must understand…'

'Oh, I understand perfectly.' Ted rose from the edge of the bed, feeling his temper flare. 'I understand that you saw Crowgarth and you knew you had no choice.'

Charlotte stood up too, pursuing him across the room. 'Just as I left you no choice but to tell me about your lectures,' she countered. 'If I hadn't confronted you on George Street that night, would you have ever told me?'

Her blue eyes were wide and beseeching and, try as he might, Ted could not tear his gaze away.

'I don't know,' he said quietly. 'I knew I needed to—I knew I could not keep being so evasive with you. But you know that I agonised over what you would think of me, if you knew all about my work.'

She nodded. 'Yes, I do know. You feared losing my good opinion, just as I have feared losing yours. But please believe me when I say that in those moments before I saw Crowgarth, I knew I was going to have to lose it—and a great deal more besides.' She shook her head again. 'And then I saw Crowgarth standing there and I knew what was at stake. I will never forgive myself if your good name is tarnished by your association with me. This is all my fault—for accepting your proposal, for promising to be your Duchess…'

'You promised to be my wife, too, not solely my Duchess,' Ted interrupted, her words seeping under his skin like poison. 'Unless, of course, the title really was of paramount consideration to you. After all, you were prepared to go to some lengths to secure the son of an earl...'

Heavens, man. What the devil did you say that for?

Charlotte's cheeks blazed to match her fiery curls. 'That is not what I meant!'

'Then tell me what you meant, Charlotte,' Ted replied, his remorse over his angry words growing in tandem with his desperation to hear her answer. To understand, for better or for worse, why she'd chosen to spend her life with him. 'Please, tell me why you were prepared to accept a convenient, loveless marriage. Tell me, truthfully, why you were prepared to accept me.'

Charlotte wiped away her tears, trying to force herself to see clearly, and to think straight. She watched as Ted's dark gaze remained intently upon her, ashamed to see how low she'd sunk in his eyes. Telling him the truth about her past had been more painful than she'd feared; not only had she ripped the veil from his eyes and forced him to see the reckless, scandalous woman he'd married, but in revealing the depths her past self had plumbed she'd caused him to question her motivation for accepting his hand in the first place. Hearing him describe their marriage as loveless had been agony, confirming, as if confirmation were needed, that she had lost his affection for ever, and before she'd even managed to find the words to confess her own.

Then you might as well tell him how you feel about him. What do you have to lose?

Nothing. There was nothing left to lose.

She drew a deep breath, trying to calm her racing heart. Trying to find the right words to explain.

'That evening in the greenhouse, when I told you I wanted to escape, I was telling the truth. Life with my mother was intolerable—you already know that. Whilst I deserved every bit of the blame she heaped on me, I knew I could no longer bear it. You gave me a way out, and when I promised I would be your wife and your Duchess, I took that promise to heart. I swore to myself that I would not let you down, that I would be a better sort of person, and would build a better life—with you. I realise now that, in doing so, I've allowed you to care for a woman who is not real.'

He frowned. 'Of course you're real.' He ran an agitated hand through his hair. 'Damn Crowgarth! Why is the Charlotte he knew any more valid than the Charlotte you are with me? Surely it is the other way around? Surely all of us learn from our experiences and our mistakes, don't we? Surely all of us change?'

'I believed I had changed.' Charlotte felt her lip tremble. 'Since arriving in Kelda, I'd tried so hard to start afresh, to learn the lessons of the past and to do something worthwhile with my life by volunteering at the school. When you asked me to marry you, I was so determined to be equal to the task, to be a steady and sensible wife and duchess. But it seems it is not possible for me to banish that wayward, impetuous side of my personality entirely. My behaviour is testament to that—after all, sensible ladies don't drink so much claret that they get tangled in the laces of their stays, or confront their husbands in the street because they've worked themselves into a state over some imagined infidelity, or indeed, accept spontaneous proposals of marriage in greenhouses from noblemen they barely know...'

'Actually, I expect all ladies do at least some of those things, some of the time,' Ted interjected. 'And I think you are being too hard on yourself, Charlotte. None of us are straightforward, and none of us are perfect.'

'Well, I am certainly not perfect,' she replied, bristling. 'As now you know.'

Charlotte folded her arms across her chest, feeling suddenly cold and exposed in her nightgown. Suddenly aware of everything, from her own exhaustion to the lateness of the hour, to the fact that she was alone with Ted in his bedchamber. Suddenly aware of just how much she wanted him to hold her and draw her close to him, even if it was for the last time.

After what you told him tonight? Don't be a ninny.

More likely he'll never touch you again. More likely he will want to separate...

That thought made her heart ache anew. In the aftermath of her revelations, she knew there was much they needed to discuss. Much which needed to be decided upon. But not tonight. She could face no more pain and turmoil tonight.

'It is late,' she began, her mouth unfathomably dry. 'I should go.'

'Don't.' Ted's dark eyes smouldered as they met hers, and she saw he felt the weight of the moment, too. He stepped towards her, reaching tentatively for her hand. 'That impetuous decision you made, to marry me,' he said quietly. 'Do you regret it?'

She shook her head, taken aback by his question. 'No, of course not. Quite the opposite, in fact. I think it is the best hasty, impulsive decision I've ever made.'

He looked genuinely, heart-wrenchingly surprised by her admission. 'Really?'

'Yes, really. I…'

Come on, Charlotte, your words have not been stolen by the Queen of the gods. Tell him. He deserves to know how you feel.

'I care for you, Ted,' she began again, brushing his cheek with her fingers. 'What I feel for you goes so far beyond our arrangement that, in fact, I think…'

Whatever she'd been about to say flew immediately from her mind as Ted captured her lips with his own and pulled her close to him. His kiss was fierce and urgent, lighting a fire deep within her belly and obliterating thoughts of anything else. She heard herself murmur as he trailed kisses down her neck, her eyes involuntarily closing as she focused solely on the feeling of his mouth against her skin, of the warmth of his hands as they sought the curve of her waist. She felt her fingers wander across his back, her confidence growing in tandem with her desire as she explored the solid, muscular details of his physique.

She heard Ted groan, sensed his need to stoke the flames as his lips reached the swell of her breasts and his hand plunged into the tumbling red curls of her hair. She murmured again, realising that she was completely lost, that she'd surrendered herself entirely to the moment and to her passions, and that wayward Charlotte was once again in control. She knew that she ought to recover her reason, that there were so many things which still remained to be said. So many questions which still needed to be asked. The same question Ted had posed to her about regrets, and other questions, too—about his feelings for her now, and about the future of their arrangement. Sensible, pressing questions, and yet she could not find it within herself to break the spell she'd fallen under. To quieten that reckless inner voice which told her to indulge in her desires tonight and face the consequences of her confessions tomorrow.

You want him, Charlotte.

'I want you,' she heard herself whisper.

His brown eyes met hers and she saw that they were filled with caution. 'Are you sure?' he breathed.

She nodded, pulling him towards the bed which beckoned behind, and making her intentions clear. In the light of dawn she would have to face up to what she'd done, to the damage wrought by her revelations. But dawn was several hours away yet; until then, they had the darkness to envelop them, to keep them from seeing clearly. Because even as she invited Ted's touch once more, even as she relished his kisses and collapsed with him on to his soft sheets, she feared that with the rising of the sun, clarity would come. Her sorry tale would sink in, and Ted would see her for what she was—a reckless woman, tainted by scandal. A mistake. A burden, to add to all the other burdens he carried around with him.

'I want you too, Charlotte,' Ted murmured.

He extinguished the candle, embracing the darkness with her as their bodies tangled and intertwined, as nightclothes were shed and skin greeted skin. All reason, all thought was swept away by a rising tide of entirely new, entirely unexpected sensations as she allowed Ted to know her completely, to take her towards a precipice she'd never known existed.

When, finally, they tumbled over it together, she held on to him tightly, hoping beyond hope that when morning came, all would not be lost. That the damage wrought by her past could yet be repaired, and that in the unforgiving light of day Ted would not conclude that he had no choice but to let his convenient bride go.

Chapter Twenty

Charlotte crept out of Ted's bedchamber into the grey light of the morning which greeted her in the hall. She shivered, wrapping her arms around herself as she hurried back towards her own bedchamber. A long corridor separated her room from Ted's and after the events of the previous night, putting that distance between them again felt necessary.

She was exhausted; unlike Ted, she had not been able to fall asleep. Instead, she'd found herself lying awake, listening to the gentle rhythm of his breathing while her mind reeled and her guilt clawed at her. Instead of behaving sensibly, instead of finishing their conversation properly and asking the questions which needed to be asked, she'd surrendered herself to her desires and thrown herself unashamedly into Ted's arms. She'd left so much unsaid and unresolved and yet now, overwrought and deprived of sleep, she felt in no fit condition to face any of it.

Still, you cannot regret last night. What a revelation...

Certainly, it was. She'd known about the intimacies between husband and wife, but she'd never contemplated the intensity of the feelings they could provoke. She felt her cheeks grow hot as she recalled the way they'd joined together, the way he'd urged her towards some hitherto unknown crescendo. The way her entire self had seemed to shatter beneath him. Revelatory? Yes—overwhelmingly so. Overwhelming because it had only intensified what she already felt for him and made her wish for things which might yet prove impossible.

Like Ted's love. Like going to his bed every night.

Indeed. As she reached the door to her bedchamber, Charlotte was forced to acknowledge that whilst she would never regret what happened between them last night, she knew that it had made matters between them even more complicated. That it had made her fear of losing him more painful and potent than ever.

'Oh! Your Grace—there you are.'

The hushed sound of Becky's voice behind her made Charlotte startle. She spun around, hoping that she did not look like she'd been ravished hours earlier.

Judging by the knowing look her maid gave her, however, her wish was in vain. 'You look much better, Your Grace. I'd just been to check on you, to see if you had recovered after feeling unwell last night. Can I fetch anything for you?'

Charlotte shook her head, beckoning her maid into her room and closing the door behind them. 'No, thank you. I think I will go back to bed and rest awhile longer.'

Becky nodded. 'You will need it, after such a tiring night—at the ball, I mean, Your Grace,' she added, her face reddening slightly. 'I will leave you to rest.'

'Thank you,' Charlotte said, trying very hard not to smile. Her mind might still have been reeling after the events of last night, but it appeared that, despite everything, some semblance of her sense of humour remained intact.

'Oh, before I go,' Becky said, reaching into the pocket of her apron and pulling out a small piece of paper. 'One of the maids was in the scullery downstairs when a man came to the servants' door and left this. It was a very unsociable hour, just a little after five, and the maid said the man gave her an awful fright. Well-clad he was, or so she said, but dreadfully dishevelled, with the smell of drink about him.' The maid gave Charlotte a pained look as she held the piece of paper out towards her. 'Anyway, he asked that she give this to you.'

Charlotte felt her heart begin to pound as she took the note. Even as she unfolded it, she knew who it was from, and she knew what it would say. She'd known ever since her eyes had met his across the ballroom and she'd seen that satisfied smile, like a hunter who'd caught his prey. Crowgarth might not have come to Edinburgh in search of her, but a cruel twist of fate had forced their paths to cross nonetheless, and now he had her in his sights.

She heard herself gasp as she read his brief letter, her mind hurriedly absorbing his message to her, conveyed in a careless scrawl. The name of an inn she did not know. The demand that they meet. The barely veiled threat regarding the damage he'd inflict upon her reputation and that of her husband if she failed to appear.

Charlotte drew a deep breath, trying to calm her nerves. This time, running away would not do. She still feared that any hope of happiness for her and Ted had been lost but, whether that was true or not, she knew she had to face Crowgarth. She had to cast off the spectre of the past, once and for all. She had to ensure that no more damage was done—especially to Ted. She owed him that much.

'What is it, Your Grace?' Becky asked.

Charlotte looked up, meeting her maid's eyes, which were heavy with concern. 'Does anyone else know about this letter?' she asked.

Becky shook her head. 'I don't think so, Your Grace. The maid gave it directly to me.'

'All right, that is good,' Charlotte replied, unsure

who she was trying to reassure more—her maid or herself. 'I need to go to a coaching inn, in somewhere called Canongate. Bryce's Inn—do you know where that is?'

'Yes, I do, but…' She watched as the furrow in her maid's brow deepened. 'Forgive me, but is everything all right? Do you want me to send for His Grace?'

Charlotte shook her head. 'No, please don't trouble the Duke. I need to dress and leave as soon as possible. There is an urgent matter I must attend to, but I should not go alone. Will you accompany me, Becky?'

She watched as her maid hesitated momentarily, as though she wanted to say something more on the subject. But then she acquiesced, nodding her agreement before bustling away to select some suitable attire for her mistress.

Charlotte sat down on the edge of her bed, feeling the first fragments of a plan start to come together in her mind. She needed to put her past firmly where it belonged, but she also needed to heed its warnings. She needed to take to heart the painful lessons which her past mistakes had taught her, and draw strength from them, too. She needed to be sensible, wise and determined Charlotte now. Quite simply, no one else would do.

Ted woke slowly, the thick curtains of his bedchamber shutting out the light and leaving him with no idea what time it was. He'd slept well, which, all things considered, seemed rather a miracle. Last night had stirred some powerful feelings within him—feelings he'd yet to wrestle with, but which, in the light of a new day, he knew he had to confront. The strength of his jealousy and fury at hearing of Charlotte's dalliance with Crowgarth had taken him aback, and had led him to say things which he shuddered to recall.

Questioning her motive for telling him her story last night had been bad enough, but questioning her motive for marrying him—that had been unforgivable. He should have apologised, there and then. He should have been clear that the true cause of his ire was that devil Crowgarth, not her. He should have told her that he understood that her actions, however misguided and full of risk, had been motivated by the trust and affection she'd placed in a man not worthy of her, not to mention a desire to please her mother and to save her family from destitution. He should have urged her to stop blaming herself, and to stop believing that she deserved her mother's condemnation for everything that had happened.

He should have told her that she deserved to be loved. That she was loved—by him.

You're a blockhead, Ted. After all, she told you that she cares for you...

Yes, she had, and in the aftermath of hearing those words, he'd completely lost his wits. Knowing that she did care for him had provoked feelings in him which, frankly, made his anger towards the man who'd tried to ruin her pale in comparison. All his passion for her, all of the lust he'd spent the past weeks trying hard to suppress had come rushing to the fore. He had spoken to her then, of wanting her, just as he had at the ball, when he'd first begun to speak about what he felt for her. He had given voice to his desire, but he had said nothing of his deeper feelings and he should have, before he'd even considered taking her to his bed. Not that he could quite bring himself to regret ravishing her so thoroughly…

Ignoring the fresh stirrings of longing which those particular memories provoked, Ted turned over, smiling sleepily to himself in the expectation of seeing fiery red curls spread across the pillow next to him, and the still-slumbering face of his beautiful wife by his side. Perhaps now she would wake, and he would kiss her, and he would say all of the things he should have said last night.

He felt his smile fade as he realised that the space beside him was cold and empty, that Charlotte had gone. That, indeed, the only hint that she'd ever been there was the ghost of her scent on the pillow.

Ted pulled himself upright, dragging his hands through his hair as he contemplated the possibilities. Perhaps she'd simply woken early and returned to her own room to dress. Perhaps she was downstairs now, enjoying breakfast before settling down in the parlour with her sewing, as she so often did.

Or perhaps she regretted what had happened between them last night. Perhaps she had interpreted it as nothing more than base lust on his part, and had fled, embarrassed, from his room as soon as she'd awoken. After all, he could hardly blame her for drawing that conclusion, could he? He'd left far too much unsaid.

Fix it now, man. Go and declare yourself to her, tell her that you love her. Tell her that Crowgarth can go to hell because all that matters to you is your marriage to her, your life together...

For once, that niggling inner voice was correct. Love—that was what this was. He loved her, and more than anything right now, he needed her to know that. Ted leapt out of bed, pulling on his nightshirt before furiously ringing the bell to summon his valet. After a few moments the young man appeared at the door, breathless and wearing a look of surprise.

'Yes, Your Grace?' he asked, rushing in while he appeared to still be chewing the last mouthful of whatever meal it was that Ted had interrupted.

'What time is it?' Ted asked.

'A little before ten o'clock, Your Grace.'

'Ten o'clock?' Ted repeated, aghast. 'I am not in the habit of sleeping all morning. Why was I not woken sooner?'

He watched as the valet's eyes shifted momentarily towards the bed before returning to his master. 'Mrs McGowan instructed me to wait until you rang for me, rather than coming in as I usually would. She said that she believed that you'd had rather a late night, and…well, that is to say…she thought Her Grace was in here with you and that you should not be disturbed.'

'I see,' Ted replied, thinking that if he had been in a lighter mood, he might have chuckled at the fact that, as usual, nothing that occurred in his home escaped the notice of his housekeeper. 'Well, Her Grace is not here,' he continued, suppressing a sigh. 'She must be resting in her bedchamber. I'm surprised she has not yet rung for Becky to attend to her.'

'Becky went into town a little while ago, Your Grace,' the valet explained. 'She told Mrs McGowan that last night Her Grace had asked her to run an errand in the morning. Said that it couldn't wait.'

'I see,' Ted said again, although the story struck him as more than a little odd. Certainly, Charlotte had said nothing to him last night about needing something urgently in town and, in any case, she'd hardly seemed in the right frame of mind to be thinking about minutiae. 'And you are certain Becky has not attended to Her Grace this morning?'

The valet looked puzzled. 'I suppose she might have. Although I'm sure she told Mrs McGowan that

Her Grace was not in her bedchamber. That was why we thought Her Grace was with you, Your Grace.'

Ted felt his temper flare. 'So you're telling me that no one in this house knows where my wife is this morning, and that the only person who might is her maid, but that she has disappeared, too?'

He did not wait for the valet to answer. Instead, Ted grabbed his long robe from where he'd draped it over a nearby chair and wrestled it over his shoulders before pulling it tightly around his waist. 'Where is Mrs McGowan?' he asked the young man, who stared at him, startled. 'Tell her that I must see her immediately.'

'She's in the kitchen, overseeing arrangements for luncheon, Your Grace. Is everything...'

The young valet did not get the chance to finish his sentence, however, as Ted all but sprinted out of the room and towards Charlotte's bedchamber. He paused outside the door, his mind racing with every terrible possibility. That the turmoil of last night had made Charlotte so unwell, her maid had been forced to go in search of a doctor. Or that by letting his desires conquer him without uttering a word about his feelings for her, he'd led her to conclude that he was no better than Crowgarth, seeking to take his pleasure with her as soon as the opportunity presented itself. That this, combined with the way he'd responded to her revelations, had proven so unbearable that she'd decided to flee with the help of her maid, and that they'd concocted this sudden errand as a ruse to escape.

If that's the case then you will go to the ends of the earth to find her, and you will do whatever it takes to make things right.

Of course he would. In any case, he reminded himself, his worst fears might yet be unfounded. She might simply be resting in her bedchamber.

'Charlotte? It's me,' he called, tapping gently on the door. 'Are you all right?'

'Your Grace!' Mrs McGowan called breathlessly from behind him. 'What is amiss? Becky checked on Her Grace earlier this morning but found she was not in her bed. We thought she was in your bedchamber, with you…'

His housekeeper's words were interrupted by him knocking again, louder this time, on the door. When again his knock received no answer, he listened at the door, trying to detect even the smallest hint that Charlotte was within. His heart descended into the pit of his stomach as he realised there was not a single sound to be heard, and that the room on the other side of that door lay still and deathly silent.

'Damn it!' he growled, turning the doorknob and pushing the door open. He could bear it no longer. He needed to know where she was. He needed to know if she really had left him, so that he could begin his search. So that he could do whatever it took to bring her back to him.

The empty room which greeted him, however, offered him few answers and many more questions. As he hurried inside, Mrs McGowan following behind him, he cast his eyes around, searching for clues. Her bedchamber was tidy, and there was no trace of a hurried departure. The bed had been made, with her nightgown laid out neatly at its foot. The delicate scent of her perfume still lingered in the air, whilst upon her dressing table, her hairbrush and hairpins still sat, as though dutifully awaiting her return. He rushed over to her clothes press, pulling open its doors to find that it was still filled with her clothing. Momentarily, his heart lifted. Perhaps she had not left him. Perhaps, wherever she was, she did intend to return.

Or perhaps she was so desperate to get away, she fled with only the clothes on her back...

'Your Grace, I think you should see this,' Mrs McGowan said, interrupting his spiralling thoughts. She held out a piece of paper to him, the colour visibly draining from her face. 'It was on the floor, beside Her Grace's bed. Forgive me, but I am afraid I did read it.'

Ted took the paper from his housekeeper's hand,

his eyes running frantically over the untidily written words etched upon it. Words which contained a demand, and a threat. Words which could have only come from one man—a man who characteristically had not troubled himself to sign his name. A man who Charlotte had feared would come for her, who would do something terrible. She'd told Ted as much, hadn't she? If only he'd listened to her—properly. If only he'd been less possessed by his seething anger and his burning desire.

'Becky told me that she needed to go out this morning, that there was something that Her Grace needed her to do,' Mrs McGowan continued, her pallor still ghostlike as she shook her head slowly. 'They must have slipped out of the house together and gone to that inn. Oh, Your Grace, I am so sorry. I should have questioned Becky's story more, I should have…'

Ted raised his hand in gentle protest. 'Please, Mrs McGowan, do not vex yourself.' He reviewed the letter once more, his jaw hardening with grim determination. 'The most important thing is that we know where my wife is—and, more than likely, her maid, too.'

He screwed the piece of paper into a ball and tossed it into the cold hearth. It could burn in there later, once Charlotte was home and safe. But first he had to bring her back to him. He had to get her away from

Crowgarth and make sure that insidious man could never trouble her again.

'I must dress at once. I must go to her,' he said, marching back out of the room. 'There isn't a moment to lose.'

Chapter Twenty-One

The moment that Charlotte stepped inside the coaching inn she regretted her decision, and that was before she'd even laid eyes upon Crowgarth. The small room into which she'd wandered was humbly furnished, with small tables and chairs spread chaotically about it, as though the proprietor had long since abandoned trying to maintain order in a place which saw the passage of so many people each day. There were a dozen or so men sitting in there, wearily nursing drinks, their chatter little more than barely discernible murmurs as they presumably awaited the arrival of the next stagecoach. She felt the weight of every pair of eyes in the room fall upon her as she hovered near the door, trying to look resolute even as her confidence faltered. She should not have come here, she knew that, but then, what else could she do?

You could have shown Ted the letter. You could have sought his help.

She shook her head at herself. No—she would not drag Ted any further into this mess of her own making. A mess which she still feared might cost her and Ted any chance of happiness, and which still threatened to do untold damage to both of their lives. She could not repair the wreckage that her past mistakes had wrought; that was impossible. But she had to find a way to stop the spectre of it haunting her. She could not spend the rest of her life looking over her shoulder, living with the threat of imminent ruin, and knowing that at any moment her kind, decent and honourable husband might be dragged down with her. Right now, as that letter had demonstrated, she was Crowgarth's plaything, and he was tormenting her for his own amusement. That had to stop—today.

'Do you want me to ask the innkeeper if Lord Crowgarth is here?' Becky asked quietly.

Their journey across town on foot had given Charlotte enough time to tell Becky her sorry tale. After all, she'd concluded, if Becky was to remain by her side throughout her exchange with Crowgarth, she was going to learn enough of it anyway. She'd had Becky dress her plainly for the occasion, and had also asked the maid to refrain from addressing her in any way which indicated that she was a duchess. Given what she was about to do, she reasoned that the less attention she drew to herself, the better.

'Yes, please,' Charlotte replied, startling at the

hacking cough of a rather unkempt-looking man across the room.

Becky gave her mistress a knowing look. 'Inns like this might have stables at the back and bedrooms upstairs, but they're little better than taverns,' she whispered. 'They're no place for the likes of you, or for the likes of Lord Crowgarth, for that matter. A man like him would usually take better lodgings in the newer part of town. Makes me wonder why he hasn't.'

'Because the stagecoach to London departs from here at two o'clock every morning, and I often find myself in need of a quick escape.'

The familiar voice of Lord Crowgarth intruding suddenly from behind them made Charlotte jump again, although her maid seemed unperturbed. Both ladies spun around to see him standing in the doorway, coatless, his fair hair dishevelled, his shirt and cravat askew, and wearing a lazy grin upon his face.

Charlotte's skin crawled as those sky-blue eyes of his drank in the sight of her greedily, and a cold dread flooded through her veins as she realised that he was blocking their only means of escape.

Instinctively, she took a step back. 'Is your father so displeased with you that he has deprived you of the family carriage?' she asked boldly, trying to ignore how hard her heart had begun to pound in her chest.

She noticed him flinch, perhaps in recognition of the knowledge which her question implied. 'My father has deprived me of a great deal,' he replied. 'But no, actually, I prefer not to travel in anything with the Malham coat of arms painted on either side of it. Draws too much attention.'

'I suppose it wouldn't do to be too noticeable, given the nature of your work,' Charlotte quipped.

Crowgarth narrowed his eyes at her. 'Someone has been telling you tales.' He looked over her shoulder, swiftly surveying the room. 'Shall we go somewhere a little more private? A duchess shouldn't be seen dead in a place like this.' He glanced at Becky. 'Your maid can wait here.'

'My maid is not leaving my side, and we are not going anywhere with you,' Charlotte replied, folding her arms across her chest. 'What do you want, my lord?'

That sly smirk crept across his face again. 'I should think that is obvious. I want what is due to me.' He feigned a sorrowful look. 'We were supposed to marry, dearest C, until you ran away from me. Now I know that ship has sailed, so to speak, but here we are, together in a coaching inn, for old times' sake.' He stepped forward, leaning close to her ear. 'I've always wanted to bed a duchess,' he whispered.

Charlotte stared at him, aghast. 'How dare you, my lord!' she exclaimed furiously. 'How could you even think…'

Crowgarth placed a single finger over her lips, silencing her. 'Do not be too hasty, madam. After all, you wouldn't want the story of our ill-fated elopement to spread now, would you?' He clicked his tongue, shaking his head dramatically. 'I imagine that husband of yours wouldn't be altogether impressed. If I remember rightly, Perry's little brother never did like to be the centre of attention. Just think how much he'd hate being the talk of society! Not to mention the damage such talk would do to his own reputation…'

Charlotte shook her head fiercely in silent protest at his blatant blackmail, feeling her face grow hot as she noticed how quiet the room had grown. No doubt their assembled audience was feasting upon the spectacle, and hanging on to every irresistibly scandalous word. Despite her earlier insistence that she was not going anywhere, she found herself pushing past Crowgarth and running back out of the door and into the dusty, bustling street outside, with Becky hurrying to follow her. For one long moment, the instinct to flee consumed her. She had to get away—from him, from his threats, from her past.

You know the only way to truly escape this is to face it, Charlotte. You must fight fire with fire. That is what you came here to do, remember?

'You know what I say is the truth, Charlotte.'

Crowgarth's taunting musical voice called after her. Charlotte paused, briefly closing her eyes as she collected herself. For once, that niggling inner voice was right. She could not allow what had happened with Crowgarth to blight her life but, most importantly, she could not allow Ted's life to be engulfed by the flames of her scandal. Ted might not love her; indeed, their entire arrangement might not survive now that he knew what sort of a woman she was. Almost nothing was certain, except for one thing: she had to put an end to this now.

Charlotte spun around to face Crowgarth, her hands planted on her hips. 'I know that spreading tales about us means you'd risk being sued for criminal conversation by my husband. Quite frankly, I don't think you would dare, my lord.'

Crowgarth laughed. 'No suit could be brought. Our liaison was before your marriage.'

Charlotte raised her eyebrows at him. 'So you say. But what if I was to say different?'

'Ha! You would never...'

Charlotte lifted her chin, giving him her haughtiest look. 'Wouldn't I? I mean, what would I have to lose, my lord? By then I would already be ruined. And you know only too well what a reckless, impetuous sort of lady I am. Who knows what sort of stories I might be driven to tell, in such desperate circumstances.'

Beside her, Charlotte sensed Becky shift uncomfortably. 'Perhaps we should go now,' she suggested.

'Oh, we will, very soon,' she assured her. 'First, I

must ensure that Lord Crowgarth understands me. I must deliver my message to him.'

He raised a curious eyebrow at her. 'Oh? And what is your message, dearest C?'

Charlotte fixed her sternest, most duchess-like gaze upon him. 'After today, Lord Crowgarth, you will never speak to me or about me again. You will tell no tales of elopements or anything else. You will never seek me out, and if our paths should cross in polite company, you will behave as though we have never met. Do I make myself clear?'

He chuckled, shaking his head at her. 'Oh, really. And why would I do that?'

She gave him a long, meaningful stare, braced to counter his threats with a final one of her own. 'Because if you do not, I will tell a story—my story, and it will be far worse than any chatter about criminal conversation. I will make sure your father and your employer know exactly what you did. I will make sure that the world knows that it was not an elopement, but an abduction. That you abducted me.'

Even as Charlotte uttered the words, she knew that they were a desperate fabrication, a final bid to silence this nefarious man on the subject of their liaison for ever. But she also knew that she had to seize control of the story somehow. She had to show him that the problem with telling a tale about something that happened in the past, for which the evidence had been erased by the passage of time, was that far worse tales could be told in return. She had to demonstrate that she was deadly serious; if he intended to ruin her, then she was going to be certain of his destruction, too.

Crowgarth's reaction, however, was one which she never could have anticipated. She had expected that he might laugh dismissively at her, or conversely grow angry, but he did neither. Instead, his face turned deathly pale, the whites of his eyes bulging as he stared at her, open-mouthed, for several long moments. When, finally, he spoke, his voice sounded hoarse and the words he said were so shocking that they were almost beyond comprehension.

'How long have you known?'

Ted hurried over North Bridge, feeling breathless as he braced himself to meet the narrow streets of old Edinburgh. As ever, the air was thick and pungent with the smoke of the city's multitudinous fires, pouring out of chimneys mounted upon rows of tall buildings which cast the ancient wynds and closes in permanent gloom. He was glad he'd decided to go on foot; the seemingly endless procession of people, horses and carts going about their business made travel by carriage painfully slow at the best of times, and today was no exception. Momentarily, Ted was reminded of an old physician he'd once known, who'd always insisted upon going about Edinburgh in a sedan chair, swearing that it was the only way to efficiently navigate the old city's filthy, crowded streets. That physician's mode of travel might have been considered old-fashioned, but perhaps he'd had a point.

A sedan chair would not have got you here any quicker, Ted. Anyway—concentrate. What are you going to do when you find that devil Crowgarth?

He huffed a breath as he rounded the corner and hurried downhill on the High Street, letting the momentum carry him towards the Canongate.

His heart and his head had been locked in battle over what to do, ever since he'd read that note. Quite frankly, his heart wanted vengeance, making his blood boil with the temptation to challenge the man to a duel, to have his satisfaction. As ever, though, his head was more cautious and altogether more considered in its response. The most important thing, he reminded himself, was that he found Charlotte and that she was safe and well. When it came to making Crowgarth answer for the pain and distress he'd caused Charlotte, then and now, well—there were probably better ways than duelling to achieve that. Both Crowgarth's father and his employer were not men to be trifled with. Some discreet but strong words whispered in their ears about the menace the man had been to the Duchess of Falstone ought to do the trick…

But if Crowgarth has harmed her, what will you do then? You know the man's character well enough to know that there is only one thing he will want from Charlotte...

Ted fisted his hands, feeling his blood heat all over again. That inner voice was right; there was only one likely explanation for Crowgarth summoning Charlotte to an inn—one entirely base, entirely carnal explanation. He thrust his hand into his coat pocket, wrapping his fingers tightly around the pistol which lay within it. The mere thought of Crowgarth's motivation made him want to shoot the man on the spot.

Spurred on by the horrifying image of that man cornering Charlotte in some grim, shabby bedchamber, Ted picked up his pace, all but running those final few yards towards Bryce's Inn. He burst inside, unthinkingly finding his way into the sparsely occupied room where men sat, drinking and waiting. A dozen or so pairs of wary eyes came to rest upon him as he worked hard to catch his breath.

'I'm looking for a lady...' he began.

'The comely redhead?' a man answered, giving him a wily grin before gulping down the last of his drink and wiping his mouth with the back of his hand. 'I'll bet you are, sir.'

Ted bristled at the fellow's impertinence. 'Do you know where she is?' he asked.

The man shrugged. 'Gone, along with a gentry

cove. P'raps a nobleman. Was hard to tell from the state of him.'

Ted felt his heart begin to race. 'Gone where?' he prompted the man. 'Where did he take her?'

The man chuckled. 'Oh, he wasn't taking her anywhere, sir. Marched out of here as freely as she'd come in, so she did, and the cove could do naught but trail behind her.' He paused, shaking his head. 'A real scapegrace, is he. Talking scandalously to her, he was. Said something about an elopement. She was all a-mort after that.'

Ted took a step forward, desperation searing him now. 'Please, if you have any inclination where they might have gone…'

The man shook his head. 'Afraid I do not, sir. The lady, she did have her abigail with her. Both looked like they wanted to get away. Perhaps she's trying to catch a stagecoach.'

Ted nodded slowly, a cold sense of dread creeping over him as he contemplated the possibilities. Perhaps Crowgarth was trying to force her into a stagecoach, with him. Or perhaps he had his own carriage and horses stabled here, ready and waiting to snatch her away…

Gripped by a fresh wave of determination, he murmured his thanks then ran back outside and deeper down the close which led to the stables where the coaches and horses were readied for their journeys.

He knew that there were two large stables in this area, both of which served as stabling for visitors as well as points of departure for coaches going south. One was here, at Bryce's Inn; the other was at The Golden Lion, a little way down St Mary's Wynd. He would search both of them, ask anyone he saw if they'd seen Charlotte and Crowgarth, and if they knew where they were going. He would find a way to follow them, then. He would follow until he found her. Until she was back safely with him.

As Ted reached the yard, however, he realised, to his great relief, that there would be no need for any of that. Instead, near to the coach house, stood Charlotte, her gaze intent upon a departing stagecoach, its driver directing its horses carefully towards the narrow lane which led to the road outside. She was smartly but very simply dressed in a green pinafore dress and white chemise, with a gold-coloured shawl which had fallen from her shoulders and hung loosely about her arms. Her head, meanwhile, was covered by a plain straw bonnet, although its brim was not quite wide enough to entirely conceal those bright red curls which the man in the inn had so impertinently spotted.

Ted could not help but think that such a demure choice of attire was deliberate, that she'd hoped to appear plain enough to go unnoticed or, at the very least, to give no immediate indication of her rank.

Certainly, it succeeded in the latter, but as to the former, it was an utter failure. As far as he was concerned, Charlotte was far too beautiful to ever look plain in anything. In better circumstances, he would have smiled at that thought. In better circumstances, he would have confessed it to her.

Stop gawping at her, man. You've a lifetime to spend doing that, after you've told her that you love her. That you never want to lose her again.

'Charlotte?' Ted called out, running towards her. 'Charlotte! Oh, thank God.'

At the sound of him calling her name, Charlotte startled and turned round to face him. She looked flushed, her eyes heavy and her expression one of deep sadness—perhaps even devastation. Ted looked back at the departing stagecoach, this time spying a familiar man with untidy sand-coloured hair seated within it. Crowgarth. He felt a lump grow in his throat as a dreadful realisation began to dawn. He recalled a question he'd asked Charlotte last night, about whether she had loved Crowgarth. Recalled, too, how she had not been able to answer him—not really.

'I don't know,' she'd said. *'Perhaps I thought I did, at the time.'*

Now, standing there, Ted feared that she did know. He imagined how, after discovering that Crowgarth was still alive, all of Charlotte's buried feelings for the man had begun to resurface. How, after being reunited with the man today, the strength of those feelings had proven too great to resist. Despite everything, despite all the harm that the handsome reprobate had done to her, Charlotte might have been unable to resist him. She loved Crowgarth, and the sorrow Ted could see upon her face was for him, and for the life she could not have with him. She remained under his spell even now, as he drove away in that stagecoach and left her to face the reality of her convenient marriage and her unwanted husband alone.

Ted curled his fists, at once heartbroken and furious with himself. What a fool he'd been, to think that Charlotte might ever love him. To allow himself to indulge in the delusion that, for her, their marriage might ever be anything more than an arrangement, hastily made in a greenhouse, in order to enable her escape.

'I cannot permit you to go after him,' Ted said, his voice low but firm as he reached her side. 'I know you will understand why that is, and what would be at stake for both of us if you pursued him.'

Charlotte blinked at him. 'What are you talking about, Ted?'

He pressed his hands together, trying hard to compose himself. 'You cannot be with Crowgarth—that cannot happen, Charlotte, no matter how much you might wish for it. The scandal would be unthinkable.

We are married, we are the Duke and Duchess of Falstone, and as far as society is concerned, we must continue to appear outwardly as husband and wife.'

He grimaced, the pain he felt in his chest almost too much to bear as he braced himself to utter the fateful words which would be the death knell for his marriage, and for all his hopes and dreams. For the love and the passion, the happiness and fulfilment which had felt so tantalisingly close that morning as he'd awoken and believed for a few blissful moments that Charlotte was there beside him.

'Privately, however, we can come to some sort of arrangement,' he continued. 'One which means we will live more separately. One which means you will not be troubled by me, or my unwanted attention, ever again.'

For a long moment, Charlotte simply stared at him, her mouth agape and her eyes wide. Then she seemed to recover herself, shaking her head slowly and drawing a deep and uneven breath.

'Yet another arrangement?' she asked, her voice tinged with sadness. 'Don't you think we've had quite enough of those?'

Ted nodded. 'I suppose so, but I…'

'The arrangement you propose won't be necessary, Ted,' she said quietly. 'I do not want to go after Crowgarth. I do not want to be with Crowgarth. Indeed, I hope that I never have to see that devilish man ever again.'

Charlotte's words caused his heart to swell with something which felt very much like hope. Only the persistent look of unhappiness etched upon his wife's lovely face prevented him from grinning from ear to ear and gathering her into his arms.

Cautiously, Ted stepped towards her. 'What is the matter, Charlotte?' he asked, his thoughts darkening as another, very different but equally awful possibility occurred to him. 'If Crowgarth has harmed you in any way, then, so help me God, I will...'

She shook her head. 'He hasn't done anything to me, except tell me the truth.'

Ted frowned. 'The truth?' he repeated. 'The truth about what?'

Charlotte looked up at him then, and Ted saw that as well as sadness, the storm clouds of anger were gathering in that mesmerising blue gaze.

'The truth about our elopement,' she said finally. 'And it is even worse than I could ever have imagined.'

Chapter Twenty-Two

For the second time in her life, Charlotte felt as though her entire world had been turned upside down. The first time she'd felt like that had been the day she'd returned to London after fleeing from Crowgarth, to discover that her father was dead, leaving her and her mother to face the trail of financial destruction he'd left in his wake.

She could still recall clearly the sight of her usually prim and proper mother, collapsed in a heap on the floor, stricken with grief at the loss of her husband and the loss of their fortune. That day, everything in her life seemed to alter irrevocably. Her perception of herself, of her position in society. Of what her future would look like. That day, she'd realised that she could no longer be certain of anything any more. Except, perhaps, for one plain and simple fact—that her decision to run away with Crowgarth had been so wrong and so injurious that it had destroyed her family. That the blame for her father's death rested squarely upon her shoulders.

That she deserved every bit of her mother's condemnation and resentment. Every cruel and poisonous word.

Yet now she knew that so much of what had happened during that fateful London Season had been obscured from her view and had been shrouded in secrecy ever since. And, worst of all, she understood now just how instrumental her mother had been in all of it. That part of Crowgarth's revelations had knocked the breath from her body, and her entire world had seemed to shift precariously yet again.

To say that her mother had never been an easy woman to live with would be an understatement, and Charlotte had long since wrestled with the knowledge of how unpleasant and scheming her parent could be. Nevertheless, the tale Crowgarth had told her had revealed a level of duplicity which was truly dreadful. Her mother had blamed her and condemned her, all whilst knowing just how pivotal her own role in events had been.

'You can tell me, Charlotte,' Ted murmured. 'In your own time. I'm here, and I'm listening.'

Charlotte pressed her lips together, glancing across the yard at Becky. Her maid had sat far enough away as to be out of earshot, but near enough to keep a watchful eye on her mistress during that fateful conversation with the rakish lord. Thank God she had not heard the tale. Her maid knowing about Charlotte's foolhardy failed elopement was bad enough, but the idea of her knowing that her mistress had acted so badly whilst being an unwitting pawn in someone else's game was altogether too humiliating to contemplate.

'My elopement was no such thing at all,' she began, her voice wavering as she struggled to maintain control. 'Lord Crowgarth was offered payment to take me away and marry me—by my own mother.'

Ted's dark eyes widened in disbelief. 'What? No, surely not.'

She nodded. 'Yes. After Crowgarth came to me and told me that his father would not consent to our marriage, it appears my mother paid him a visit and made him an offer he could not refuse.'

'The scoundrel,' Ted hissed. 'Is there nothing that man would not do for profit?'

Charlotte shrugged. 'I think it had less to do with profit and more to do with his debts. Crowgarth admitted that his father was making life difficult for him at the time, refusing to pay his debts if he did not marry the heiress that he'd selected for him. Given that he was disinclined towards the match, my mother's scheme proved to be a perfect solution to his problems.'

Ted nodded slowly. 'So the wretch really did plan to wed you, then?'

'No—my instincts were right, at least about that,' Charlotte replied bitterly. 'In her apparent desperation, my mother agreed to pay him before the deed was done. Once he had the money, he took me away as agreed, but it seems he never intended to do anything more than ruin me.' She curled her fists, pressing them against her cheeks. 'And there I was, oblivious to it all, believing that we were going to marry, when all the time I was being abducted without even knowing it. When I think about how he must have been laughing at me...'

Ted took a step closer, placing a tender hand upon her arm. 'None of this is your fault, Charlotte.'

She shuddered. 'Do you know, he even knew all about what had happened in Lowhaven? My mother had painted a really colourful picture for him, telling him what a mess I'd made, and how she could see I was making a mess of things all over again. That was her justification for offering Crowgarth money—that I was too useless to secure a husband on my own.'

Ted's jaw hardened. 'Your mother's actions were nothing to do with you and everything to do with her own desperation and ambition,' he said. 'Surely, you must see that. And as for Crowgarth...' His gaze shifted briefly towards the narrow lane, from which Crowgarth's coach had long since disappeared. 'I could kill him for what he has done to you. And as for choosing to tell you all of this now, and choosing to torment you with it…'

She drew a sharp breath. 'Crowgarth didn't choose to tell me, as such. I suppose you could say that, unwittingly, I tricked him into a confession.'

Ted frowned. 'Tricked him how?'

'I decided to counter his threats with some of my own,' she explained. 'I told him that if he breathed a word to anyone about our failed elopement, I would tell the world that he had abducted me. I did not know that he had, of course—I was trying to ensure that he left us alone, for good. I could see immediately that my threat had hit a nerve. The next thing I knew, he was begging me to join him in the stable yard, where we could talk more privately and he could explain everything. His confession came pouring out, after that.'

Ted gave her arm a gentle squeeze. 'That is impressive, Charlotte. And extremely brave.'

She shrugged. 'Is it? I threatened him with what I believed was a lie. That lie leading to the truth was mere happenstance.'

'You did what needed to be done to protect yourself and to stand up to the man,' Ted insisted. 'You have absolutely nothing to reproach yourself for.'

'Perhaps.' Momentarily, she clenched her jaw, anger swelling within her as she thought about Crowgarth's revelations once more. 'I wish I could claim that his confession was contrite. However, I think it was mainly an act of self-defence. He wanted to ensure that I knew his version of events, and to persuade me that he was also a victim—of his father's cruelty and my mother's machinations.' She crossed her arms, hugging her shawl tighter around herself. 'I was not persuaded, of course, and I told him so. I also admitted to him then that until he'd confessed to it, I had known nothing of the plan which he'd concocted with my mother to abduct me.'

'And what did he say to that?'

'In truth, I think that was when he began to panic,' she replied. 'He begged me then—to reveal nothing of what he'd told me to anyone, not even to you. There was a sort of desperation, even fear, in his eyes, as though he saw that the balance of power had shifted. That for the first time since I'd first had the misfortune to meet him, it was me—and you, as my husband and as a duke—who could make trouble for him, and not the other way around.'

For a long moment Ted stared at the narrow lane, as though the power of thought alone could summon back that stagecoach which had whisked Crowgarth away. Anger bubbled away in the pit of his stomach. Anger that he had arrived a moment too late and had been deprived of the chance to confront the wretched rogue himself. Anger that he had not been able to personally make all the ways in which the Duke of Falstone could cause trouble for him abundantly clear. Anger that he had not been here to protect Charlotte when he ought to have been. Although he had to concede that his protection had not been necessary. The way in which Charlotte had cleverly and confidently dealt with Crowgarth had been nothing short of admirable.

'I'd say that Crowgarth's fear was justified,' he said in the end. 'Since I would dearly like to make the man's life a living hell. In fact, I am still sorely tempted to do so. I'm sure both the Earl of Malham and Lord Sidmouth would be very interested to hear about his kidnapping exploits. I'm sure they'd also both readily agree to the imposition of a lengthy exile, in the circumstances. Somewhere remote—St Helena, perhaps. He can go and keep Bonaparte company…'

'Ted.' Charlotte reached out, touching him softly on the arm. 'That won't be necessary. It is over. He has fled, and I dare say the fear of reprisals will be enough to prevent him from so much as saying my name ever again.'

Ted nodded, a very different sort of heat possessing him in response to her touch. He placed his hand over hers. 'You're right. More than likely, he will flee to the Continent anyway, just as he did in the aftermath of abducting you.' He regarded her carefully. 'Unless, of course, that particular story your mother told you was not true...'

At the mention of her perfidious parent, Charlotte gave Ted a pained look. 'No, that part was true. His intention was to take his pleasure with me, then abandon me to my fate and flee the country. It seems that once he had that money from my mother in his pocket, the temptation to evade his creditors instead of facing up to his debts proved too great, and no doubt he intended to remain at a safe distance from my mother and the ensuing scandal, after breaking his agreement to wed me.' She winced. 'Obviously, I ran away from him before he could enact the first part of his plan, and so he proceeded to the nearest port and boarded a vessel as soon as he could.'

'Damnable scoundrel,' Ted hissed. 'So, what then—he fled and spread a rumour that he'd perished at sea to conceal his whereabouts?'

'I believe there was an incident at sea, and a rumour did spread, although he said it did not originate with him. However, he admitted that it had suited him to let the uncertainty over his fate hang for a while.'

'I'm sure it did,' Ted mused knowingly. 'Although, of course, an heir cannot stay dead for ever. Not if he wishes to inherit one day.'

'Exactly.' Charlotte gave him a grim smile. 'I presume that by the time Crowgarth reappeared, my mother and I had left London for Kelda, which is why we never heard that he still lived. Unless, of course, my mother did hear of it and kept the truth from me. After everything I've learned today, frankly, I would not put anything past her.'

The sorrow in Charlotte's voice made Ted's heart lurch for her. Her mother's behaviour, and indeed her treatment of her daughter, had been nothing short of appalling from start to finish. Charlotte deserved so much more than that. She deserved kindness, respect, affection. She deserved love—his love. An unwavering, unconditional, everlasting love which he would pledge to her, as though they were standing before an altar, making their marriage vows all over again.

'So now you know everything,' Charlotte continued, oblivious to the powerful feelings currently raging inside of him. 'Now you will understand that I meant it when I said that I hope never to see that man again.' She looked at him, those blue eyes of hers at once beseeching and filled with hurt. 'I cannot believe that you thought I wanted to go after him, that I wanted to be with him.'

Ted took another step closer, cupping her cheek with his hand. 'I am sorry. When I saw the look on your face, the way you were watching Crowgarth as he left, I'm ashamed to say that I jumped to the wrong conclusion.'

She furrowed her brow at him, searching his gaze.

'How could you even contemplate the idea of me caring for Crowgarth, after everything he has done? After the way he has treated me? That is not rational, Ted.'

He caressed her cheek with his thumb. 'You're right, it's not. But one thing I've had to realise, Charlotte, is that I am not always particularly rational around you.' Despite himself, he felt the ghost of a smile creep on to his lips. 'If you recall, I was rather provoked by Henry's lusty behaviour towards you, and he is my friend. My flirtatious, licentious friend, but a friend nonetheless. Crowgarth is my worst enemy,' he concluded, his smile fading now. 'The thought that you might still have feelings for the wretch, irrational as it was, was also unbearable.'

'Crowgarth is your worst enemy?' she repeated.

'Of course he is. He has done you a great deal of harm. Never mind making him Napoleon's gaolmate—if I ever see him again, I will kill him.'

She raised her eyebrows at him. 'I think that is the third time I've heard you threaten violence towards the man. What would Dr Edward Scott say, I wonder?' she asked, giving him a playful smile. 'Since he was always so committed to preserving life.'

Her teasing made Ted chuckle. 'I think the good doctor would make an exception for a duke who sought only to protect his duchess.' He brushed his fingers over her cheek once more, still holding her gaze with his own. 'For a husband who wanted to protect his wife.'

'I see,' she breathed. 'Still, I think that the doctor would be surprised, since that duke is usually so calm and sensible.'

'No, he isn't,' Ted replied. 'He just hides his feelings well. Too well, perhaps.'

The sound of a horse whinnying loudly behind them intruded, startling them both. Ted offered Charlotte his arm, and together they walked out of the stable yard and back towards the bustling High Street of the Canongate. There was still so much more to discuss, Ted knew, and so much more he needed to say. But not there, amongst the stables, surrounded by horses and ostlers. Not in the place where Charlotte had had to endure Crowgarth's confession.

If he was to make a confession of his own, if he was to speak to her about all those feelings he'd concealed, too well and for too long, then he would choose another place. A favourite place—high above the city, where he intended, finally, to declare his love for her, and to express his hope that one day, Charlotte might be able to love him, too.

Chapter Twenty-Three

Of all the things which Charlotte might have expected Ted to say to her as they left that coaching inn, asking her what she wore on her feet was not one of them. Nor did she expect that upon hearing her inform him that she wore boots, he would turn to Becky and instruct her to return to Charlotte Square and inform Mrs McGowan that the Duchess was safe and well. That instead of returning to Charlotte Square too, he would take her by the hand and lead her in the opposite direction entirely, down to the bottom of the Canongate's main thoroughfare. To where the street seemed to widen and the tightly packed dwellings of the ancient town seemed finally to fall away, giving way to the fields beyond.

'Where are we going?' she asked.

Ted gave her a mysterious smile. 'Up,' he replied, pointing to the imposing cluster of hills which loomed above them. 'Unless you do not wish to? Only, I thought we might both benefit from some air.'

Charlotte agreed, surprised to realise that the idea of a walk appealed to her far more than the thought of returning home. Perhaps it was the hope that fresh air and the gentle breeze could calm her frayed nerves and whirling thoughts. Or perhaps it was the temptation to believe that they could somehow delay the inevitable; that for a little while, at least, they could avoid either reckoning with the past or confronting the future. That they could simply be together, in the present, thinking of nothing more than putting one foot in front of the other as they made their ascent beneath a brightening sky.

'This hill is known as Arthur's Seat,' Ted said breathlessly as they reached the summit a while later. 'When I worked here, I was in the habit of walking up here often, of just sitting at the top and watching the town below.'

Charlotte watched as Ted stood, looking uncharacteristically dishevelled, his hair teased into disorder by the wind, his coat long since removed, his cravat loosened and his sleeves rolled up to his elbows. She smiled, thinking how handsome yet how unlike a duke he looked. It occurred to her that this was exactly how Dr Edward Scott might have looked after a busy day at the lying-in hospital. She went to stand by his side, following his gaze over the patchwork of browns and greys which comprised the city, punctuated only by the smoke which snaked from its many chimneys.

'It is very peaceful up here,' she observed. 'I imagine it was just what was needed, after a difficult day with your patients.'

He nodded. 'Some of my colleagues found solace in a bottle of something strong, or the arms of a mistress, but I always found it here. Life in Edinburgh, with all those streets and all those people, it has a tendency to swallow you up, to consume you.' He slumped down wearily on the ground before laying his coat down and inviting her to sit beside him. 'It can make it difficult to see clearly. Up here, I always found some perspective.'

'I dare say perspective is exactly what is needed, after today,' Charlotte replied, sitting down next to him. 'Although I'm not sure I can find it, even at the top of a hill.'

Ted frowned. 'You have had a terrible shock, Charlotte. Things were not as they seemed at all, and it will take time for you to come to terms with that.'

'That is only partly true,' she countered quietly, removing her bonnet and placing it on the ground beside her. 'Hearing that my mother schemed with Crowgarth was upsetting, but I know her too well for that to have shocked me. And I might have been a pawn in my mother's and Crowgarth's games, but

I made my own moves, too. It is still true that I decided to go with Crowgarth; I cannot absolve myself of responsibility for that. Nor can I pretend that my actions did not contribute to my father's death. My mother was not wrong in that respect.'

'I disagree,' Ted insisted. 'You weren't responsible for your father's ruin, just as you weren't responsible for his demise. Your mother was entirely wrong to lay the blame at your feet—especially given she was no innocent bystander.'

Charlotte swiped at the single hot, plump tear which slid down her cheek. 'The belief that it was all my doing has haunted me. That night at the inn, when you heard me cry out in my sleep—I was dreaming about my father. About the sight of him slumped lifelessly over his desk. My mother described the scene to me in such vivid detail so many times…'

Ted moved closer, placing his hand over hers. 'You have to forgive yourself. Young ladies run away to elope every day, and while that often results in anger and panic, I don't believe it usually causes death. Your father's life was falling apart. He'd ruined himself and his family—and as for your mother, paying a man to kidnap and marry you! In different ways, they were all gambling with your life, Charlotte.'

Charlotte closed her eyes for a long moment, pressing her lips together and collecting herself. Ted was right. Of course he was right. She'd spent her whole life trying to fulfil the wishes of her family, trying to follow the course which had been laid out for her. Allowing her path to be forged by the machinations of others, or by the consequences of their ruinous choices. Until that evening in the greenhouse, when she'd leapt feet first into the unknown and had begun to navigate her own course, on her own terms. Terms she'd agreed with Ted. Terms which seemed woefully inadequate in light of the feelings she now had for her convenient duke...

Inadequate for you, perhaps. You don't really know how Ted feels now, or how he will feel once the truth about you has sunk in.

'I never asked how you knew where I had gone this morning,' Charlotte said in the end, unable to muster the courage to address the question of feelings just yet. 'I presume you must have found Crowgarth's letter?'

Ted nodded, his expression growing stormy for a moment. 'I did. I wish you had come to me, Charlotte. I would have dealt with him. The nerve of the man, writing to you and threatening you like that...' He shook his head. 'I was so worried about you.'

'I did not want to drag you any further into my mess,' she explained. 'I wanted to deal with my own mistakes, once and for all. I am sorry that I worried you. When I received that letter, I promised myself that I would deal with Crowgarth calmly and sensibly, that I would not take any risks. I formulated a plan to warn him off, and I took Becky with me so that I wasn't unaccompanied.' She pulled at her pinafore, smiling shyly. 'And I wore this—the plainest, least duchess-like item of clothing I own. I tried to draw as little attention to myself as possible. I was trying to fix things, and cause no further harm to you.'

Ted returned her smile, giving her hand a squeeze. 'I like the less formal attire. It suits you. Especially the straw bonnet.'

She laughed at that, prodding his crumpled shirt sleeve. 'And I rather like this more relaxed incarnation of Ted, if I'm honest.' She felt her smile begin to fade as she held his gaze, her eyes searching his for a hint of meaning, a glimmer of hope. 'I will understand, Ted, if you cannot forgive me for what I've done—today and in the past. If you cannot look beyond my disgraceful behaviour, my involvement with Crowgarth, the fact that I married you without telling you about any of it…'

'If I recall, confessions about our respective pasts never formed a part of our agreement.' Ted's dark gaze grew serious. 'There is nothing for me to forgive, Charlotte.'

'But…'

Before she could say another word, Ted drew close, capturing her lips with his own. The kiss was soft and tender at first, as were his fingers when they brushed under her chin and across her cheek, causing shivers to cascade down her spine. Her eyes fluttered closed and she heard herself sigh as Ted deepened the kiss, his hands wandering to tease the curls which had already been loosened by the wind. All thoughts of being sensible melted away, replaced by a visceral, desperate sort of instinct as Charlotte pulled Ted closer and lay back on the ground. She murmured again as she felt his lips trace a path down her neck before being frustrated by the collar of her chemise.

The obstacle seemed to bring Ted to his senses. 'Forgive me,' he said breathlessly, touching his forehead against hers. 'I'm not sure I can be trusted around you. Especially not after last night.'

The reminder of sharing Ted's bed made that strange, potent feeling course through Charlotte once more. 'It is fortune then, that I am already your wife,' she replied softly. 'That is, if you still wish me to be...'

'Of course I do, Charlotte,' he said, returning to sit before offering her his hand and pulling her upright. 'In fact, the thought of not having you in my life...' He paused, shaking his head, apparently searching for the right words. 'This morning, when I woke up and first discovered you had gone, I admit I feared the worst. The thought that you might have left me was unbearable. Not that I would have blamed you. Not after the way I behaved.'

Charlotte's mouth fell open and for a long moment she stared at him in surprise. In the aftermath of receiving Crowgarth's note, she'd been so consumed by the need to deal with her past, to rid herself of the man and his threats, that she'd never even considered that Ted might have thought she'd gone for ever. And as for the idea that Ted might have given her cause to leave him—that was just unfathomable.

'You really believed I'd left you?' she repeated in astonishment. 'But...why?'

Ted dragged his hand through his hair, trying to find the right words to explain himself. Everything he'd wanted to say to her that morning, before he'd discovered she was gone, came rushing to the fore—a chaotic mess of thoughts and feelings racing around inside his head. He needed to put them to order. He needed to speak plainly. He needed to leave no doubt in Charlotte's mind as to exactly how he felt.

'Last night, when you told me what happened with Crowgarth, I admit I was shocked,' he began. 'I admit too that I allowed my feelings about the man to affect my judgement, and I said some things to you which I should not have said. I questioned your reasons for telling me your story, and I was wrong to do that. As far as you were concerned, Crowgarth had risen from the dead and you were frightened. Instead of comforting you, I condemned you, and as for questioning your motivation for marrying me…' He pressed his lips together for a moment, collecting himself. 'I am truly ashamed of that. When I realised you were gone, I thought it was my words and my actions which had driven you away.'

'Oh, Ted.' Charlotte reached over and took hold of his hand, placing it in her lap. 'Your reaction was nothing more than I deserved.'

He shook his head. 'I disagree. Then, to make matters worse, having behaved so badly towards you, I took you to my bed…'

'Actually, I think you will find that I took you to your bed,' Charlotte countered, the most becoming hint of a blush staining her cheeks.

Despite the serious nature of their conversation, Ted found himself chuckling at that. 'All right,' he conceded. 'But still, I should have apologised to you first. I should have said so many things to you.'

Charlotte eyed him quizzically. 'Such as?'

He drew a deep breath. 'Such as—what happened with Crowgarth was a mistake, Charlotte, but you should not allow it to cast a shadow over the rest of your life. All you wanted was to do as your mother had asked and to save your family from ruin and, in doing so, you placed your trust in a man who was not worthy of you. You made a mistake, but you made it with the very best of intentions, and when you realised your mistake and saw Crowgarth for what he was, you ran from him. One mistake does not mean that you are undeserving of happiness. You deserve to be loved, which is just as well because I love you, Charlotte—deeply, eternally and without reservation. And I very much hope that one day, you might be able to love me, too.'

He watched her closely, his heart thudding in his chest as she contemplated his words.

'I'm afraid that *one day* won't be possible, Ted,' she began, those blue eyes of hers seeming to sparkle as a smile broke across her face. 'Because I love you already. I love you now—so very much. However, I'm not sure that deep and unreserved love was part of our arrangement.'

He grinned at her before pulling her closer to him, wrapping his arm around her shoulder. 'Yes, well, all of this—you and me—it has gone far beyond that arrangement we made, hasn't it?'

She wrinkled her nose slightly as she glanced up at him. 'Oh, I don't know about that,' she replied. She placed a single finger on her chin in mock contemplation. 'What was it that we agreed to, again? Something about getting along well enough together, and having a companionable marriage, wasn't it?'

Ted laughed, placing a brief kiss on the tip of her nose. 'Yes, it was something like that. I'm not sure we have done very well at it, though. Or at least, I haven't—unless being unable to take my eyes off you every time you walk into a room counts as getting along well? Or lying in bed at night wishing you were there with me counts as being companionable?'

Charlotte raised her eyebrows suggestively. 'Or unlacing my stays counts as helping me to escape?'

Ted groaned. 'Don't remind me. That was absolute torture. How I stopped myself from taking you to bed there and then, I will never know.'

'Now that I know what that is like, I think I wish you had.' She paused, biting her lip, the colour in her cheeks deepening by the second. 'Sorry—I am not sure why I said that.'

Ted regarded her carefully, confused by her apparent retreat from the flirtation they'd been enjoying. 'Hopefully because it's true?'

He heard her draw a deep breath. 'Of course it is, but saying it aloud like that is the sort of thing the old Charlotte would have done. The wayward Charlotte—the one who...who Crowgarth called a harlot. That day, at the coaching inn, when I refused his advances and right before I fled from him, that's what he called me—Charlotte the Harlot.' She shook her head slightly. 'Those words have haunted me ever since.'

Ted placed a gentle kiss on top of her head, holding her close to him. 'Crowgarth was being cruel, Charlotte. He was lashing out at you when you would not give him what he wanted. There was nothing wrong with who you were then, and there is nothing wrong with you now. There is nothing wrong with expressing your passions and desires. Or stealing a peek at your husband's scarred body while he changes for bed,' he added mischievously.

Charlotte covered her face with her hands. 'I was so embarrassed when I let it slip that I'd seen that scar,' she murmured through her fingers.

'Don't be. I think that was the moment when I started to hope that there could be something more than friendship between us,' he confessed. 'Although I quickly talked myself out of it, of course. The thought that in forging that agreement with you I'd accidentally made a love match seemed ridiculous.'

Charlotte reached up, kissing him firmly on the lips. 'I think that perhaps the signs were always there, ever since that day when we walked together by the stream, and you wrapped your greatcoat around my shoulders. The way you looked at me...'

'Actually, for me the first sign came sooner than that.' Ted gave her a pained look. 'You might recall earlier that day, you and Elspeth walked in on a rather heated conversation between me and my mother.'

Charlotte nodded. 'Yes, I do remember that. You looked so flustered and so provoked, and excused yourself very quickly. Elspeth told me later that she believed you'd been arguing over the matter of you finding a bride.'

'We had. My mother was pressing me over the matter, as usual, urging me to go to London and put myself at the mercy of the marriage mart. In response, I threatened to marry the next eligible young lady who walked through Chatton's door. Moments later, you walked in. Fate was clearly laughing at me that day. As was my mother, of course.'

Charlotte's brow furrowed. 'Is that why you asked me to marry you? Because of your threat?'

'No! Of course not, although I dare say my mother is still convinced that is the reason. I do wonder if it was serendipity, though. You'd looked at me so warily that day that it drove me to prove to you that I wasn't some dreadful ogre, to try to make amends by inviting you for dinner. Then I saw how unhappy you were and…that night in the greenhouse, I really had not planned to propose to you. But the look I saw in your eyes, as though you were fighting with yourself to maintain control over emotions you did not wish to acknowledge, and those words you said, about playing the cards life dealt you—I felt such an affinity with you, then. I wanted to help you, whilst knowing that by becoming my wife, you'd be helping me, too.' He kissed her cheek. 'It was easily the best and most impulsive decision I have ever made.'

Charlotte smiled at him. 'I'm glad you asked me, and I'm glad I said yes. I've spent so long berating myself for my impetuous tendencies, but since marrying you, I've learned that sometimes my instincts are worth paying attention to.' Briefly, she turned her gaze away from him, staring down at the city below. 'I never thought it was possible to be as happy as I have been, these past weeks with you.'

Ted placed another kiss upon Charlotte's lips—a long, lingering kiss, filled with promise. 'I intend to spend my life making you happy, Charlotte,' he whispered. 'Yesterday, when I told you that marrying you has made being the Duke feel more bearable, I was not being entirely truthful.'

He saw those beautiful blue eyes of hers widen slightly. 'You weren't?'

'No, I wasn't.' He shook his head at himself. 'I've spent so long resenting my inheritance, believing it had robbed me of my happiness, of my purpose. I was so fixated on what I'd lost and yet I realise now that the life I had, alone and wedded to my work, was never perfect, because you were not a part of it. I may never have wanted to be the Duke of Falstone but I am glad that I am, because becoming the Duke and returning to Chatton meant that I met you. My life with you is so much more than bearable, Charlotte. It is complete.'

'Oh, Ted.' Charlotte traced her fingers across his cheek. 'But surely you are not going to give up on your vocation entirely? There must be things you can do through patronage, just as you do for the lying-in hospital here. Or there are charitable works, or lecturing…'

He smiled at her. 'I believe my lecturing days may be almost at an end. I have one more to deliver here, and frankly I will be glad when it is done. However, the idea of some sort of charitable endeavour does have merit, perhaps serving Kelda and its environs.'

'When we return to Chatton, you could speak to Mr Deane,' Charlotte suggested. 'I'm sure he would have some suggestions.'

Ted nodded. 'That is a good idea. There is much work to be done on the estate, too. I've spent a lot of time dealing with the mess which Perry bequeathed to me, and now I must ensure that the estate is running as well as possible. There are people who depend upon me, and I owe it to them—my tenants, my family.' He smiled. 'You.'

Charlotte grinned at him. 'For a man who says he was not born to be a duke, you certainly sound like one. And, of course, I will help you in any way that I can.'

'I was not born for it, but perhaps I am growing into it. Again, I believe much of that is because of you.' He squeezed her hand in appreciation. 'Speaking of returning home,' he continued, giving her a cautious look. 'What do you wish to do about your mother?'

He watched as Charlotte's expression darkened

and he could see that she was giving the question some thought. 'Mama has often complained that Aunt Maud's cottage is too small and damp, and altogether bad for her health. I find now that I quite agree with her. I think we should find them both somewhere much more pleasant and comfortable to live, as long as it is at a sufficient distance from Chatton.' She looked at him warily. 'Does that sound acceptable?'

'It is far more than she deserves, Charlotte, but if that is what you wish then of course it is acceptable.'

'Oh, don't worry. First, I will make sure she knows exactly why she is to live at a distance from me,' Charlotte replied. 'But the past is the past, Ted. I want to live for the future now. Our future, and our children's future.'

'Children?' he repeated, managing somehow to keep his voice suitably quizzical even as his heart swelled with what felt suspiciously like joy.

She nudged him playfully. 'Yes, children,' she replied, laughing softly. 'Don't tell me you've forgotten your mother's lecture on the purpose of marriage already? The Dukedom needs heirs, remember.'

Ted laughed too. 'Well, if it is our duty…' he began, punctuating his words with yet more kisses as together they lay down under the sunlit sky. 'Then who are we to argue?'

Epilogue

Summer 1820

'I would tell you to ensure that my brother does not work too hard, but truly you are no better,' Elspeth said, eyeing Charlotte sternly. 'Ever since you returned to Chatton, the pair of you have been relentless.'

Behind them, the last of Elspeth and the Dowager Duchess's luggage was loaded on to their carriage by several rather flushed-looking servants who were scurrying back and forth. It was a hot day for travelling—so hot, in fact, that Ted had urged his mother and sister to delay their journey for a few days, when it might be cooler. The Dowager Duchess, however, was resolute—plans had been made and would not be changed. She had friends she wished to visit, and places she wished to see. And, ultimately, a dower house that she wished to find and to purchase, so that both she and Elspeth would have a home of their own.

'I shall miss you,' Charlotte said, throwing her arms around her friend in her usual impulsive manner.

'Do not change the subject,' Elspeth replied, although she was laughing and embraced Charlotte, too. 'But of course, I will miss you too, sister.' She wrinkled her nose playfully as she stepped back. 'It still feels odd to call you that.'

'Who are you calling odd, Elspeth?' the Dowager Duchess asked as she hurried past, casting a scrutinising eye over the pile of portmanteaus and ensuring nothing had been forgotten.

'No one, Mother.' Elspeth rolled her eyes at her parent, before giving Charlotte another of those stern looks over which she had such complete mastery. 'Promise me you will not exhaust yourself. I could leave you some good books, if you need an excuse to sit and rest more?'

Charlotte laughed. 'You know that I am not an enthusiastic reader. I'm far more inclined to sit down with some sewing.'

Elspeth made a face. 'Spoken like a woman who has yet to discover Lord Byron.'

'What's all this about Byron?' Ted asked as he wandered out of Chatton's front door to stand at Charlotte's side. 'Quite why that man makes all the ladies swoon, I will never understand.'

'Not all the ladies,' Charlotte countered, slipping her arm around Ted's waist. He responded in kind, drawing Charlotte close to him and placing a kiss lightly upon her forehead.

Elspeth clicked her tongue in mock disapproval. 'Oh, Lord, can the pair of you not wait until Mother and I are safely away?'

Charlotte smiled at Ted, who gave her an amused, knowing look in return. Since their return from Edinburgh, they'd enjoyed their time with Ted's mother and sister; nevertheless, the idea of having all of Chatton House to themselves was very appealing. No more snatched kisses in the parlour, or brief, passionate encounters in Ted's study when he was supposed to be working through the mountain of papers on his desk. And no more counting the minutes until his mother retired for the night so that they could hurry off to his bedchamber…

'You will write often, won't you, Ted?' the Dowager Duchess asked as she joined them for the final farewells. 'I want regular news about this hospital plan of yours.'

'Mother, don't encourage them!' Elspeth interjected. 'I have just been telling Charlotte that they both work too hard. It is a worthy endeavour, but even so…'

Charlotte and Ted exchanged another glance. Elspeth was right; these past weeks they had both thrown themselves wholeheartedly into bringing the plan Ted had formulated with his friend, Mr Deane, to fruition. Having settled upon founding a small hospital to serve Kelda and the scattered villages of this remote corner of Northumberland, the three of them had been busy, writing letters to garner support for the idea, working to secure suitable premises and furnishings, and embarking on the search for suitably trained people as well as apprentices to serve within its walls alongside Mr Deane. When they were not doing that, Ted was busy with the day-to-day business of running a vast estate, and Charlotte had more than enough to occupy her as the mistress of Chatton, especially now that she was also taking over the patronage of the School of Industry.

For the most part, Charlotte had not found any of it tiring. She enjoyed undertaking her duties and she relished working with Ted, witnessing his evident passion for the medical world, and sharing in his joy at doing something to improve the lives of people in Kelda and beyond. Their endeavours had brought them closer, and Charlotte didn't doubt that she loved him more than ever. Although, if she was honest with herself, recently she had felt a little wearier than usual, and a little sickly in the mornings, too—two facts which had given her pause for thought…

'I dare say the pair of them will do just fine,' the Dowager Duchess said with a smile which made it clear she'd noted their silent communication. 'Come then, Elspeth—our carriage awaits us, and our summer holds the promise of many adventures to come.' She stepped forward, embracing Ted then Charlotte in turn. 'And I mean it when I say that I want news—any and all news—from you both,' she said, giving them each a meaningful look. 'I've left you a note of our itinerary and where we will be staying, so you will find it easy enough to write.'

'Yes, all right, Mother,' Ted answered her with affectionate impatience. 'Any and all news. Now, off you go, before it grows too late to depart at all.'

After several final goodbyes, the Dowager Duchess and Elspeth set off down the long driveway which wound its way through the Chatton estate before meeting the road beyond. Charlotte and Ted stood hand in hand, watching as the carriage grew smaller, the clopping sound of the horses' hooves grew more faint and the sight of hands waving farewell out of the windows became indiscernible. It was only then, when the carriage was little more than a smudge of paint in the distance, that Charlotte turned back to Ted.

'Any and all news,' she repeated, chuckling. 'In Dowager Duchess speak, I do believe that means that she wants to know the moment I am with child.'

Ted raised an eyebrow at her, his dark eyes brightening with amusement. 'My mother has never been renowned for being subtle,' he replied. 'But she means well.'

Charlotte nodded. 'She does. She has been very good to me, these past weeks—not least in passing on the benefit of her experience of being the mistress of Chatton. It has been nice to be treated so kindly, to be given advice and guidance, and not to be berated or made to feel like a burden.' She glanced towards the horizon, where the Dowager Duchess's carriage could no longer be seen. 'On reflection, I feel a little bit guilty now.'

'Guilty? Why?' Ted asked.

Briefly, she chewed her lip, before glancing up at him and placing a hand gingerly over her belly. 'Because I do think it is possible—I mean, there have been signs that…'

She saw the most enormous grin spread across Ted's face as the penny dropped. Before she could utter another word, he pulled her into his arms, laughing as he lifted her off the ground and spun her around.

'I'd like to remind you that I may be in a delicate condition,' she teased, laughing too now.

'Oh—yes, of course.' Carefully, he put her down, although his hands remained upon her waist as he regarded her. 'This is just the most wonderful news.

How certain are you?' he asked, his joy evident in his dark gaze. 'Are your courses absent? Have you been feeling particularly fatigued, or experienced any nausea? It will be too soon to feel the quickening—I suppose we cannot know for certain until then...'

'Can the Duke please ask Dr Scott to calm himself,' Charlotte replied, chuckling. 'It is too soon to be absolutely certain, but I think it is very likely that I am with child. I am sorry, I think now that I should have shared my suspicions with you sooner, and that we should have told your mother before she departed.'

'No, absolutely not,' Ted replied, still grinning from ear to ear. 'She would have been insufferable and likely would never have left. I will write to her with the news, once we are sure.'

Charlotte nodded her agreement. 'I suppose I ought to write to my mother then, too,' she replied, her heart lurching painfully at the prospect.

'Hmm, yes, I suppose you must.' Ted gave her hand a gentle, reassuring squeeze, his smile fading now as he regarded her cautiously. 'Have you heard from your mother of late?'

Charlotte felt her breath catch in her throat—partly at the question, but mostly at the memories it provoked about that awful conversation they'd had, not long after Charlotte and Ted had returned to Chatton. The way her mother's face had paled, the moment Charlotte told her that Crowgarth still lived. The way she'd thrown herself upon her daughter's mercy, weeping and wailing as Charlotte confronted her with the truth about the so-called elopement.

'How could you, Mama?' she'd cried. 'How could you try to bargain with the devil?'

'I had to do something!' her mother had sobbed. 'The heir to an earldom was about to slip through your fingers, and we were facing ruin! I knew that time was running out, that there would not be another opportunity for you to make such an advantageous match.'

'Advantageous?' Charlotte had repeated, incredulous, as the tears streamed down her face. 'I was a reckless fool to have fallen for Crowgarth's charms, to wilfully ignore the whispers about his reputation! When he told me that he couldn't marry me, you should have regarded that as a lucky escape. Instead, you were willing to manoeuvre me into causing a scandal and spending my life trapped in a miserable marriage to a rake, and for what? All so that I would be a countess one day, and in the hope that the Earl of Malham would take pity on his poor daughter-in-law's family, and clear Papa's debts?'

Her mother's noisy sobs had been all the confirmation that was needed of the truth in those words. 'What does any of this matter now?' she'd asked, growing defensive then. 'You did not marry him, and everything I feared has come to pass. Your father is gone, Charlotte—he is dead and has left me with nothing!'

'It matters, Mama,' Charlotte had replied, more quietly this time. 'It matters that you were willing to sacrifice my happiness for your ambition, and to repair the damage Papa had done. And it matters that you allowed me to believe that Papa's death was all my fault. I think that is the part which hurts the most—you stood by and let me shoulder all the blame and all the guilt for what happened. Indeed, you blamed me, despite your own involvement, and despite everything you knew. How could you do that to your own daughter?'

She'd received no further answers, and in the end she had concluded that she might never understand her mother's reasons for behaving the way that she had. She'd taken a long, hard look at her surviving parent then, hunched over her walking cane, her thin frame more shrivelled than ever as she sobbed, and she'd decided that enough was enough. In the aftermath of her father's death, her mother had made Charlotte suffer, but it was clear that she'd suffered, too. The woman she'd been since their arrival in Kelda—increasingly bitter, wilfully isolated with her sister and hopelessly reliant upon her many tinctures—was a woman in pain. A woman stricken with grief over all that she'd lost—a husband, a comfortable life, and a fortune. And perhaps, Charlotte had thought, a woman stricken with guilt.

Charlotte's suggestion of finding somewhere more suitable for her mother and Aunt Maud to live had met with no resistance, and while such a house was sought for them both ladies had departed their little cottage to stay with Uncle Matthew. Her mother had appeared to understand Charlotte's need for distance; indeed, given everything her daughter now knew about her past actions, Charlotte suspected that distance was exactly what her mother had wanted, too.

'Not a single word since she left,' Charlotte replied, finally answering Ted's question. 'Just that short letter from Uncle Matthew, informing me of their safe arrival.'

She saw the hint of a frown gather between Ted's eyebrows. 'Do you mind that she hasn't written?'

Charlotte shrugged. 'I'm not sure. Sometimes I think that I do wish to hear from her, but then you should be careful what you wish for, shouldn't you?'

Ted wrapped his arm around her shoulder, pulling her close to him as together they turned around and walked back towards the grand entrance to Chatton House. 'Oh, I don't know,' he replied, kissing the top of her head. 'I suppose that depends upon what your wish is.'

Charlotte cast him a playful glance. 'Really? And what is it that you wish for, Your Grace?'

'Nothing,' he replied, giving her one of those smiles which seemed to illuminate every feature of his handsome face. 'My wish was already granted, you see. Many weeks ago in a greenhouse, when a beautiful lady agreed to marry me. And do you know what the strange thing about that wish was?'

'No,' Charlotte said, unable to stop herself from grinning. 'What was it?'

He kissed her again, on the lips this time. 'It was a wish that I did not even know I'd made—a wish for love, and happiness, and a life spent with you.'

'That is strange,' she replied, still smiling. 'Whereas I wished for one thing and got something else entirely.'

'Oh?' Ted asked. 'And what was that?'

Together they walked into the great, wide hallway of their home where, not so long ago, Ted had stood, pointing angrily towards the door just as Charlotte had hurried in from the rain. Where their eyes had met for just a moment longer than they ought to, leaving their thoughts to linger upon each other ever since.

'I wished to escape,' she said finally, leaning her head against his shoulder as they sauntered down the hall. 'But somehow I ended up exactly where I belong.'

* * * * *

MILLS & BOON®

Coming next month

THE FORTUNE HUNTER'S GUIDE TO LOVE
Emma-Claire Sunday

'We're still in this together, right?' Sylvia quickened the pace of her handheld churn.

'Yes, but I assumed I'd be playing a more...advisory role.'

'But courting is...it's a whole production! Usually there's a *team* of people preparing a young lady to catch a husband. I'll need you for promenades, and dates, and hair and makeup of course—'

'I didn't realise your courtship rituals were so complicated.' Hannah finished filling her barrel, then gripped its handle and spun.

'Well, what about you?' Sylvia asked. 'What are your courtship rituals? If you don't care about appearances, how do you attract suitors?'

'Who says I don't care about appearances?' Hannah's face was serious.

'Oh—' Sylvia stopped churning, her hands now over her face. 'I'm so sorry, I didn't mean to imply— You just don't, you don't curl your hair or anything, but—but you are quite comely. Really beautiful, I think.'

Hannah held her expression for just a moment longer, then broke into a wide grin. 'Of course I don't care about *appearances*, Sylvia. But now I know the best way to get a compliment out of you is to just let you talk.'

Sylvia gasped, embarrassed but glad that she hadn't actually insulted Hannah. Still, she decided it was best to stop talking for now. She listened to the scrape of damp wood against the butter-making jug, the squish of cream going solid. Flecks of white splashed across her hands. Her armpits dampened with the sweat of hard work. She sighed.

'Do you actually like them?' Hannah eventually asked.

'Who?'

'The suitors. The men. Do they make you feel...*smitten*?'

'Of course they do,' Sylvia said, but her words were more automatic than genuine. She was becoming too exhausted to be anything other than honest. 'Or, they *will*. They'll make me feel smitten, enamoured, enchanted, all that...but no, not yet.'

'Why not?'

'I had no suitors while in mourning, and the year before I was too young to take the whole thing seriously. This year—this was supposed to be my year.'

Hannah nodded. 'The year of falling in love?'

'Exactly. The year of falling in love. But now...now it's the year of fortune-hunting.'

Continue reading

THE FORTUNE HUNTER'S GUIDE TO LOVE
Emma-Claire Sunday

Available next month
millsandboon.co.uk

Copyright © 2025 Emma-Claire Sunday

COMING SOON!

We really hope you enjoyed reading this book. If you're looking for more romance be sure to head to the shops when new books are available on

Thursday 17th July

To see which titles are coming soon, please visit
millsandboon.co.uk/nextmonth

MILLS & BOON

FOUR BRAND NEW BOOKS FROM
MILLS & BOON MODERN

The same great stories you love, a stylish new look!

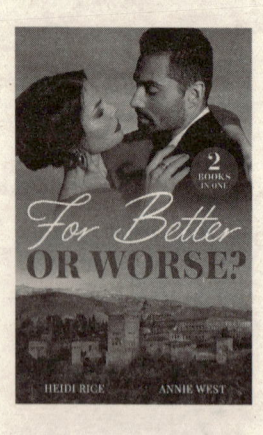

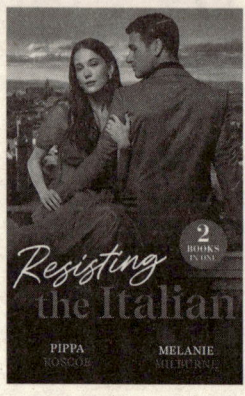

For Better or Worse?
Heidi Rice / Annie West
2 Books in One

Demand for 'I Do'
Sharon Kendrick / Jackie Ashenden
2 Books in One

Resisting the Italian
Pippa Roscoe / Melanie Milburne
2 Books in One

Mediterranean Heirs
Caitlin Crews / Bella Mason
2 Books in One

OUT NOW

Eight Modern stories published every month, find them all at:

millsandboon.co.uk

LET'S TALK
Romance

For exclusive extracts, competitions and special offers, find us online:

- **f** MillsandBoon
- **X** @MillsandBoon
- **◉** @MillsandBoonUK
- **♪** @MillsandBoonUK

Get in touch on 01413 063 232

For all the latest titles coming soon, visit
millsandboon.co.uk/nextmonth

afterglow BOOKS

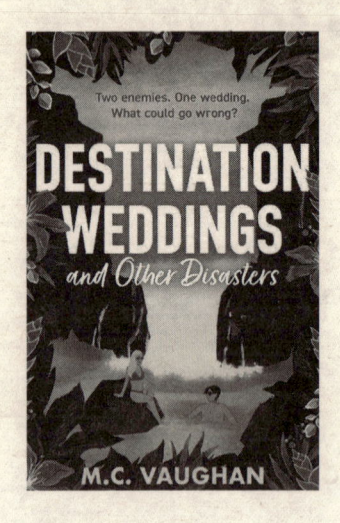

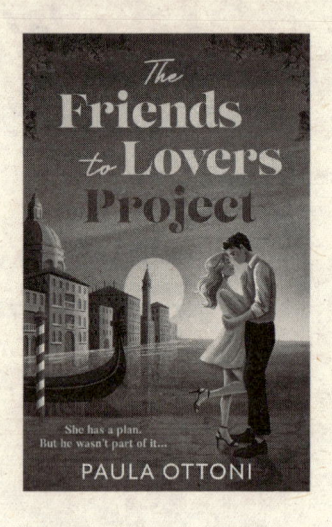

DESTINATION WEDDINGS and Other Disasters
Two enemies. One wedding. What could go wrong?
M.C. VAUGHAN

- ✈ International
- ♥ Enemies to lovers
- (♥) Forced proximity

The Friends to Lovers Project
She has a plan. But he wasn't part of it...
PAULA OTTONI

- 👫 Friends to lovers
- ✈ International
- △ Love triangle

OUT NOW

Two stories published every month. Discover more at:
Afterglowbooks.co.uk